Winners Losers

Published by Snowy Day Publications 2017
Hardy, Virginia 24101

snowydaypublications@gmail.com
Copyright 2017 Chuck Lumpkin
All Rights Reserved

ISBN-13: 978-1977529459
ISBN-10: 1977529453

Cover Photo by
Samantha Jane Richardson

Edited by Sue Patterson

Chapter 1

Marty & Denise Jenkins

The morning was like every other in the Jenkins' home. Marty got up at 6AM, showered, put on his coveralls, fresh from his wife's laundry basket and went into the kitchen for his breakfast. Denise, his wife of nearly fifty years, was already in the kitchen. Their two kids were grown and had families of their own, so it was just the two.

"Marty, you look great this morning. Do you have a meeting?" Denise always complimented her husband to give him confidence to face another day in the factory. She had heard from some of the wives that many of the workers would be made redundant in the near future. She did not want Marty worrying about his job.

"Thanks hon, we have some orders that must be finished today before we break for the weekend and there may be some customers roaming around the plant. The boss wants us all to look sharp when customers come around."

Marty finished his breakfast. His lunch pail was waiting as usual with his surprise for today as he always told his coworkers. His wife always made something different, or at least it seemed different. Denise walked with him to the front door as she did every morning for as long as memory served.

"You be careful and eat all of your lunch" said Denise as she gave him a peck on the cheek.

Marty looked deep into his wife's eyes and knew she was concerned about his job. He was at least five years away from retirement. Although his house was paid for, he had little savings and if he lost his job, they would be hard pressed financially. He knew of friends his age that had lost their jobs and never were able to find employment again. Most had to mortgage their homes to meet obligations.

"You have a nice day hon. I'll see you tonight." With that he put on his cap, opened the front door and walked to his fifteen year old car. He named his car 'Bertha'. *Come on Bertha, don't let me down today*, he thought. The old car kicked over and began to purr. He eased it into gear and backed out of his short drive into the road. The plant was not far away. He had driven this same route for years and knew all the tradesmen that were along the way delivering their wares. He waved at Mike the milkman and Johnny the newspaper boy.

Marty pulled into the plant's large car park and pulled into his favorite spot under a large tree. At one time, the car park would have been full, but now days it was less than half full. He carefully closed the door and headed into the plant.

The day was hot but the plant's ventilation system kept the shop floor as cool as possible. He waved at a couple of his work mates. They all liked Marty. He was always upbeat and never complained. If anyone needed assistance, Marty was always available to help.

Marty had been busy all morning sorting out various components that went into the assembly of the orders. It was break time when a voice came over the loud speakers for all workers to assemble for an announcement. Marty had an inkling what was about to happen. He feared for some of his coworkers that had less seniority.

The workers assembled in front of the loading dock. The boss came out and read ten names. "If your name was read, please report to the office." With that the boss left the loading area.

There was a murmur. All knew what was about to happen. Those whose name was called were to be made redundant. Several of the workers had their head down and some wiped a tear from their cheek.

Marty was very thankful his name was not among those read. He knew two of the workers and they had started work only a couple of months after he started. He knew if there was to be more layoffs that he would be in the next group.

The boss made another announcement. "All workers will be required to work an extra hour today in order to meet the deadline for the order to be finished."

Marty shrugged. An hour was not that bad, at least he still had a job.

The day was uneventful and the order was completed when the whistle blew for the end of the day. It had not been a happy one.

Marty gathered up his lunch pail and walked with all the other workers to the car park. He dreaded going home and telling Denise what had happened. She would worry and he did not like for her to worry. He headed to the pub as he did every Friday after work.

§

Marty pulled open the huge oak door and was greeted with a wall of thick cigarette smoke hanging like a dingy curtain. The Duke of Wellington was tucked in between two dilapidated warehouses in Botany Bay; the pub was nearly as old as Sydney itself. On Friday nights, most of the workers stopped on the way home for a pint and Marty was one of the regulars.

Most of the patrons wore their work clothes. Marty's coveralls bore grease stains and a thick layer of dust. A dented lunch pail dangled from his left hand. He hung-up his sweat stained cap along with his lunch pail on a coat hook near the door.

Arnold, his best friend, watched as Marty ambled toward the ancient bar where his friends had already gathered, nursing their pints and shouting at each other. Someone shouted something to Marty, but the roar from the chatter made it difficult to hear anything, he nodded to be polite.

"Marty you're late! Must have bought a fist full of lottery tickets this week, eh", shouted Arnold, slapping him on the back, which produced a little puff of dust.

In a subdued voice, "No mate, just the one ticket as usual", said Marty looking down at the stained wooden floor that probably had not seen a broom in the past decade.

Arnold stared at Marty. "Why so glum mate?"

"The plant is suffering. The boss made ten of me mates redundant this week. Lucky this time around, but you mark my word; I'll be in the next round." Marty turned his head towards the little group standing next to Arnold. "You lot wait and see. The foreman made us work an extra hour to make up for the ones leaving. That's why I'm late." They all shook their heads in sympathy and turned away to avoid eye contact. Times were bad.

"Sorry to hear that mate", said Arnold who was president of the local union. He had heard rumors that Marty's plant was to close in two months. Arnold knew Marty didn't have much saved and his pension would be meager at best. He couldn't get up the nerve to tell Marty.

Arnold needed to divert Marty's gloom. Being a super fan of the Sydney Swans, Arnold said, "My Swans are going to destroy Fitzroy. Gonna watch the game tonight?" Marty, a die heart fan of Fitzroy, stared into his pint without comment. Arnold's face pulled down in a frown. *Marty has a real problem. I just can't bring myself to tell him the plant is closing and he will lose his job.*

The barman turned on the TV for the weekly lottery drawing. Pint glasses clinked as they were put down on the bar. Lottery tickets pulled from pockets sounded like the rustle of leaves. All stared in silence at the screen mounted above the bar.

The picture flickered on. "Good evening everyone" said the announcer, "Get ready for this week's lottery drawing. There was no winner from last Friday's drawing so the jackpot this week will be four million dollars, for six correct numbers in a row. Let's get started.

The sound of the first ball rolling down the chute filled the room. All eyes were glued to the TV. "The first number is eight."

Marty yelled out, "I've got an eight". His friends shook their heads.

Arnold smiled and told one of the mates, "Maybe this will bring Marty out of his funk."

The next ball seemed to take forever to roll to a stop. A Seven filled the screen. "I've got the a seven too", yelled an excited Marty. Arnold along with the others groaned loudly as each looked for a seven on their own ticket.

Marty took a sip of his pint and watched as the third ball rolled down to the end of the tray. The sound seemed much louder than normal. The ball stopped but the number could not be seen. The announcer turned the ball so the camera would show an eleven. Arnold looked over at Marty's ticket. "Hey mates, Marty has the third number too!" The entire pub broke into a polite applause and a few groans.

The fourth ball began its journey and bumped the stop at the end with a loud click. The ball had 14 printed on its side. Marty looked at his ticket. He had 14. "I…I can't believe this, I've got number 14 too!" All chatter stopped. The only sound was some-one slurping a beer and the sound of the fifth ball rolling down the chute.

"22" said the TV announcer.

Arnold looked at Marty's ticket, "Marty has 22! That's five in a row." The crowd collected around Marty as the sixth and final ball popped out of the basket and began its roll. It stopped but so the camera could not see the number. Not a sound was made in the bar.

The TV announcer turned the ball. "And the final ball is three."

Marty looked up at the screen and then at his ticket. Print-ed clearly on the ticket was the number three. Marty's knees gave way. Arnold grabbed him and helped him over to a stool. Marty's knuckles had turned white from clutching the ticket.

There was dead silence. Marty looked up at the faces staring down at Australia's newest multi-millionaire. "Pints for all", he yelled. The room erupted with cheers.

§

Old Bertha purred all the way home. Marty was grinning from ear to ear. *Denise will be so happy. No worries about a job anymore.*

Marty pulled into his drive. He skipped up the two steps to his front door and opened it as he did every night. He hung up his cap and took his lunch pail into the kitchen. Denise was busy washing some dishes and pots. She turned to greet Marty with a smile and a "Hello."

"Hon, I've got news to tell you. I think you should come into the lounge and sit down."

Denise's face turned white as a sheet. She just knew that Mary had lost his job. She wiped her wet hands on her apron and followed Marty to the lounge and took a seat in her favorite chair. *Marty doesn't act like he is worried about anything,* thought Denise.

"Hon, I am going to resign my job on Monday. Now before you begin to worry, I want to show you something." He took out the lottery ticket and handed it to Denise.

Denise looked at the ticket and back at Marty. "So, it's a lottery ticket like every other you have each week. What's so special about this ticket?"

"We won the lottery. I don't need the job anymore."

Denise looked puzzled. "How much did you win? A few thousand?"

Marty had a huge grin on his face. "Not a few thousand, but a few million. Four million to be exact."

Dense threw her hands to her face. She sat staring at the ticket then at Marty. "My heavens, oh my goodness. Are you sure?"

"Yes, it's true. We are now millionaires."

Dense jumped up from her chair and ran to Marty with a huge hug and kiss. "What do we do now?"

"We front up to the lottery board and present our winning ticket. We will go first thing Monday morning. Arnold told me they open at 10 AM. He's going to call them and inform them that I won and will be calling in to collect my winnings. I'll call the plant and tell them I'm not coming in and that I'm retiring."

"Are you sure you want to retire?"

"Yes. Arnold told me tonight that the plant will be closing in a few months anyway. This came as a miracle. We are truly blessed."

§

On Monday morning, Marty phoned the plant and told his boss he would not be returning. The boss did not ask why. He actually seemed relieved.

"Okay, the boss didn't seem upset," said Marty. The phone rang. It was a voice he had not heard before. "Mr. Jenkins, this is Sir Rodney Stonebridge of the Australian lottery board. I received a call from your mate Arnold Strong that you may have the winning lottery ticket."

"Yes sir, I have the winning ticket."

"Please keep it in a safe place and come to our office this afternoon at 2 PM. We will examine your ticket. If it is the winning ticket you will be presented with your winnings."

"Thank you Sir. My wife and I will be at your office this afternoon. Can you give me the address?" Marty wrote the address down on a pad and disconnected the call.

Denise was standing very quietly with her hands constantly wiping away nonexistent dishwater. "Who was that?"

"That was Sir Rodney Stonebridge from the lottery board. He wants us to come to their office this afternoon at 2 PM. They are located at Olympic Park. That's about a forty five minute drive."

"Oh my, what am I to wear?"

Chapter 2

Winners

Marty parked in front of the lottery board's office. He went around to the passenger door and opened it for Denise. She wore a beautiful floral print dress. Marty had on a striped suit and red tie. They were like teenagers at their first dance as they walked hand in hand up the stairs to the large revolving doors.

They entered the lobby and saw an information desk with a young man typing on a computer terminal. "Yes may I help you?"

Marty looked at Denise and smiled. "Yes, we are here to see Sir Rodney Stonebridge. We have an appointment for 2 PM."

The young man pressed some buttons on his phone and nodded. He spoke to someone and hung up. "Sir Rodney will be down in a moment. Please have a seat."

Marty and Denise sat down in the comfortable chairs to wait. In a few moments a tall handsome man approached them with his hand extended. "I am Rodney Stonebridge, and I believe you are Mr. and Mrs. Jenkins."

Marty took his hand and gave a firm handshake. "Yes sir, I'm Marty Jenkins and this is my wife Denise."

"I am very pleased to meet you. I'm sure you are excited and want to know what will be happening today. First let me congratulate you on winning one of our largest jackpots. We will be checking your ticket shortly and then if all is proper, we will have the awards ceremony. Please follow me."

Sir Rodney ushered Marty and Denise into a large room with several people at computer terminals. "Give me the ticket and we can verify that it is the winning ticket."

Marty took the ticket from his wallet and handed it over to Sir Rodney. "This will only take a few seconds." He handed the ticket to one of the computer operators. The operator keyed in the ticket number. A printer whirred alive and a document spat out into the tray. The young female operator handed the document and the ticket back to Sir Rodney. "Well, your ticket is the winning ticket. Please sign here and here." He handed one copy to Marty. "Now we will go upstairs to the board room for the awarding of the prize."

The lift ride up to the board room was quick. Marty and Denise held hands. When the car stopped, Stonebridge waved the two out to a plush hallway with thick carpet. Several people were entering a room with large double doors. Stonebridge indicated that was their destination.

Several photographers snapped their pictures. There were lots of people standing around the large room. Waiters were weaving in and out of the crowd with trays filled with all sorts of drinks and canapés. There was excitement in the room. Denise was stunned. Marty squeezed her hand for reassurance. He recognized several of the men. Some were political office holders and several well known TV celebrities. One was the well known celebrity that read out the lottery numbers each week. The reporters were shouting questions. Marty was overwhelmed. Stonebridge politely moved Marty and Denise away from the surge of reporters. More pictures were snapped.

Several minutes went by before a large portly man stood on a low dais and announced the award ceremony would begin. Marty recognized him as the Deputy Prime Minister. He addressed the crowd as if he were running for office. Finally, he introduced Sir Rodney Stonebridge as the chairman of the lottery board. Stonebridge moved to the dais and looked out over the crowd while the photographers snapped his picture.

Ladies and gentlemen, it gives me great pleasure to announce there is a winner of the second largest lottery in our history. Mister and Mrs. Marty Jenkins please come forward. Marty and Denise walked through the throng and stepped up on the dais. Marty had a huge smile. Denise was very nervous. Stonebridge turned to the crowd, "Mr. Jenkins presented the winning ticket and it has been verified. As you know, there is no tax on winnings of the lottery. The cheque I am holding is for $4,000,000 payable to Marty Jenkins. Lights flashed as photographs were taken of Sir Rodney Stonebridge handing Marty the cheque.

"I am very nervous" said Marty to the crowd. There was laughter. "I thank the board for making this all possible. Thank you." Stonebridge took Marty by the arm and introduced him to all the dignitaries. Denise stayed as close to Marty as possible. She didn't know any of the people and the way they pushed and shoved to get to Marty was disconcerting. After several minutes of handshakes and photo sessions with the dignitaries, most of the press group left.

Marty was approached by someone he knew very well. Not personally, but had seen on TV for years. The man congratulated Marty. They shook hands. A photographer asked for a pose. The picture was snapped. Marty was near speechless in front of the celebrity. "I watch you every Friday night," said a very nervous Marty. The celebrity smiled and left Marty.

Marty noticed he had a brochure in his hand. He didn't remember where it came from. He put the brochure into his jacket pocket without even looking at it. Sir Rodney smiled. He took Marty aside and told him that many of the winners had help with financial matters from professionals. He suggested that Marty seek professional help on how to invest his winnings.

Marty told Sir Rodney that he had read recent stories in the press pointing out that most of the lottery winners had lost most of their winnings due to poor investments and the lottery board should provide assistance to their winners. Sir Rodney said he did not feel that was necessary; a private firm could handle that chore.

Marty and Denise left the Lottery Board meeting and giggled a lot on the way home. Denise kept looking at the cheque. She had never seen that many zeros on a check before. She finally said, "What are we going to do with all this money?"

Marty was concentrating on traffic. "I think we should take Sir Rodney's advice and find a professional." He remembered something. He reached into his jacket pocket and pulled out the brochure. "Someone gave this to me. Take a look at this. Maybe they can help." He handed the brochure to Denise.

"It's from Secure Pacific Investments. They are located in North Sydney. It says here they specialize in managing funds for individuals and businesses. Maybe we should give them a ring and see what they can do to help us. I'm scared of making the wrong decision."

"We should listen to what they have to say. Maybe they can make investments that will make our winnings grow." He laughed. "Not that we could spend all the money in our lifetime. It would be great to setup a trust for our kids and grand kids."

Denise smiled and reached over and held his hand. "I love you. Always thinking of others. We'll call this company first thing tomorrow."

§

Fredric Peters expected a phone call from his boss that informed him of the possibility of the Jenkins' contacting him for investing their winnings. If they had not contacted him within three days, he was to personally contact them and go to their home. That would not would not be necessary.

Marty Jenkins called Secure Pacific Investments the next day and made an appointment for Wednesday.

On Wednesday Marty and Denise parked in a car park on Clark Street and took the lift up to the offices of Secure Pacific Investments. They walked into the offices and met Fredric Peters.

"Let me get you a refreshment" said Peters.

"No thank you" said Marty. Denise shook her head no.

Peters looked the two over carefully. He had years of experience of sizing up a mark. The couple appeared working class with near zero knowledge of investments.

"How does this work?" asked Marty.

"First you make a list of firms you feel would be good safe investments. You pick the investment and we make it happen. You will receive quarterly statements showing the activity of your investments. We take a very small percentage of your investments as our fee." Peters watched as they absorbed what he was saying.

Marty nodded. "Do you provide a list for us to pick from?"

"Sometimes we provide the list, but mostly our clients provide their own list and we assist by making the purchases for them. If you have trouble making a list, then we can provide a list of possible investments."

"We don't know any firms to make a list. We would like for you to provide us a list to pick from", said Marty.

"That will be fine." Peters opened a desk drawer and took out a sheet of paper with several names of firms. "Here is a list for you to look over. Do you have the cheque the lottery board gave you?"

Denise opened her purse and took out the cheque and handed it over to Peters. Peters examined the cheque and handed it back to Denise. "You will have to endorse the check over to Secure Pacific Investments. I will place the cheque in our trust account under your name. I suggest that you keep some of the money for your personal use. I suggest $250,000. I will write you a cheque from your trust account for that amount. You can then deposit that in your own account at your bank. Mr. Jenkins please endorse the cheque to Secure Pacific Investments while I write your check."

Peters made sure they endorsed the cheque over to Secure Pacific Investments. Peters wrote a cheque and handed it to Marty. He looked at it and handed it to Denise to put in her purse.

"Mr. Peters, when do we have to select the investments from the list?" asked Marty.

"You can do it now or anytime you wish. We will make the investments as soon as you select. Until then your money will remain in your trust account."

Marty looked over at Denise. "Let's go ahead and make the

selection. I don't know any of these firms."

"I suggest you select the top three and add any that you would like," said Peters.

Denise, thinking about their youngest son, looked over at Marty, "How about that Queensland mining company? Geoff is starting a job there soon. I think we should invest in his company, maybe $25,000?"

"Mr. Peters do you think you could add the mining company to the list for $25,000" asked Marty.

"Sure I can do that. I will purchase those shares this afternoon." Peters smiled. *This is going great.*

Marty and Denise left Secure Pacific Investments and went directly to their neighbor hood Westpac bank. They deposited the $250,000 into their account. The bank manager came out personally and congratulated them on winning the lottery.

Marty and Denise went home feeling they were financially secure for the future. They had enough cash in the bank to take care of day to day expenses. They had investments that would grow and provide a secure future for their children and grand children. What could go wrong?

Chapter 3—Nigel Bowman and Mark Young

Nigel Bowman was known as the 'Tall Man', a shade over 2.1 meters. His sandy hair always seemed in disarray. He prided himself on keeping fit and he enjoyed sport but was not as a player just a fan. His wife of 18 years had become adjusted to the unpredictable schedule for a detective of the elite Australian Fraud Bureau. They lived in a new section of Canberra that was home to many government employees.

"Honey, are you going out of town this week?" asked Marie.

Nigel finished tying his tie. "I don't think so" he yelled back. "Why do you ask?"

"We have been asked to dinner by Bonnie and Walter on Wednesday night."

"Oh. As far as I know I'll be in town." Nigel liked Walter, but could do with less of Bonnie's jabbering on about politics and the 'mess' as she called parliament.

Chapter 3

Nigel Bowman and Mark Young

Nigel Bowman was known as the 'Tall Man', a shade over 2.1 meters. His sandy hair always seemed in disarray. He prided himself on keeping fit and he enjoyed sport but was not as a player just a fan. His wife of 18 years had become adjusted to the un-predictable schedule for a detective of the elite Australian Fraud Bureau. They lived in a new section of Canberra that was home to many government employees.

"Honey, are you going out of town this week?" asked Marie.

Nigel finished tying his tie. "I don't think so" he yelled back. "Why do you ask?"

"We have been asked to dinner by Bonnie and Walter on Wednesday night."

"Oh. As far as I know I'll be in town." Nigel liked Walter, but could do with less of Bonnie's jabbering on about politics and the 'mess' as she called parliament.

Marie made a note to call Bonnie and accept the invitation. She knew Nigel and Walter enjoyed watching rugby together.

Nigel came into the kitchen and sat down at the small table in the breakfast nook. The morning paper was laid out as it always was beside his plate. He scanned the headlines and turned to the sport page. "Hum, seems the Sydney Swans are having start up problems this year. They normally have won all of the preliminary games by now." Marie didn't answer knowing full well he was just talking to himself.

Marie placed breakfast on the table and took the other seat. She looked out of the bay window at the beautiful garden she took so much pride in. Her time was spent mostly gardening. They ate in silence as she observed her garden and Nigel read the paper.

"Hum, here is an article on Sir Rodney Stonebridge. It says he running for a seat with Labour with an eye on the PM position."

Marie looked back at Nigel and smiled. She knew nothing about politics, except what Bonnie told her.

They finished breakfast and Nigel put away the paper and pulled on his suit jacket. He was handed his briefcase by Marie. "Honey, you have a good day."

"You too sweetie." Nigel went out the side door to the government furnished car.

The drive to work was not far. The traffic in Canberra was light compared to Sydney or Melbourne. He always said that life was too short to live in either of those cities. He knew that Marie loved the parks and openness of Canberra.

Nigel parked in his designated space. This would be the second week of classroom work. He was being brought up-to-date on computers, new forensic techniques and modern law-enforcement gadgets. Some of the gadgets were like something from James Bond. Most of the technology he had only heard of a few months before the classes.

Nigel walked up the stairs to the police building entrance. The classrooms were on the first floor. He went up the stairs and down the hall to his classroom. There were several other officers from many different cities and divisions standing near the coffee machine chatting. He joined the group and made himself a cup of coffee.

"Nigel, I hear there is a promotion to Senior Inspector in the wind for you", said one of the plain clothes detectives.

"Maybe, I've not been told yet", said Nigel with a grin.

"Well good luck mate."

A woman came into the room and called the class to order. She was the third lecturer for these sessions. She introduced herself as Inspector Joyce Mathews. "Good morning. For the next day or so we are going to be learning about financial fraud. Most of you may refer to this type of crime as 'White collar' crime. When executives of companies create schemes to steal the company's assets that is what we call White Collar crime."

"Fraud schemes are very elaborate in some white collar crimes. Some are just simple theft. We are going to examine some actual cases. You will follow the leads and try to come up with a solution to those cases using the techniques you have learned over the past several weeks. I will ask you to pair up and each team will be given the exact same facts in an actual case in chronological order of their occurrence. The first team to come up with a technique to solve the case will receive special recognition at the graduation exercise." Joyce looked around the class and noted that there were only a handful of uniforms; the others were detectives from all over Australia.

The group looked at one another with anticipation of the competition. The uniformed group paired up with a detective to make it a level playing field. Nigel Bowman was paired with one of the youngest looking of the uniformed group.

"I have the facts of the case on these forms. Each form contains only the facts that lead to the actions actually taken by the investigators. You must provide the investigative techniques that lead to solving the case. Before you open the next section of the packet, write down your investigative techniques on the forms provided. There is an answer form for each section. Good luck." Joyce Mathews began giving out the forms, one to each pair of students. "Each packet has steps the actual case took. Please do not read ahead and come up with your own actions to solve the case."

Nigel extended his hand to his partner. "I'm Nigel Bowman."

"I'm Mark Young" said the young man. "I've just finished law school and I'm applying for a position with the Attorney General's office and hope I won't keep you from winning."

Nigel smiled. "I don't think you will slow us down. You'll do just fine." He slapped Mark on the back. Mark looked relieved and smiled.

Detective Mathews reached Nigel and Mark. She handed Nigel the packet of paper and looked at Mark. "You are lucky; you are with one of the most decorated detectives in Australia, a real Sherlock Holmes." She winked at the two and moved on to the next group.

Mark looked at Nigel with wide eyes. "Wow, I bet you've solved a lot of cases."

"A few," Nigel let that line of conversation drop. "Let's read the initial findings and then decide on a direction to take with the investigation." Each read the opening to the case and the initial findings. They went section by section and wrote down all of the theories and techniques they would use to solve the case. Mark handed in their answers.

Mark had no way of knowing, but this short course on fraud would play a major role with his career in the future.

Nigel slipped out of the classroom to his small cubical on the fourth floor. His boss was waiting for him.

§

Nigel's boss saw him enter the large room used for all of the fraud bureau detectives.

"Nigel I need to speak to you about your partner. Let's go to your cubical." His boss knew this was not going to be news that Nigel wanted to hear. "Your partner has been reassigned to Perth and will be moving next week. I'm sorry for such a sudden move, but an opening came up in Perth and as you know he and his wife are originally from Perth."

Nigel looked at his boss. The news was a shock. His partner had given him no indication this was in the works. They had been together for four years. "I can't say I'm thrilled, but he deserves a chance to return to his home town. I'm happy for him. How long has this been in the works?"

"It just happened late yesterday. I got a call from Perth that they had an opening and wanted to know if I had anyone to recommend." He looked at Nigel for a reaction.

"Yes, well that's why I didn't know. He and his wife are from Perth and I've heard him say that he wished an opening would come so they could return. I'm happy you chose him. He'll be very happy. Who do you have in mind to assign as my partner?"

"I think you have already met your new partner. She has been conducting the fraud classes." He watched Nigel's face at learning his new partner was a woman.

"I just left that class. I'm impressed with her knowledge of modern police technology, especially when it comes to fraud. I'm looking forward to working with her."

"Good, detective Mathews will report to our division tomorrow."

Chapter 4

Complaint

Two years later:

The Superintendant of Australia's elite Federal fraud squad sat at his desk with his chin in the palm of his hand. Someone with a lot of pull had instructed him to send out his best people on what he considered a wild goose chase. He had summoned his best two.

"Have a seat. Can I get you anything?"

"No thanks Sir" said Nigel Bowman as he folded his tall body into a chair in front of the desk.

The Superintendant looked appraisingly at Nigel, who had a habit of turning his wedding ring with his right hand when he was seated in the Superintendant's office.

"Nothing for me either", said Joyce Mathews. She held several degrees from the University of Sydney, one in criminal justice, one in accounting and a Master's degree in financial management. She was still the only female in the department. Twice married and twice divorced, she was well thought of in the department and had made Senior Inspector.

These two have been together for over two years. They really work well together. They deserved their promotions to Senior Inspectors. The Superintendant pulled at his ear to break his rambling thoughts. "The Attorney General's office wants us to check into a complaint lodged by a couple in Sydney. They claim their lottery winnings have been stolen by an investment firm that was recommended by someone connected to the Lottery Board." The Superintendent raised his eyes towards the ceiling.

Nigel sat still. He had heard of other cases where lottery winnings had flown the coop and the winners ended up broke. "Superintendant, how much money did they invest?"

"A shade under 4 million dollars and according to the complaint, most is gone."

"Wow! When did they win this lot?" asked Joyce who normally sat and listened without comment.

"They won the national lottery two years ago. The couple's complaint says they have repeatedly asked the investment firm for an accounting, but are only given a bunch of undecipherable spreadsheets. They engaged an accountant and he told them that he could not make heads or tails of the information either. The couple holds the Lottery Board to blame, claiming someone connected to the board recommended the firm."

"Did the AG say if there has been a crime committed?" asked Nigel.

The Superintendant thought for a moment, "I'm guessing, but I think the Attorney General wants to get to the bottom of the allegations and determine if a crime has been committed, primarily because of the large amount of money involved and the constant newspaper articles blasting the lottery board's lack of concern for its winners. I don't think it will look good for the Lottery Board if the complaint is true and became public."

"Did the AG's representative give any instructions as to how they thought the investigation should be conducted?" Nigel was not born in a sheep pen; he knew that if politics was involved, the

AG had to cover his backside. He thought, *if there is substance to this, the AG will want favorable press showing his aggressive investigation. Elections were only a few months away.*

"No instructions, just check into the matter and determine if the couple's claim has any merit and if a crime has in fact been committed." He threw a thin folder with the particulars over to Nigel.

"Okay Superintendant, we'll give it a go. What's the time frame for us to report back on this?"

"Take as much time you need, but I should think that an interview with the couple and the investment firm should be enough to smoke out any problems."

§

"No, I've not heard of anything about an investigation concerning any of our client's investments", said Fredric Peters managing director of Secure Pacific Investments. A frown appeared on his face as he listened to more. He was a short heavyset man with a pock marked face and short wavy black hair. He picked a piece of lent from his expensive suit, which was the latest fashion. He straightened his tie from one of Sydney's elite men's clubs, never mind he had never set foot in it.

The voice over the phone said, "I heard some talk about a complaint lodged by Marty and Denise Jenkins. I think you should be prepared to answer any inquiry made." The deep voice was stern and to the point.

"Okay, that's not a problem boss", said Peters, a smooth talker who had sold investment opportunities in real estate that didn't exist, shares in new companies never formed and even shares in plays and movies that were never produced. Peters was hired because of his past and his special skills. He made well above the going salary for his position and enjoyed many perks. He didn't need petty schemes any longer. This was the big time. His boss never came to check on him; in fact his boss had never even set foot in the company offices. He knew his boss well and so did most of Australia, but in fact had never really met the man. Peters had been hired over the phone.

Peters put the phone down. He grinned as he thought about their scheme. *It's like taking candy from a babe.* Oh how I love this job. He was very careful to document how his clients chose all the investments, even if they were not aware they were choosing only the ones he wanted them to select. Peters looked out of his window on the eighth floor that faced the Sydney harbour. The bridge was busy today and he could see cars backed up at the toll booths. There was talk of a tunnel someday.

§

Nigel and Joyce left the Superintendant's office and returned to their small but comfortable cubical. Their desks faced each other. On the wall were two of Australia's highest police commendation certificates awarded to Nigel and Joyce by the Prime Minister.

Nigel slumped down in his swivel chair and pitched the folder onto the top of his desk. He said, "Here we go again, chasing after the political football to cover somebody's backside. Make the call to the Jenkins' and set up an appointment this afternoon and I'll get us on the Canberra-Sydney flight. I'll read over the case file and collect some names and addresses."

"Okay, should I make reservations for over-night accommodations?"

"That's a good idea. Given the time, we could be there too late for the last fight back." He'd have to phone his wife and inform her he would be out of town on a case, again. After 18 years, she accepted his last minute dash out of town as a normal part of their marriage. Nigel pulled a dog-eared map of Sydney from his desk drawer. He loved Sydney, but it was too big and noisy for his wife who never failed to tell him how she loved the small town atmosphere of Canberra with its clean streets and parks.

Joyce made an appointment for 16:30 with the Jenkins'. She phoned her mum to pick up her nine year old son from school. Her mum loved to keep him while Joyce had to go out of town on assignments.

The flight to Sydney was short and arrived on time. A detective from the Sydney office had delivered an unmarked car and waited until they arrived. He turned over the keys, got Nigel's signature on the receipt, and left with another detective.

"I'll drive and you navigate", said Joyce.

Nigel unfolded his dog eared map. "I studied the map and it looks straight forward to me. About a ten minute drive according to the map. Take the M-5 to Southern Cross Drive follow through the tunnel, turn left onto Botany Road and their street is just off to the right. When we get close I'll give you the house number details." As they drove, Nigel noted the dozens of modest homes and businesses were along the way.

Nigel and Joyce parked in front of the small neat home of Marty and Denise Jenkins. Nigel observed the house and the neighborhood. "Well it doesn't appear they spent any winnings on buying a mansion", said Nigel as they walked to the front door. Nigel pressed the button and heard a melodious chime from within the house.

The door opened, "Yes, may I help you?" said Denise Jenkins, a small petite woman with small wire rimmed glasses which gave her a grandmotherly look. She was wearing an apron with white baking flour showing in spots.

"I'm Inspector Bowman and this is Inspector Mathews. We have an appointment".

"Oh yes, do come in we've been expecting you. Marty is in the back watching the game on the telly. I was fixing our tea. Give me a minute and I'll fetch him." She hurried off down the hallway.

"This is a charming little place and neat as pin. Can you smell that bread baking? Reminds me of my own mum baking bread for Sunday tea." said Joyce.

A man of about sixty years, in a monogrammed work shirt, returned with Denise and introduced himself as Marty Jenkins. "Please, can we offer you something?"

"No thank you Mr. Jenkins", said Nigel. "We are here to ask a few questions about your complaint filed with Attorney General's office." Nigel and Joyce sat down on the sofa.

"Oh yes! Well, Denise and I are very concerned about our investments. We have some money left from the original payout mind you, but our investments are a mystery to us."

"You say you got an original payout. How did you receive your payout?" asked Joyce.

"When we met with the managing director of our investment firm, he gave us a draft for $250,000 when we turned over our lottery cheque for four million to him."

While Joyce was speaking with Marty, Nigel picked up a framed picture on the coffee table of two boys in their teens. He looked around at the appointments in the room. *Nothing fancy, old style TV, furniture seemed comfortable and well used and the house in general appeared to be twenty to thirty years old but very clean and neat.*

"So you actually got a cash payment of $250,000", said Joyce.

"Yes, we deposited it to our account in the Westpac branch near here. I was about to be redundant from work, the plant was closing you see, so the money was a God send. We are very frugal people and have most of it still in our account. My pension doesn't amount to much."

The questions and answers went on for about thirty minutes. To Joyce it was apparent the couple was not conversant with financial matters. Marty explained to Nigel and Joyce why they thought their winnings were being embezzled by the firm recommended by someone they thought was from the Lottery Board. During the questions it came out they had selected their investments from a list provided by their investment firm. They were receiving quarterly reports from the investment firm, but their oldest son, a bookkeeper, said he couldn't understand them and advised seeking the advice of a chartered accountant. Marty said he had called Mr. Peters, of the investment firm, for his help, but was told the papers were self-explanatory. Not happy with the explanation, he and Denise filed the complaint.

"Mr. Peters is the managing director of the investment firm?" asked Nigel.

"Yes, he is the only one we have talked to at the investment company."

"Can we see your papers from the investment company?" asked Joyce.

Denise looked at Marty and nodded. She went to the back of the house and returned with a small metal box. "These are all the papers we have received from the investment company." Joyce studied one of the spread sheets. She unfolded a document from the box that was a Secure Pacific Investment agreement. She saw that the Jenkins' had signed it authorizing the firm to engage investments on their behalf.

"Mr. Jenkins, do you mind if we take these to our office and make copies?" Joyce asked.

"No, of course not, you do what you want with them; they're no good to us."

Nigel and Joyce thanked the Jenkins' and assured them the police were looking into their complaint and would be back in contact in a few days. They left the Jenkins' house and drove to the Hilton hotel in the Rocks area of Sydney. They Checked in and agreed to meet for dinner later.

Chapter 5

Secure Pacific Investments

Fredric Peters began the task of preparing for any inquiries that may come up about the Jenkins'. He phoned the Napier Horse Auction in New Zealand and spoke to the office manager. He posed as one of their customers from Bangkok. "I want to thank you Miss Thurman for taking your time to speak with me. Some of my competitors are jealous and may try to find out what I purchased. Have you received any queries for any information about our transactions?"

"No sir. I've not received any calls. This is our off season and I'm the only one in the office." said the office manager. She knew that Bangkok was the source of many purchases.

"Okay, thanks", replied Peters hanging up the phone. He pulled open the drawer of a large file cabinet and retrieved a file of information labeled Marty and Denise Jenkins.

Peters picked up the phone and called a number in Singapore. "This is Mr. O'Brian, pass code 8790. Do you have any mail for me?"

"Hold sir, let me check", said the voice on the phone. "Yes sir, there are two letters, one from the Singapore Fidelity Bank and another from Telecom."

"Okay, forward the letters to the usual postal box." He disconnected.

§

"These mud bugs are lovely, I am hungry," said Joyce. She looked through the glass wall of the main restaurant on the mezzanine into the lobby of the Sydney Hilton directly below. It was full of patrons busy checking in and pulling their bags up to the counter.

"They are that. I always enjoy the Sydney mud bugs when we come here. Have you had time to digest the paper-work we got from the Jenkins?" He took a sip from his wine glass.

"Well, I couldn't make much from them. I have never seen anything like these documents that are meant to be reports for investments." Joyce used her serviette to tap at the corners of her mouth. "I have read all of the documents and made copies."

Nigel paused and placed his fork on his plate. "Is there anything sticking out as fraudulent?"

"Nothing specific in itself, but if this is the type of accounting they provide to their investors, then they are asking for trouble, but poor reporting in itself is not illegal, only stupid." Joyce turned up a corner of her mouth in disgust.

"What about the agreement document, does it have anything that indicates fraud?"

"Odd thing about that document. The Jenkins' signed a document that gives Secure Pacific full authority to invest their money into anything it desires and absolves Secure Pacific from any losses that may occur. Each transaction is charged a fee which is surprisingly very small in relationship to the amount of the transactions. So in a nut shell, the Jenkins' have no cause to complain, as I interpret the agreement. On first look, I'd say we're chasing after nothing" said Joyce.

"Hummm, tomorrow let's pop around to Secure Pacific and interview the managing director. I'm thinking along the same lines and maybe this is going nowhere. The Jenkins' may be victims of their own incompetence in matters of investments. I'll phone the investment firm first thing in the morning and make an appointment", said Nigel.

"Why call and warn them we are coming, let's just drop by tomorrow."

Nigel raised his eyebrows and nodded okay. They finished dinner, had a drink at the bar in the lobby, and retired to their respective rooms for the evening.

§

Peters made a call to Singapore. "Hello, Mr. Chung, this is Fredric Peters in Sydney. How are you today?"

"I'm fine Mr. Peters, what can I do for you?"

"I need you to be prepared to answer a few queries that may be posed in the near future. This concerns the company in Singapore."

"Ah, you are referring to Asian Investments. Yes what questions will be asked?"

"Most likely they will want to know if you are the managing director of course and possibly board members names and the normal kind of corporate queries. You may say that you are the managing director but nothing more. Tell them it is a private company and confidential. Call me if you get any queries." He broke the connection and sat back to ponder any other areas they may probe into. Because Peters paid Chung well, Chung would follow instructions to the letter. There should be no problem if someone contacted Singapore. The probe would most likely end with a phone call or two.

§

"I love the breakfast buffet at the Hilton", said Nigel as he consumed his breakfast.

"Lovely," said Joyce. "Have you looked up the address for Secure Pacific?"

"Yep, just across the bridge in North Sydney, right on High Street and left on Clark Road. Just up the hill. It shouldn't take us but 15 minutes to get there."

"If I remember right, parking is a bugger along Clark Road. I'm not sure if there is a car park on Clark Road." said Joyce.

"If not we'll park in a red zone and put up our Official Police business sign."

Joyce saw Nigel come through the revolving door to the covered drive. The car was waiting. Nigel drove. "You got any coins for the toll?"

"Yep, here you go. Don't you ever carry coins?"

"Nope, they punch holes through my pockets and make a bunch of noise when I walk—very annoying", said Nigel. "Besides, my wife collects all my coins each night." Joyce shook her head and smiled.

They drove across the bridge and turned right into High street. Joyce saw a traffic policeman writing tickets for cars with expired meters. Turning left on to Clark Road Nigel spied an empty parking space on the left just up from the address of Secure Pacific. Parked, they entered the building and read the directory mounted on the wall. The lift was waiting and Joyce pressed the eighth floor button.

The entrance to the Secure Pacific Investments, Ltd. was a smoked glass door. There was no lobby, only a medium size room with two desks and file cabinets. Three glassed in cubicles opened off the room; one had a man working at a desk. He appeared to be in his early forties with a full head of well-groomed short wavy black hair. As they entered the main room, he looked up.

"May I help you?"

Nigel stepped to the door of the cubicle, "Yes we are here to see Mr. Peters."

"I'm Fredric Peters."

"Mr. Peters, I am Inspector Bowman and this is Inspector

Mathews. We would like a bit of your time."

"Sure, have a seat. What can I help you with?"

"We are investigating a complaint made by a lottery winner. The complaint alleges that your firm may have mishandled the investments for a couple named Jenkins", said Nigel.

"I see. I'm not sure if I know exactly to whom you are referring; let me bring up their data." Peters turned and typed into his computer. "Ah, here we are Marty and Denise Jenkins. They have made several investments through our firm. I'm afraid with somewhat unsuccessful results. Of course this is confidential information", said Peters.

"Mr. Peters, the quarterly reports that you sent to the Jenkins' are hard to understand. Would you mind going over them with me?" said Joyce.

"Miss Mathew is it? I must have permission from the Jenkins' before I can discuss their account. "

"Come now Mr. Peters, we are here to investigate a complaint. We can do this with your cooperation or we can get a court order. Of course there would be a public record of that and the press is very diligent latching onto these kinds of things", said Nigel.

Peters looked at the two without any emotional clues. "Inspector Bowman, I assure you that if you were an investor with our firm, I would treat your account the same. I will be glad to phone the Jenkins' to get their verbal permission with you and Miss Mathew as witnesses. Would that be satisfactory?"

"Make your call Mr. Peters, and its Inspector Mathews", said Nigel.

Joyce sat and watched the body language of Peters. He was cool. No sign of deception. Nothing to indicate he was lying. She watched him read the number from his computer screen for the Jenkins'. They answered and Peters pressed the phone's speaker button.

Peters asked, "Mr. Jenkins, Inspectors Bowman and Mathews are here inquiring into your account. Do you give them permission to view your account records?"

Marty's voice came through the speaker, "Yes sir. They can

look at anything that is ours and you may discuss any of our business with them."

"Thank you Mr. Jenkins. That will be all." He pressed the off button to disconnect the line. "Now what is it you would like to know about their account?"

From her small case, Joyce took out the paper-work the Jenkins' had given them. "I would like to go over these spread sheets with you and have you explain what they mean."

Peters smiled and said of course. They spent the better part of 20 minutes discussing the spread sheets. Joyce made some notes and Nigel sat trying to follow the conversation.

Joyce said, "Mr. Peters, it seems to me that all of their investments have been either very bad or are about to tank. What do you have to say about this?"

"Well, I am very concerned about their poor choices. The Jenkins' invested almost all of their winnings with an Investment firm in Singapore. The firm in turn invested heavily into race horses owned by a horse breeding company in Hong Kong. The Hong Kong firm failed and eventually the horses had to be sold off and brought only a fraction of their purchase price. The company was wound up after only a few months in business. Their account value with the Singapore investment firm plunged to nothing. Their investment in mining shares in Queensland turned out to be a very long shot that eventually failed. I'm afraid they have very little left in their account."

"Mr. Peters, who made the selection list of firms for investing?" asked Nigel.

"I'm assuming they made up the list. I rarely get involved in the selection of investments; I only handle the transactions for the client and register the shares", said Peters.

Joyce noticed Peters left eye twitched as he spoke. "So, you say that the Jenkins' had their own list to make their investments", asked Joyce.

"Yes, I don't know where they got their list."

Nigel looked at Joyce and said, "Thank you Mr. Peters. That is all for today. We will be in touch and let you know how the investigation is going."

Peters looked at Nigel and said, "Thank you Inspector. Please phone or pop by anytime. I'm here to help."

"Oh, by the way, how many employees do you have?"

"It's only me. We have a very small clientele and I can handle all that is necessary."

Nigel and Joyce got up and shook hands with Fredric Peters. They proceeded to the lift. Abruptly Nigel turned and walked swiftly back into the office and right up to Peter's desk. "Sorry I thought I left my note pad. Oops, apparently not, here it is in my coat pocket." As Nigel walked up to Peter's desk, he heard Peters say, "They threatened to get a court order. What was I to do?"

Nigel returned to the lift and caught up with Joyce. "Well, he has someone that he gets instructions from. I heard him speaking to someone about our threat to get a court order. I'm not sure what to make of this whole thing. I can't see any laws broken."

"The Jenkins' say that the selection list was prepared by Peters, Peters said that he did not have any knowledge of where the selection came from. We have someone not telling the truth, but why?" said Joyce.

"Personally, I believe the Jenkins'. With the exception of the mining company, I don't think they would have a clue that the Singapore firm existed. Peters on the other hand has every reason to disavow any knowledge of the list. It would tie him directly into the selection process. It's the classic their word against his." said Nigel.

"Maybe the Jenkins' are embarrassed by the poor choices and are looking for someone to blame. Don't forget, the investment agreement gives Secure Pacific every right to invest the Jenkins' money anyway they want and not be held accountable for any losses. Given that, why would Peters care if we knew he produced the list or someone else?" asked Joyce.

"Let's go to the Company Registration Office and look up the Secure Pacific Investment company", said Nigel.

§

They walked down the steps of the Australian Company Registration Office. "Well, their paperwork only showed that Peters is the registered agent and a shareholder but that was about it. The company was formed a month before the Jenkins' engaged the firm."

"I'm wondering if they have other clients and if so, did they win the lottery also?" asked Joyce.

"Good question, how do we find this out?" asked Nigel.

"We could try to get a search warrant to check Secure Pacific's files, but we're not even sure if a crime has been committed."

"Okay, let's check in at the police Head Office and see what we can dig up on Peters. He seemed too smooth and pat for my taste" said Nigel.

They arrived at the Sydney police head office and were assigned the visiting detective's office. A small inter office with no windows. There was one table with a computer terminal and two chairs. The walls were bare with the exception of a large cork board on the back wall. Nigel spread out his case folder and logged into the police network. He brought up a search engine, and typed in Fredric Peters. It took only a blink of the eye to register a hit. The information showed many complaints filed against Peters from petty larceny to major fraud. There was only one conviction and that was for a minor charge of cheque kitting three years ago. He was a person of interest in a major fraud scheme of a local bank a month before Secure Pacific Investments was formed. No charges were ever filed for a lack of evidence. "Well, it appears Mr. Peters is a very careful man. Not one major conviction and only one arrest. He comes close to the edge but has never been charged with anything major" said Nigel.

Joyce made notes from the screen. She looked up, "I think we may have something. Peters represented a car as being his and tried to borrow $20,000 against it from the bank that filed the fraud complaint. They could not confirm that Peters owned the car and the loan was never completed. There is no record of him ever owning or registering a car. I think we may have leverage to check into the particulars of the vehicle. It may have been stolen. The investigating detective is named Macfarlane. There is no record he checked out the car registration since the loan was never completed. I'll phone the bank and make an appointment. They should have all the registration information about the car."

"Great, I'll talk to the detective in charge of the investigation and get his take on Peters. Let's meet back here in an hour" said Nigel.

Nigel called the watch commander and inquired into detective MacFarlane who investigated the complaint filed by the bank. He was told the detective was in the squad room at the moment. Nigel went to squad room and found MacFarlane.

The detective couldn't remember much about the case. "It was a two day thing that was closed because no real crime had been committed. We could not prove that Peters had stolen the car. The vehicle was reported missing, but then it turned up at the owner's house a week later," said MacFarlane. Nigel thanked the detective.

§

Joyce phoned the bank and asked if they could fax over a copy of the loan papers pertaining to Peters' application for a loan. The police case files had a loan number which made the inquiry fast. Within a few minutes a clerk came in with the fax. The car was a Rover, one year old with a registration plate number YKJ-359. Joyce entered the registration number into the police automobile registration system. It returned the owner as Abraham Weinstein of Rush Cutters Bay. Joyce entered the name into the system and it came up with a complaint filed by Mr. Weinstein a week before Peters made an application for the loan. Weinstein reported his car missing. A week later he withdrew his missing car complaint.

Nigel came into the small office and took a seat. Joyce looked up from her note writing and said, "I may have something. It appears the car Peters represented on the bank loan application as his car was actually a vehicle reported missing a week prior to the date on the application. I checked the stolen vehicle file and the car was not listed as stolen, strange? I was about to phone Mr. Weinstein the owner when you came in." Joyce punched in the phone number listed for Mr. Abraham Weinstein. It rang.

"Hello, this is Abe" said a voice.

"Mr. Weinstein, this is Inspector Joyce Mathews with the police. I would like to ask you a few questions about a complaint you made a few years ago regarding your missing automobile."

"Yes, I filed a complaint. What questions do you have?"

"Our records show that your car was never listed as stolen. Can you explain what happened to your car?"

"Well, I'm not sure what happened to it. It was missing for a week or so, then one morning I went out to get the paper and there it was right back in front of my home. It had a full tank of petrol and appeared to have been thoroughly cleaned. I was never sure who took it, but they sure took good care of it" said Weinstein.

"Did the police check the car after it was returned?"

"I phoned them and said it had been returned. They never contacted me after that."

"Okay, Mr. Weinstein, thank you for your time. Goodbye", Joyce hung up the phone.

Nigel was looking at Joyce for an update. She told him about the car being missing but then returned all clean and full of petrol. "I think we have enough to get a warrant to check Peters' credit cards and phone records with regards to the loan application listing a car not belonging to Peters. Even if the case is a few years old, it was never resolved. It's a cold case and we are checking it out."

"I'm not sure. It seems we are on a wild goose chase. We don't know that a crime has been committed. How do we justify checking on an old missing car case and tying it to the Jenkins case?"

"Right, well let's do this, check with the Attorney General's office and get a feel for how to proceed. If they say go for it, then we can most likely wrap this up by tomorrow and go home" said Joyce.

Nigel phoned the AG's office in Canberra. The Deputy AG said to proceed to determine if a crime had been committed and he would get a warrant faxed within the next hour to check out the phone and credit card records of Peters. The fax arrived at 3 pm. By 4 pm they had all the phone and credit card records faxed to them. Joyce noted that Peters had four credit cards and two phones. She checked the dates on the credit cards with respect to purchasing petrol on the dates of the missing car. One of the credit cards showed a purchase of petrol at a station near Darlington Point, not far from Weinstein's home. Another card showed a purchase of a car wash the same day.

Nigel said, "This proves nothing. It only shows he bought fuel and had a car washed. It doesn't say it was Weinstein's car. But, it is strange that Peters appears to have needed money and then abruptly abandoned the idea. This occurred near the same time Secure Pacific was registered."

Joyce had a worried look, "I know, and under the circumstances it gives us reason to suspect Mr. Peters of something, but what? I checked out the phone number he called at the time of our visit to his office. He called a mobile number that is one of those pay as you go phones, totally untraceable. The same number appears several times. There are many calls to Singapore and Hong Kong. Also two calls to New Zealand. I think I would like to call these numbers and check out who they are."

"Yep, if we get a connection to the Jenkins' case then we proceed. If not, we close the case.

Chapter 6

Preparation

Fredric Peters made a phone call to a number in Bangkok. He spoke only three words, "Call me back". Peters settled back in his desk chair and watched the traffic cross the "Coat Hanger", the nick name for the Sydney Harbour Bridge. After several minutes his phone rang. He answered on the third ring, which was the protocol. "Fredric Peters speaking, may I help you?"

A voice with a Thailand accent said, "Do you need help?"

"Yes, I need preparations for an exit. I will need first class tickets with open dates issued in the name of Barry O'Brian from Sydney to Singapore, on to Hong Kong and then to Bangkok. Set these up and overnight to the usual address. Your fee will be transferred in the next few minutes."

"You will have the package tomorrow morning." The call terminated.

Peters opened his safe and took out a new mobile phone and several documents. They were bank statements. He checked the balances and phoned the banks. He started transferring funds. If he had to move fast he wanted the money to be in a place only he could get to it. He made the regular transfer to an account that was not under his control. Peters assumed it was an account for his boss, even if it was in Vanuatu. He wanted everything to look normal. If things smoothed out he could always reverse the funds to their original accounts. There had not been any new Lottery winners signing up in the last few months. The fun had all but gone from the scheme. The totals were approaching over ten million dollars. Maybe it was time to move on. He had that prickly feeling things were happening and not to his advantage.

§

Joyce placed a call to the unlisted number. She used the police system phone that would not show its number on the caller ID. She heard the ringing tone.

"Hello, what do you want?" said a deep resonant voice crisp and almost rude.

Nigel was on the line listening. His eyebrows went up. He signaled to Joyce to hang up. She disconnected the call. "Who was that, did you recognize the voice?" said Joyce.

"I think I know that voice. I guess we can say we have found a connection to Jenkins. Wow, you never know where these things lead."

Joyce sat and stared at the case folder. "Now what? Whoever that was doesn't prove anything and I still can't see where a crime has been committed" said Joyce. She doodled on her writing pad. Nigel reached over and wrote a name on the writing pad. Her eyebrows went up. "Oh crap, this is going to be sticky."

"We have to get the Jenkins' to identify who told them to use Secure Pacific. Let's get a few pictures of the lottery board members and take them by the Jenkins' to see if they can identify him" said Nigel.

That evening, armed with the pictures, Nigel and Joyce went to the Jenkins' home. Marty studied the pictures for several minutes and pointed to one, "That's the man from the Lottery Board that gave me the brochure. Denise what do you think?"

"Yes, but it's been so long. I just don't know." She wrung her hands and looked down at the floor. "I'm so sorry, but I just can't accuse someone if I'm not positive."

"That's okay Mrs. Jenkins. I'd rather you be in doubt than point out the wrong person", said Joyce.

Marty stared at the picture. "I'm sure that is 'em. He was the one that gave me a brochure about Secure Pacific Investments" said Marty. "Denise, get the photo album." Denise went to a closet in the hall and took out a thick photo album and handed it to Marty. Marty turned several pages until he pointed to a picture. It was of himself posing with a celebrity. It was clear the man was handing Marty a document of some sort.

Nigel looked at Marty's eyes. They did not waver. "Do you know this man's name?"

"Everybody knows 'em. At the time, I did not know who gave me the brochure, but I'm certain of it now." Marty stared at the pictures. "There were lots of people and photographers snapping pictures. I was so confused and overwhelmed, I forgot it was 'em, but I know 'e is the one that gave me the brochure and we posed for pictures. I was so nervous that I don't remember what I said to 'em. I do remember that Sir Rodney told us to seek professional advice. He didn't say any particular firm. When we were driving home, I remembered the brochure in my jacket pocket. I gave it to Denise to look over. We called Secure Pacific Investments on Tuesday morning."

§

Peters' phone buzzed. "This is Peters, may I help you?"

"Did you give out my special mobile number? I just received a call and the person hung up. I never receive calls on this phone except from you" said the deep voice.

"No, I'd never give out your number" said Peters.

"Well, it bloody well had not been you." The phone clicked off. Peters sat thinking. *The boss is getting paranoid with the investigation going on—probably just a wrong number. I think the Inspectors are done anyway. Nothing they can prove.*

§

Nigel phoned the AG's office and spoke to the AG's personal assistant first thing the following morning. He explained the results of showing the pictures to Marty Jenkins. The AG's PA was shocked.

"One of the persons identified by Mr. Jenkins is a personal friend of the AG," said the personal assistant. He told Nigel to sit tight until he could speak to the AG. He would call back in about an hour with instructions.

Nigel went to the break room for tea. He fixed two cups and took them back to the borrowed office.

Joyce was working on the computer tracking some of the other phone numbers on the list. She reached and took the tea. "I think there is a lot going on but for the life of me, I can't find a crime committed. Even if our new suspect did give the brochure to the Jenkins', and even if they lost all of their money, there is no clear crime committed. If we can find other lottery winners who also were encouraged to use Secure Pacific Investments by our suspect, then we have more smoke but no fire. Somehow we have to tie him to Secure Pacific Investments."

"Was the brochure in that box of stuff we got from the Jenkins'? asked Nigel.

"I think so, let me look." She opened the box and rummaged through its contents. "Yes here it is. What do you need it for?"

"Maybe there is a finger print or even better DNA. That would be conclusive evidence that the brochure was given to Marty Jenkins at the awards ceremony. Let's have it checked out by the lab." Joyce carefully placed the brochure into an evidence bag with a note to identify the finger prints and any DNA available. She rang the office clerk to come and fetch the bag and have it sent to the lab.

"Let's check out the overseas numbers and see where that

leads," said Joyce.

The phone rang. "This is Nigel Bowman." Nigel listened and reached for his pad. He jotted down some information and hung up. "Well that was the AG's office. They want us the dig up all we can but to keep it to ourselves and only the AG's office. He gave me a special number to call with reports. What do you make of that?"

"It sounds to me like we have turned over the proverbial rock and things are squirming to get back out of sight. I think we have a real serious case of political fallout and if we aren't very careful and cross every tee, we may be the ones trying to find a rock to crawl under."

"My feelings exactly. We need to document every single thing we've done so far, and then list all the theories and a procedure to run down every lead" said Nigel.

A knock on the door was the clerk to collect the evidence bag.

They spent the better part of the morning writing on 3X5 cards and pinning them to the cork board. They posted a do not disturb sign on their office door and pushed the lock button to keep any eyes from seeing their notes and theories. They were careful not to put any names on the board.

"Well that's the best we can do without more information. I don't think we want to interview our new suspect until we are sure he is really involved. The lab report should confirm if his finger prints are on the brochure. Let's start with the New Zealand connection."

Joyce punched in the New Zealand number from the list. They both could hear the ringing tone on the speaker phone. A female voice answered. "Napier Horse Auction, Miss. Thurman speaking."

"Miss. Thurman, this is Inspector Joyce Mathews with the Australian Police, we are running down items in a case here. We ran across your phone number and would like to ask you a few questions."

"Why sure. What can I do to help?"

"Can you tell me about your business?"

"Sure, we auction race horses for our clients. Many of them are sent overseas, especially to the United States."

Joyce paused, "Miss Thurman, over the past couple of years, have there been any large purchases of horses by any Australian company or individuals?"

"No, nothing comes to mind. We did have a few horses purchased by some men in Bangkok. Those purchases were very unusual as they never were here to personally bid."

Nigel and Joyce looked at each other. Joyce said, "Miss Thurman, can you get permission to fax us the names of the individuals that purchased the horses and any documents that are associated with those transactions?"

"Sure, I have the authority to release to you that information. It's fairly common in this business to cooperate with the authorities. Many horses are stolen and are hard to track down. Horses don't have serial numbers or license plates you see. I will fax you all I have by Tomorrow."

"Thank you very much Miss Thurman. What was the largest purchase over the last two years?"

"That's easy; a Hong Kong company purchased, in a private sale, fifty horses for $3 million Australian dollars. They were new clients of ours. The horses they purchased never left our lot and they were resold a few months later to company in Bangkok. The price they got caused them a substantial loss on the sale. I guess that is why they are no longer in business. The odd thing is the Bangkok firm never claimed their stock. The horses are still here."

"Are you saying that the horses sold to Hong Kong then resold to Bangkok have never left your premises?" said Joyce.

"Yes that is correct. Our company has received payment for the feed and upkeep for the past year and half. Our client has not instructed me what to do with the horses. I have repeatedly requested disposition, but I've been told to keep them on our lots till further notice."

"Who did you contact for payment of the upkeep?" asked Joyce.

"I'll have to dig that up. I'll include those documents with the others and send them to you. Give me a fax number."

Joyce gave her the fax number, thanked her and hung up. She sat for a few seconds staring at the cork board. "It seems the horses were not important. It's really looking like a definite money laundering scheme."

Nigel said, "Until we receive the auction company's information, we can pursue the other information on our list. Let's check out this Singapore firm, Asian Trust. It's on the quarterly reports given to the Jenkins'. They opened a large account in that company, nearly their entire winnings."

Nigel placed the call to Asian Trust but with little satisfactory results. Mr. Chung was polite but didn't answer many questions. He explained that under Singapore law, his company was private and he could not reveal who the shareholders were or who was on the board of directors.

"I have been giving a lot of thought about the investments made on behalf of the Jenkins. If this is fraud, we need to follow the money. If we can prove the money came back to either Peters or our suspect, then we have fraud. Let's work up a theory to launder money using race horses," said Joyce.

For the next few hours Joyce drew diagrams and wrote theories of how the money laundering could have been pulled off.

Nigel looked at his watch. "Let's quit for the evening and go have dinner."

Joyce rubbed her forehead and nodded agreement. She phoned the Hilton and extended their rooms for two more days.

Nigel locked the borrowed office and posted a do not disturb sign on the door. He told the watch commander they would be back in the morning and not to allow anyone, including the cleaning crew into their temporary office. Nigel drove up York Street deep in thought. Joyce sat quietly thinking about the money trail. They arrived at the Hilton and turned their car over to the valet to park.

"Let's meet for dinner in half an hour and talk about the money trail", said Nigel.

Joyce nodded and said nothing. They took the lift to their floor.

Nigel called the Canberra office to check in with the Superintendent. They chatted for a few minutes and Nigel disconnected. He looked at his watch and noticed that it was time to meet Joyce in the restaurant for dinner.

§

"I checked in with the Superintendent and updated him on where we were without revealing our suspect's name. I told him we would give the case two more days", said Nigel.

"I've been thinking about the money trail. If we are going to make a connection with either Peters or our suspect, then we will have to have a bank identify them as the owner of an account where the money was transferred", said Joyce.

"Yes, that will mean we will have to go to the banks. Before the Superintendent will give us permission to pursue that lead we will have to come up with some reasonable evidence that will warrant the expense and time. I'm not sure this is going anywhere but let's give it a go."

They ate dinner and retired to their respective rooms. Nigel made a list of questions that had to be answered before they could approach the Superintendent. He turned off the light and slept soundly.

§

Joyce and Nigel ate breakfast in near silence. Nigel pushed back from the table and pulled out his note pad and read off the list of questions to be answered before they could approach the Superintendent with the request to chase the money.

"Those are questions that are going to be hard to answer in 24 hours", said Joyce.

"I know. I thought we could each take a couple of questions and work independently. If we break every two hours for a review of what we have accomplished, then we could speed up the process and not spend too much time on each thread."

"OK, I'll take the horse auction and the Hong Kong company connection. You take the company in Singapore and the Bangkok connections. If our theory on the money trail is correct then we should be able to nail down something by lunch time", said Joyce.

They finished their breakfast, retrieved their car and drove to the police head office. They checked in with the watch commander and walked down the hall to the borrowed office. It took several minutes to review the money trail theory. Each sat and began to make notes on their approach to solve their individual threads to the case.

Joyce phoned the Napier Horse Auction. Miss Thurman was very cooperative and looked up the copies of the cheques that were sent from the party in Bangkok for the upkeep of the horses. Joyce made note of the bank and routing codes that were on the deposit slips. "Miss. Thurman can you fax copies of the cheques made out to the Hong Kong firm and copies of the cheques from Bangkok for the original purchases?"

"Yes Inspector Mathews, I'll send them with the other documents."

Nigel phoned the company registration office in Bangkok. He identified himself and asked to speak to the officer in charge. The man explained that under Bangkok law, he could not discuss the information over the phone; only an in person request would be accommodated. Nigel hung up and made notes. His next call was to the Singapore Company Office where he asked for information about Asian Investments. He got almost an identical reception as he did from Bangkok. He reviewed his notes and decided to call the mining company in Queensland.

"This is police Inspector Bowman. I'm calling in reference to some stock purchase transactions made through an investment firm here in Sydney. I would like to know three things. One, does the company's share registry show shares issued to either Mr. and Mrs. Jenkins or to Secure Pacific Investments of Sydney, two, can you look up the transaction and give me the banking information available for depositing the cheque for the transaction and three, can you give me a copy of the company cheque register for the past three years?"

"I will need to have a written request to present to the creditors committee, the company has been put into receivership and the next meeting will be in three weeks", said the man on the phone.

"What about if I get a court order and search warrant today, do you think you could then process the request?" asked Nigel.

The man hesitated a few seconds and said, "That won't be necessary. Fax me the request and I will send you the information this afternoon." He gave Nigel his fax number.

Nigel hung up the phone and made notes of the time and the three questions. He looked up and saw Joyce smiling as she was writing rapidly on her note pad. She looked up and winked.

Joyce hung up her phone. "Well now, I think I may have a strong lead to the money. A fax will be here shortly with copies of the cheques issued to the auction house by the Bangkok individuals and the Bangkok firm. She is sending us the auction house cheque issued to the Bangkok firm. The Hong Kong firm used a wire transfer, but she has the information that will tell us the banks used in Hong Kong."

"Well done. I've got to fax a request for some info to the mining company in Queensland. It seems the creditors have taken over and I spoke to one of their representatives. He indicated he would have the information available this afternoon. The company registration office in Singapore and Bangkok are dead ends, they will only reveal information if the request is made in person."

Chapter 7

Money Trail

A clerk in the Singapore government's Company Registration office hung up his phone and immediately placed a call to a local mobile phone. The clerk told Chung about someone's attempt to find out information about Asian Investments.

"I see nephew, thank you for your information. You did the right thing. Sometimes our investors get upset if we reveal too much information about them. You have a nice day", said Chung. He hung up and dialed a number in North Sydney.

Peters calmly received the information from Chung. He thanked Chung and sat back in his comfortable chair and stared out the window at downtown Sydney. He began to think. *Is now the time to get out? Are things getting too close?*

§

The police office clerk knocked on the door and handed Nigel a stack of faxes. Nigel saw they were from the horse auction house in New Zealand and handed them over to Joyce.

Joyce sorted them into two piles, Bangkok and Hong Kong. Well this will take some time to sort out who paid what to whom. I'll use the cork board to place the various faxes on a timeline.

Nigel nodded and picked up one of the faxes to examine. "The original purchase of horses came from four individuals in Bangkok. It appears they have the same bank but different accounts. Good idea to map this."

Joyce took 3 X 5 cards and wrote the four names and the dates of the purchases.

Nigel stood back and noted that the purchases were for two to five horses each over a two month period. The fifty horses totaled AUD $100,000. "Now put up the deposit tickets and cheques so we can see the trail of money."

Joyce spent several minutes matching faxes to the timeline. The picture was becoming clearer as to how the money flowed.

Nigel studied the board. "Okay, the first $3.5 million went from Secure Pacific Investments to Asian Investments in Singapore, which was the Jenkins' opening their account."

Joyce consulted Peter's phone records. "From these records, I can't tell if any of these calls from Peters are faxes, most likely not. I would guess that the Secure Pacific Investment's fax machine is on a hard wired phone line."

Nigel was rubbing his hands together. He did this when he was excited about collecting evidence. "We've nailed down the money trail to purchase the original lot of horses. According to the auction house, all the cheques came from four individuals who happened to have accounts in the same bank in Bangkok."

Joyce nodded. "This fax pinned to the auction house shows a deposit from the Hong Kong Horse Breeders of $3 million into the auction house's account in Auckland. This occurred only a week after the last of the 50 horses were purchased."

Nigel picked up a document. "So the $3 million Asian Investments sent to Hong Kong to purchase shares in the Breeding outfit is the most likely source for the Hong Kong firm to purchase the 50 horses from the four gents in Bangkok."

"The four gents in Bangkok bought these horses off the auction floor. I wonder who bid for them," said Joyce.

"Maybe Miss Thurman would remember how they acquired the bids."

"I'll phone her now", said Joyce. She phoned New Zealand and pressed the speaker button. Miss Thurman answered on the second ring. "Miss Thurman, this is Inspector Mathews again, I have a question, and do you have a moment?"

"Why yes Inspector Mathews, what can I help you with?"

"The four gentlemen from Bangkok who purchased the fifty horses, how did they bid for them?"

"They sent us faxes and give me instructions to bid on their behalf. Each gentleman gave a cap of AUD $2,000 per horse and no more than 3 horses at each auction. I gave the faxes to the auctioneer. The auctioneer started each auction with that bid as a reserve. If there were no takers for a higher bid, then the horse was sold to one of the gentlemen from Bangkok until they each had purchased three horses," said Miss Thurman.

"How did the Hong Kong firm purchase the 50 horses these gentlemen acquired?" asked Joyce.

"If I remember correctly, I received a fax from a man who said he represented the Bangkok gentlemen. That fax should be in the group I sent you. The fax contained a document with proper authorization for the man to act on their behalf and was signed by each of the four clients. The fax stated they had reached an agreement to sell to a Hong Kong company the horses in mass without an auction.

"A Hong Kong bank transferred on behalf of Hong Kong Horse Breeders, $3 million dollars. The proceeds, $2.91 million, after our commission, were to be sent to an account at a Bangkok bank. This happens sometimes when a group of horses are purchased for speculation and then sold off to one buyer in a private sale. We still get our commission and the sale is recorded as a private auction. This is what happened in this case.

"A few months after the Hong Kong company purchased the group of horses, they informed me that they had sold the group off to a Bangkok company. The Bangkok company sent me a cheque in the amount of AUD $100,000 and I wrote a cheque for that exact amount to the company in Hong Kong. My boss felt so bad about the loss of nearly $3,000,000 by the Hong Kong Horse Breeders that he decided not to charge a commission on the resale." Miss Thurman cleared her throat and said, "That's all I remember."

"Thank you Miss Thurman, you have been very helpful", said Joyce. She pressed the button to disconnect.

Joyce sat looking at the cork board. "Wow, those were some convoluted transactions. What do you make of it?"

"Well, I think it is definitely an elaborate laundering scheme. Most of the money ended up in Bangkok. How do we tie all of this back to Peters?" Nigel scratched his head.

"We have to verify that Peters owned or had access to the accounts in Singapore, Hong Kong and Bangkok. Let's start with trying to trace the phone number used to fax these bidding instructions." Joyce pulled a couple of the faxes from the pile. She wrote the fax numbers on cards and pinned them to the board.

Nigel looked at the board. "Well there is no connection between the fax numbers as I can see. They are all different."

"Let's send a fax to each of the numbers. We can make the faxes look like a wrong number. Maybe the receiver will respond." Joyce wrote on her note pad, Dear Stephen, we haven't heard from you and are wondering if all is okay, Mum. She read it to Nigel.

Nigel raised an eyebrow. "That is short, doesn't say anything—good"

Joyce wrote the four fax numbers on the top of the note and walked to the desk of the office clerk. "Please send this fax to each of these numbers and if any response comes phone me immediately?" She handed over the note sheet with the four fax numbers.

She returned to the small office. "Okay, now let's grab some lunch and wait."

At an office in Bangkok, four different fax machines spat out the same identical fax message. The clerk looked puzzled. The faxes were in English so she took them to her boss. He read them, each said the same thing. Someone seemed worried about their love one. He told the clerk to send a fax back saying they have a wrong fax number, and inform them that this is a public fax office.

§

While Joyce and Nigel were at lunch, Joyce's mobile rang. She answered. She produced a wide smile and thanked someone and hung up. Nigel sat and stared at her. "Well?"

"That was the office. We got a response from the faxes; all were delivered to the same public fax office. This is now getting interesting" said Joyce.

They sat in silence and finished their lunch. They walked down York Street and took a short cut through a shopping mall back to the police building. When they entered a young man was seated in the waiting area and got up and approached them.

"My name is Mark Young; I'm from the AG's office. He looked at Nigel. "I remember you, we took a fraud class together. I would like to speak to you two in private."

Nigel looked at Joyce, nodded and motioned for the young man to follow them to their office. Nigel borrowed a chair from an empty desk and brought it into their office and closed the door. He offered the young man the seat and he and Joyce sat down. Nigel asked, "Yes I remember that class. In fact Inspector Mathews was our instructor. What can we do for you?"

"I was asked to work with you on the Jenkins case."

Nigel looked at Joyce and Joyce said, "In what way do you want to work with us?"

"I'm not sure. I am a law clerk now in the AG's office. I've really not had any opportunity to work directly with the police before. I was told to keep notes, report twice a day and assist in any way that I could."

"I see, and who gave you these orders" asked Nigel.

"The Attorney General himself" said Young.

There was a moment of silence as this sunk in. Joyce cleared her throat and asked, "Do you have the authority to issue warrants?"

"Yes, in the envelope with my credentials is a document the AG gave me with authority to do whatever is requested by you to gain as much information about this case as possible. I don't have a clue what the case is about, but the AG made it perfectly clear that it is to be treated confidential."

Nigel said, "We have reason to believe that a couple who lodged a complaint against the Lottery Board has been scammed out of three and three quarter million dollars. We have not determined who is actually involved with the exception of one person. There are many overseas connections, but so far we can't prove anything. We have only learned what appears as a money laundering scheme involving the use of race horses, which has accounted for most of the money the Jenkins' lost. We have traced the money from Sydney to Singapore, to Hong Kong, to New Zealand and finally to Bangkok."

Joyce said, "And, to make the matters worse we have discovered a suspect that is a personal friend of the AG and seems to have some connection to the scam."

Mark Young blinked his eyes. It was obvious to both Nigel and Joyce that the AG has chosen not to reveal much.

Nigel said, "Mark, we haven't formed a plan yet, so let us work a while and get things sorted out and meet back here in two hours."

Mark got up, shook hands with Nigel and Joyce and left the office.

Joyce said, "Maybe we can use his authority to our advantage. Let's get a search warrant to look at the books of Secure Pacific Investments.

"Okay, let's create a timeline from the info on the cork board. Then we will know the dates to search for in the files. The warrant should include the computer files too" said Nigel.

They worked for most of the two hours and came to the conclusion that Secure Pacific Investments may hold the key. Mark returned right on time. He took his seat. Nigel went over the details of the timeline. "We found an old case that involved the managing director of Secure Pacific Investments. We had enough evidence to get a warrant to retrieve his phone and credit card records. We interviewed him without any real success. There is a question of who actually created the investment list for the Jenkins', but that was not important because of the agreement giving Secure Investments total control over all investments."

Joyce spoke up, "I made notes of phone calls from Peters' records on those dates. There was not much in the way of phone calls. But, after our visit to Peters' office there was one local call, one to Bangkok, one to Singapore and one to New Zealand and we have the faxes from Bangkok with the bidding instructions."

They each looked a long time at the timeline and the credit card lists and the phone call list. Nigel said, "That looks suspicious but doesn't point to anything we can prove."

Mark raised his hand as if he was in a class room. Nigel said, "Yes Mark. You don't have to raise your hand, just ask the questions, you're part of the team now."

Mark's cheeks turned red. "What if the four individuals in Bangkok do not exist and the instructions for the bidding came from this person Peters to someone in Bangkok who then resent the instructions via fax to New Zealand? If we had access to Secure Pacific's phone records, we could check out any fax numbers to Bangkok and see if any are to the Public Fax Office." Joyce smiled and nodded at Nigel.

Nigel said, "Now that is good thinking. If we can prove that a fax from North Sydney was delivered to the public fax office in Bangkok and resent by someone with the instructions to purchase the horses in New Zealand then we have a very good start on pinning down Peters' connection to the horse scam. Mark, can you come up with a search warrant to give us access to their phone records?"

"Yes, I can issue a warrant for all their phone records as a matter of police an inquiry."

"Great, then let's get on it", said Nigel.

Within an hour, the police clerk came to the tiny office with a fax with the Secure Pacific Investments phone records for the past two years. Nigel took the list and matched the dates with the faxes from Bangkok to the auction house. Each bidding date was matched with a fax from Secure Pacific. The fax number to Bangkok was the same in each case.

Joyce said, "I'll send the same fax we did this morning to that number and see what happens." Joyce opened the door and went to the office clerk's desk and handed her the same note with the fax number in Bangkok that appeared on the Secure Pacific's phone list. Nigel thought about what would be the most important information they could uncover from a search of Secure Pacific. He started a list. Cheque register, cancelled cheques, correspondence, other lottery winners.

Mark watched as Nigel made the list. He asked, "What is that list for?"

"We will need a general search warrant to look for these items at Secure Pacific. Do you think you can get a warrant that would cover that range of things?"

Mark stared at the list. "Why are we looking for these items? I mean if I am to get a judge to issue a general search warrant, I need to know the reason we are looking for these items and what crime has been committed. A phone list is easy, this will be almost impossible without a definite crime."

Joyce reentered the room. She heard the last part of Mark's question. Nigel looked at Joyce and nodded. Joyce said, "As we have explained, we suspect a major fraud has occurred and have reason to believe the Jenkins' have been victims of Secure Pacific Investments and others. The evidence we have is circumstantial at best, but it seems that all of the investments made by the Jenkins' have lost money. The companies the Jenkins invested in were recommended by Secure Pacific, although they said they had nothing to do with the selection process. The faxes to two of the overseas locations are for the people and companies that are involved in the money laundering scheme and are the same as the locations of the investments made by the Jenkins'.

Nigel said, "Hold off on trying a general search warrant just yet. Maybe by tomorrow something will turn-up you can use."

The phone rang. Nigel ~~reached and picked up the phone~~ answered it. "This is Bowman." Nigel listened for a minute or so. "Thank you and could you fax that information to me. Yes to the fax number I gave you this morning." Nigel hung up. "That was the receiver for the Queensland Mining Company. The Jenkins' did own shares in the mining company. The shares were purchased through Secure Pacific Investments. The amount was AUD $25,000. The company went bankrupt two weeks after the shares were purchased. There were over one thousand shareholders and twenty three creditors who will most likely end up with nothing. They are faxing over a list of the creditors and the shareholders with the number of shares held by each."

Joyce said, "I don't see any sign of a scam involving the mining company. The amount is so low compared to the other transactions. I wonder when the trades were made."

Nigel consulted his notes, "The same day as the Jenkins' deposited their cheque with Peters. Let's call the Jenkins' and ask how the choice for the mining shares was made." Joyce picked up the phone and called the Jenkins'.

"Mr. Jenkins, this is Inspector Mathews. I would like to ask you a question about the purchase of some mining shares the day you met with Mr. Peters." Joyce listened, thanked Mr. Jenkins and disconnected. "Mrs. Jenkins wanted to buy the shares because her youngest son was to start work with the mine after school was out. This was the only purchase request given to Peters."

"Okay, so the mining investment can be removed from the money laundering list.

A knock on the door was the office clerk with a return fax. It was the same public fax office in Bangkok. "This proves only one thing, Secure Pacific Investments and the four individuals are using the same fax office", said Joyce.

Mark spoke up, "The dates could not have been happenstance. There has to be a connection."

"I agree, let's check out this tomorrow. I think that is all we can do today. Mark plan on being here tomorrow morning at 09:00. Think about how to get a general search warrant for Secure Pacific

Investments," said Nigel.

They locked and left the office for the night.

Chapter 8

Escape

Peters left his apartment at 08:00. He got to the office and sat for a few minutes sipping his coffee. He received the package containing his new passport and airline tickets. The time had come. He copied all of the files from the computer to a tape back-up and then erased all of the hard drive. He took two folders from the file cabinet. Closed and locked the front door. He exited the building and looked up and down Clark Street for anyone that may be watching him. He saw no one and continued to the car park. The boot of his car contained a bag he had packed the day before just in case he had to make a dash, which he knew would be soon, but not this soon. He pitched the Secure Pacific door keys into the rubbish bin as he passed.

It took him 45 minutes to reach the airport and park in the long term car park. Peters struggled with his piece of luggage even though it had casters. He pushed it from the car park to the shuttle bus stop.

The bus driver helped him put the bag in the rack. He would

tip the driver a twenty so the driver would remember him. There were several stops along the way to the international terminal. The departure hall was on the upper level and the bus stopped in front of the second door which indicated United Airlines, Qantas and Japan airlines. Peters tipped the driver and said, "Off to the big smoke, America. " He smiled and retrieved his bag.

"Thank you sir, you have a lovely trip to the states", said the driver looking at the twenty with a large smile.

The bus pulled away and Peters took a two dollar coin from his pocket and inserted it into the machine that released a baggage trolley. He loaded his bag and started pushing the trolley toward the other side of the huge departures terminal. If anyone asked the driver of the shuttle bus, he was going to America, probably on United Airlines. Peters was now off to a new life. His latest bank statements showed nearly ten million dollars in the bank. He knew that his ex-boss would be furious, but what could he do, certainly not call the police. His long hours of planning this moment of escape were being executed.

Peters walked up to the window for an exit Tax stamp and slid his passport and airline ticket through the slot to the officer. The officer collected the cash for the stamp and placed the stamp on the back of his airline ticket and one on the back of his passport.

Peters proceeded to the Singapore Airlines counter and presented his first class ticket and fake passport in the name of Barry O'Bryan. He requested a seat to Singapore on the earliest possible flight. He had looked at the departures board and saw a flight out in three hours. The ticket agent made an inquiry on his computer and told Peters there was a seat available. Peters unzipped the side pocket of his bag and removed a thick envelope that contained a large amount of Singapore dollars and some other items and then placed the bags on the conveyor belt. The bag weighed over 100kg, but because he was flying first class the agent ignored the over-weight. The ticket agent examined his passport and ticket and issued his boarding pass.

Peters went to the men's room and removed all of his ID, Aussie currency, and credit cards from his wallet. He threw the

Australian coins into the rubbish bin. Nothing was to remain that belonged to Fredric Peters. This had to be a clean break and he planned never to return to Australia. He took all of the articles removed including his old passport and placed them into a plastic zip lock bag. He placed the plastic bag into a large manila envelope.

Peters exited the men's and walked swiftly to the DHL shipping box along the back wall of the huge international terminal. He removed a standard document size shipping envelope from the stack and inserted the manila envelope. He opened the envelope he had retrieved from his bag and removed the computerized shipping label. He pulled the paper protector from the adhesive backing and stuck it on the area indicated. The address was in Malay. He dropped the package into the DHL box. He was now Barry O'Bryan.

O'Bryan proceeded to the guarded door leading to the immigration hall. The guard looked at his boarding pass and passport with the exit stamps. The guard nodded and motioned for O'Bryan to pass.

The next hurdle was the first test of his new Singapore passport at the immigration desk. He went up to one of the kiosks type desks that contained all of the exit forms necessary. He filled out the form and put it inside of the fake passport. The lines at the check point were very short, only a couple of people at each. The immigration clerk routing people to the lines pointed to a line with two elderly people. He walked up and stood behind the red line. It took no more than a minute for the immigration officer to motion him forward. O'Bryan placed his passport on the counter. The immigration office looked at the form, checked all the boxes and then looked at the passport.

"This your first trip to Australia?" The entry stamp showed that O'Bryan had entered Australia 60 days ago, well within the 6 months which the visa stamp indicated.

O'Bryan had anticipated that with no other entry stamps he would not have traveled any place else. "Uh, yes sir." The immigration officer flipped through the crisp pages and reached for his hand stamp to indicate the time and date of departure from

Sydney, Australia. The stamp made a loud clunk when the officer depressed the plunger. O'Bryan smiled at the officer and picked up his passport and headed to his gate. He was now free of Australia, his ex-wife, his boss and Fredric Peters. The past was no more and he had $10 million dollars in the bank.

§

Mark Young was on the phone early with a judge and presented the evidence of the faxes and the dates. He smiled as he hung up the phone. The judge owed many favors to the AG. The warrants were on their way and should be in the police building within the hour.

Nigel and Joyce were getting off the lift when they spotted Mark sitting in the waiting room on the fifth floor. Nigel waved Mark to follow them down the hall to their borrowed office. Joyce inserted the key and opened the door. Nigel went through and hung up his jacket. "Well Mark, did you get a good night's sleep and ready for the crunch of today?" Nigel saw a faint smile appear on Mark's mouth.

"Yes sir, I am staying at my sister's and we had a very pleasant dinner and evening." Mark looked very relaxed compared to yesterday's meeting.

"We need to review what we need to accomplish today and map out a schedule", said Joyce.

A knock on the door made Joyce stop in mid-sentence. She was standing next to the door and turned and opened it to a courier standing with a large envelope. She took the envelope and signed the receipt. The envelope was addressed to Mark Young. She handed it to Mark.

Nigel raised an eyebrow and looked toward Mark. It was thin. Mark removed the flap and pulled several pages out and examined the top page and looked at the signature at the bottom of the last page. He handed the document to Nigel.

Nigel read the top and looked at Mark and Joyce. "Mark you are a surprise. You must have worked hard to get this." Nigel handed the document to Joyce.

"Now we can map out our schedule today, starting with serving this warrant to Mr. Peters." She continued to read. "Mark this is brilliant. You covered all the items on our list. Congratulations, you have earned your place on our team. Thanks."

Mark's cheeks were slightly red. "Yes, I collected on a favor." He looked embarrassed.

Nigel extended his hand shook Mark's hand and gave him a pat on the back. "Well done."

Joyce took out her note pad to make a schedule for the day. She stopped. "Maybe we should make the schedule after we return from serving the warrant. We may find something that will alter the course of the investigation."

"Good idea", said Nigel. He looked at his watch. "Half past nine. Let's head over to North Sydney now and get this over with. I'll phone the watch comander and request a uniformed officer to accompany us."

They met the police officer in the car park. They took separate cars because Nigel was not sure how long they would be and didn't want to tie up the officer any longer than necessary.

When they arrived at the eighth floor, they found the door locked and the office dark. The officer radioed back the situation. A lock smith was dispatched.

Within an hour they opened the door. Joyce found the computer useless with the wiped hard drive. The metal filing cabinet was locked and took the lock smith only a few minutes to pop the lock. It became obvious that some files were missing. The hanging folders were still separated and empty. There were several other folders with names. Nigel wrote down all the names.

Mark walked around the office and checked the other cubicles. There was nothing in the desks and there were no other filing cabinets. He walked over to the coffee table and saw some mail lying on the top. He picked up the mail and noticed the envelopes were from a local bank in Sydney.

"Nigel, I think I have found something." He handed the envelopes to Nigel who used his finger to rip open the flaps. Nigel removed several pages from each envelope. After scanning each page he handed them over to Joyce who did the same.

"This one appears to be a local account and shows deposits of various amounts that could be fees and cheques written for utilities, rent and other minor bills. The other one is a trust account and contains only a few thousand dollars. There are several wire transfers to a bank in Vanuatu that almost depleted this account", said Joyce.

"Let's give this place a good toss", said Nigel.

They opened and examined all the drawers and cabinets in the office. There was not much. It became obvious that Peters had vacated with some files. They told the police officer to have the lock changed and seal the door with crime tape pending further investigation. Nigel, Joyce and Mark returned to the police building.

Nigel looked over his notes. "I'll call the Lottery Board and see if any of these names were winners." He consulted his note book and made the call. After reading several of the names, it became obvious that all were lottery winners. "Some were for only a few thousand. Most of the list is for amounts over a hundred thousand. The total is almost six million. That's a lot of money. It still doesn't prove a crime was committed. But it does bring into question as to why most if not all of Secure Pacific Investment's clients are lottery winners."

§

Chapter 9

New Identity

Barry O'Bryan, A.K.A. Fredric Peters, sat back in his first class seat and enjoyed his Scotch. He was now on his way to a new life without financial worries. His bank account was in Bangkok and he had moved all the money to that account. No one knew of this account and only one person knew his current identity. He was safe.

He arrived in Singapore and cleared immigration and customs without incident, claimed his suit case and pulled it to the door labeled Taxi Waiting Area. O'Bryan checked into the Imperial Hotel at 20:00 and went to dinner. It was Thursday. He had a few loose ends to tie up before the weekend.

The next morning, Barry O'Bryan packed his suit case and pulled it to the door. He phoned the front desk to have a porter come and get his bag and take it to the lobby. An hour later, O'Bryan went to the lobby and claimed his suit case from the concierge counter, made his way through the automatic doors and waved for a taxi. No one paid him any attention. The ride was short to the shopping mall. He rolled his suit case to the area that contained lockers for shoppers to store items they didn't want to haul around while shopping. He placed his suit case into one of largest lockers and took the key.

O'Bryan made several phone calls from a public phone in the shopping mall. One was to Asian Investments. He instructed Chung to meet him for lunch at a restaurant in the mall.

O'Bryan waited at a table in the back of the Restaurant. Chung joined him a few minutes later. O'Bryan told Chung that the company was being wound up and to dispose of all bank documents, corporate documents, phone bills and faxes. He handed Chung a cheque for $50,000, the balance remaining in the Asian Investments account, and told him to enjoy a vacation. O'Bryan was careful to pay for the meal and drinks with cash.

O'Bryan returned to the atrium in the mall and made another phone call. This one was to a local number. The call lasted several minutes. He looked at his watch. He had an hour. He walked through the mall and entered several of the shops, but didn't make a purchase.

He retrieved his bag from the locker and waited at the north entrance. He saw the dark green car approach slowly. O'Bryan stepped from the shadows and waved at the driver. The car pulled to the curb and he got in the rear seat. The driver placed his bag into the boot. The car pulled away from the curb and moved swiftly towards the causeway. Not a word was spoken.

The car pulled up to the border station. An officer viewed their documents and waved the car through. After forty-five minutes, the car pulled into a gated community and came to a stop at a modest home sitting on several acres of wooded land. There were several other homes on the cul-de-sac. The driver exited and opened the door. "Will you need the car anymore today Mr. Sutton", asked the driver.

O'Bryan/Sutton shook his head as no and exited the car. He walked to the front door and removed a collection of keys from his pocket. He entered the foyer and placed his brief case on the table along with a newspaper from the hotel. He walked to the large lounge and to the bar that took up most of one wall and fixed himself a Scotch. Larry Sutton sat drinking his Scotch and looked out upon his private wooded wonderland. He could barely see the homes on either side. He had purchased the property a year ago and had only visited it on two occasions. He had been careful to make his exit plans well in advance of ever needing them. He used the name Sutton only once before and that was to establish his Malaysian residence and hire a staff to take care of this property. The staff assumed he was just another rich man that traveled the world and rarely visited his one of many homes.

O'Bryan/Sutton finished his drink and walked to the den/office and inserted a key from his collection into the center drawer of his desk. He removed a mobile phone and charger. He plugged in the phone to charge. The phone charge indicator show it was charging, he punched in a number. A female answered. "This is Larry; I'm home and will be here for a few days. Would you like to have dinner while I'm here?" The female voice had an Asian accent and responded with a yes. "I'll have the car pick you up at 6." He pressed the off button.

§

The woman put down her private mobile phone and smiled. She knew the call would be coming. She had spoken to Bangkok earlier and confirmed that Peters/Sutton would be arriving this evening. She had already made the necessary arrangements with her office. It appeared Peters had finally made his move.

§

Barry/Larry walked to the foyer and retrieved his brief case and returned to the den/office. He removed four data tapes. He copied all of the data to an external hard drive. He picked up his phone and entered several numbers. A buzzing sound was emitted from the bookcase behind his desk. A door swung open revealing a large wall safe. He opened the safe and placed the tapes and the external drive on the top shelf. He removed a large bundle of US dollars and closed the safe and the secret door in the book case. Looking at his watch, he noted he had a couple of hours before his company was due for dinner.

O'Bryan/Sutton went to the master bedroom suite and opened the walk-in closet doors. There were racks of suites, shirts and drawers full of clothing. He stripped and showered. He dressed in a casual pair of cream colored slacks and a black silk shirt. Looking in the full length mirror, he was ready for his guest.

Sutton went to the kitchen and opened the freezer with shelf after shelf of all sorts of meats, breads, vegetables and desserts. He chose a couple of rib eye steaks and a couple of packages of veggies. He normally had a cook prepare his meals, but had not requested the cook when he phoned to alert the staff he was returning. In his other life, he did all the cooking after his wife left him. He actually enjoyed cooking. It would be a simple meal, steak, a pre-baked potato, also from the freezer, and veggies. A bottle of select wine and that should complete the evening. No dessert, he knew his company did not eat desserts. She said her husband liked her girly figure. He picked up the in-house phone and called Wong to pick up his guest. Wong knew the address.

§

Nigel hung up his jacket and settled into one of the chairs around the small table in the borrowed office. Joyce and Mark seated themselves. Joyce made a few notes on her note pad.

"I think Peters has bolted. Let's talk to the watch commander and see if we can get some assistance in tracking down Peters", said Joyce.

Nigel picked up the phone and called the watch commander. Nigel explained what had happened and requested assistance in checking out Peters' home. The last known address for Peters' was in Botany Bay. The watch commander said he would dispatch someone to check on Peters' house.

"Okay, we believe Peters has bolted. We found nothing that indicated a crime had been committed in his office. We have only suspicion that he was laundering money invested by lottery winners through off shore accounts. We cannot establish that he had control of any of the companies or accounts where the money transfers were made", said Joyce.

Nigel sat looking at the cork board that contained a probable may have diagram of the how the money flowed. "What if Peters has left the country? Where would he go?"

"Why don't we check with the airlines for any one with the name of Peters checking in or with reservations for any flights to Bangkok, Hong Kong or Singapore", said Nigel.

Mark said, "I can help do that. I'll work at one of the empty desks down the hall." Nigel nodded and Mark left the room.

Nigel drummed his fingers on the desktop. "You know, this is getting us nowhere. We have no evidence of a crime, we can't find a connection between Peters and the money, we don't know who controlles the bank accounts and owned the off shore companies. What's our next step?"

"If Peters is at home with an illness, it will solve the no show at the office. If on the other hand, he is not to be found, then we have probable cause to issue a warrant for his arrest. I think we should wait until it is confirmed that he is not in his residence and then get Mark to issue a search warrant for Peters' home", said Joyce.

The phone rang. Nigel snatched it up and listened. "Thanks." He put the phone down. "That was the watch commander; no one is at Peters home. A neighbor said she saw him yesterday afternoon loading a suite bag into his car."

"Okay, let's get Mark on the search warrant for Peters' home", said Nigel. He got up and walked down the hall to where Mark was on the phone. Mark hung up the phone and made a note on his pad.

"Mark, we need a search warrant for Peters' home, can you make those arrangements?"

Mark reached into a pile of papers on his desk and handed one to Nigel. It was a warrant for the arrest of Peters. "No search warrant is needed. Once the arrest warrant is issued, it is an automatic search warrant for anything belonging to Peters", said Mark.

Nigel looked over the document, smiled and patted Mark on the shoulder. "How did you get the warrant so fast?"

"When I left your office, I thought that it would be faster to get an arrest warrant issued for theft than anything else. He has taken documents from the firm's office and destroyed their database. It was apparent to me that he was the most likely suspect, since he was the only employee. I have the authority to issue arrest warrants. I got the plate number issued for his company car and put out an alert."

Nigel stood there looking at Mark. "Amazing! Any luck with the airlines?"

"No, none of the overseas airlines have any tickets issued to Fredric Peters or any reservations. I just finished with Qantas."

"Let's go back to the office and give Joyce the news", said Nigel.

They went over everything they had discovered. Nothing pointed to a crime. All they had were suspicions and strange transactions. The phone rang. "Yes this is Joyce Mathews." She listened and made some notes. "What time was the ticket issued? Okay, thanks." She hung up the phone and smiled. "It seems that Fredric Peters' car was found at the long term parking at the airport. The parking ticket was still on the dashboard and the car was unlocked. The patrol officer said she could read the ticket through the windscreen and the time stamp was yesterday at 14:15."

"Well, he didn't leave the country under his own name. There is no record of any ticket issued to Fredric Peters. Do you think he just dumped the car and is still in the country?" asked Mark.

"I think he left the country, most likely to Bangkok, Singapore or Hong Kong. I think we should head for the airport", said Joyce.

They parked their car in the same lot as Peters' car. They went over the car carefully but found nothing that would indicate his whereabouts. Mark talked to the gate attendant without getting anything that would help. Mark walked back towards Peters' car when he noticed the shuttle bus. He flagged the bus down. The bus pulled over and Mark identified himself and showed the bus driver a picture of Peters. The bus driver smiled and said, "Yeah, I remember him. He tipped me a twenty for helping with his luggage. He said he was going to America and I let him off at United's gate."

Mark walked back to where Nigel and Joyce were finishing up going through Peters' car. "Peters' was here and took the shuttle bus to United Airlines. The bus driver recognized his picture because Peters' tipped the driver a twenty. The driver said Peters was headed to America."

"Then he is traveling under an assumed name, which means he has a fake passport. I think we need to talk to airport security and take a look at some surveillance recordings", said Nigel.

The three got into their car and drove to the main international terminal and parked in an area marked for police cars only. Nigel went to the main security desk and identified himself and asked to speak to the supervisor.

A thin man of about fifty walked from the office and asked if he could be of assistance. Nigel explained they needed to see the recordings from yesterday afternoon from about 14:15 onwards. The man told them to follow him and took them to a darkened room filled with screens showing almost every inch of the huge terminal. The supervisor indicated a small room off the main room with a large screen TV. He explained how the controls worked and started the timeline from 14:15 yesterday.

There were six different frames on the large TV. Nigel said he would take the two over each other on the far left, Joyce take the two in the middle and Mark take the two on the far right. They watched for fifteen minutes. Mark said, "Hey I think I spotted him. Is that him at the Singapore counter?"

Nigel pressed the stop button. He zoomed the frame to nearly the entire screen.

"That's him", said Joyce.

They noted the time as 14:40pm. Nigel pressed the play button and the picture resumed but only the frame with Peters. They watched him hand over a ticket and present his passport. Peters unzipped one of the bags and removed a large envelope and placed it in his briefcase. The ticket agent issued the boarding pass and placed the bag on the conveyor belt. Peters left the Singapore counter and walked out of the frame. Nigel pressed another button and the six frames reappeared. None contained Peters. He pressed another button and six more frames appeared.

Joyce said, "There he is going toward the men's." Nigel zoomed in and confirmed that it was Peters. They watched as Peters went into the men's room. He came out after six minutes. He looked around and walked toward the shops area of the great hall. Nigel had trouble following Peters because he was unsure of the sequence of the cameras. He stopped the recordings and pressed the frame button several times before Peters' image appeared.

Nigel pressed the resume button and they watched as Peters walked to a DHL box and retrieved a shipping envelope from the supply under the box. Peters took an envelope from his briefcase and removed from the envelope a shipping label. He pealed the backing from the gummy side and placed the label on the DHL package and placed the envelope into the shipping package and pressed the seal. He pulled open the box and inserted his package and went to the immigration hall doors. He showed the guard his passport and boarding pass and disappeared into the hall. Technically he was no longer in Australia.

Nigel, Joyce and Mark sat back in their chairs as the camera lost Peters' image. No security cameras were allowed in the immigration hall.

"He had this all planned out in advance. He had a preprinted shipping label and a fake passport," said Mark.

"Let's go to the Singapore counter and talk to the ticket agent. We have the exact time he was at the counter. We should get the name of the passenger," said Nigel.

When they arrived at the ticket counter, there was no one around. There were no flights for several hours. A TV monitor indicated that Check in would begin in two hours. Joyce saw a door to the Singapore Airlines office. She knocked on the door. A young woman answered the door. Joyce showed her credentials, had a brief conversation and returned to the counter where Nigel and Mark were standing.

"It seems the agent will not be on duty for another two hours. I asked if they could identify a passenger from the time the boarding pass was issued. The office clerk said she didn't know, but I should check back in two hours."

Nigel looked at his watch. "What else can we do? We know he boarded a Singapore flight under an alias with a fake passport. We don't know which flight and the name he is using. Mark, do you know the regulations regarding getting a flight manifest?"

"I don't think we need a warrant. We now have a definite crime committed. If we indicate that a fugitive may have taken a flight to evade capture with a false passport, then I think they will release the manifest."

Joyce was thinking about the facts they had so far. "If he is headed to Singapore then it is most likely the money is there too. We must get to Singapore, if that is where he is headed."

Nigel turned to Mark, "Call the AG and tell him what has happened. Peters is on the run and we think he is headed to Singapore where the money is. We will not have proof of this for another two hours. We need permission to go to Singapore and pursue Peters."

Marks pulled his mobile phone out and made the call. He was on the line with the AG for over ten minutes.

"The AG says to wait until we have evidence that Peters actually boarded a flight to Singapore, then to call him back for further instructions."

They went to a coffee bar and relaxed until Singapore Airlines ticket counter opened for business. Nigel went up to the ticket agent and showed his identification. He told the agent that he needed to interview him involving a fugitive that may have boarded a flight yesterday. There were several people in line for check in. The agent looked at the credentials and picked up a phone. He spoke several seconds and replaced the phone. He said to Nigel to give him a few minutes until a relief agent came. Nigel nodded and stepped back behind the roped off area. Within 10 minutes the young ticket agent came out and introduced himself to the group and asked what he could do to help.

"We need to know if you remember processing this man." Nigel showed the agent a picture of Peters.

"Yes, I recognize this man. He had a first class ticket to Singapore. He is a Singapore citizen."

"He had a Singapore passport?" asked Nigel.

"Yes, it was unusual, because it had only one stamp of entry to Australia, a 6 month visa and one stamp of exit from Singapore. It was the man's first use of the passport."

"Do you remember the name on the passport?" Nigel had his fingers crossed.

"I remember it was an odd name. It was Scottish. An O' something. I can look it up. We have the entire manifest for yesterday's flight still online."

The Agent returned behind the counter to a position unoccupied. Nigel, Joyce and Mark stood in front of the counter as the agent typed. "Ah, here it is a prepaid open ticket. The name is O'Bryan, Barry." The agent looked up and smiled at Nigel.

"Was the ticket a round trip or one way" asked Joyce.

"It was a one way ticket with two open segments, one to Hong Kong and one to Bangkok."

"Jackpot ", said Nigel. "Thank you."

Mark removed his mobile phone and punched in the AG's number. Mark confirmed that Peters had indeed caught a flight to Singapore and was using an alias of Barry O'Bryan. The AG gave the go ahead to pursue Peters to Singapore. Mark turned to Nigel and Joyce and said, "We have the AG's blessing to pursue Peters."

"We?" said Nigel.

"Yes" said Mark. "The AG was adamant that I accompany you and offer any assistance. He also said he will place a call to the Singapore AG and call in a few favors as he called it."

"We need to return to the office and make arrangements", said Nigel. "I'll call the Superintendent."

"What about the grunt work here? We need to ask the watch commander for some feet on the ground", said Joyce.

"Let's make a list of things that need following up. The watch commander will need to know what these feet on the ground are needed for."

They returned to the borrowed office and worked for the best part of an hour. Nigel went to the watch commander's office with a long list of follow up leads. The watch commander was not happy, but agreed to furnish two detectives.

§

The Frank Lithgo, the watch commander sat for a few moments, picked up his phone and called the police head office in Townsville. "Hey Rufus, this is Frank in Sydney."

"Frank, what can I do for you?"

"I'd like to collect on a favor you owe me. How about you send me two detectives to help out in a case we have down here", said Frank.

"I do have two that I can loan you for a few weeks, but you pick up the tab for housing and transportation."

"Done deal. Send them on down. Fax me their personnel info", said Frank. He grinned as he disconnected the call.

Rufus sat back and smiled at the thought of getting rid of two goof-offs for a few weeks. He phoned the bull pen and asked the two to come to his office.

Sir Rodney Stonebridge hung up his office phone with a frown on his face. He sat thinking. After a few minutes, he made a call from his personal mobile phone. "The police just phoned with a list of all the lottery winners that invested in Secure Pacific Investments. I think you should question Peters and find out what the hell is going on." He didn't wait for a reply.

Chapter 10

Favor

The dinner and afterwards had gone well. It was a beautiful morning. O'Bryan/Sutton fixed breakfast and sat the food on a small table on the patio. "I've got a favor to ask you", said Sutton.

"Yes, anything Larry", said the beautiful Asian woman sitting across the table.

"I need two credit cards on your bank with a limit of USD $20,000 each. I will deposit USD $80,000 into each of the accounts to guarantee the credit. The monthly bills are to be paid from the deposit."

"Oh, I don't see a problem with that. It's a simple transaction. I presume you want overseas type cards, Visa and Master Card. You'll have the cards tomorrow. Have Wong pick them up at the bank." *So this is exit time. I will notify Bangkok.*

Her family owned the bank for over a hundred years. She inherited the bank from her father and although she did not appear to participate in the day to day running of the bank, she could make things happen. Malaysian banks were not regulated like Singapore banks.

"Wong will take you home. I want you to know how much I've enjoyed our time together." She smiled and finished her breakfast. Sutton handed her an envelope containing USD $160,000 in cash.

"Larry, I cherish the day we met at that conference in Hong Kong. Let's not wait so long the next time." She smiled and gave him a peck on the cheek and left for her ride home.

Gwen Leong got into the car and waved back at Sutton as the car moved out of the drive. She took out her mobile and punched in a Bangkok number. "He is on the run. He gave me $160,000 to cover credit card purchases. He must be planning something big."

Peters/O'Bryan/Sutton's plan Phase One had been executed. He would get the credit cards tomorrow and then be on his way to Hong Kong.

Sutton worked most of the day on plans. He completed his paperwork by 16:00. He dismantled the computer and placed it in the secret safe. It was getting late and his stomach was protesting the lack of food. He made his way to the kitchen. He pulled open the freezer door when his mobile phone rang.

"Hello."

"Larry it's me. I got the cards and Wong can pick them up first thing tomorrow. They will be with the manager."

"Thank you so much. I'll have Wong there by 10:00. I miss you already."

"Until we meet again, bye." The line clicked and went dead.

Larry pulled a few items from the freezer. Satisfied his meal selection was complete he placed them on the counter top to thaw out. He went to his bedroom and began to pack his clothing for the week or so he would be in Hong Kong. It was a business trip, so he would not need casual attire. After selecting the suits, shirts and ties, he closed the case and took it to the front hall for Wong to put in the boot of the car. He phoned Wong in the guest quarters and told him to pick up a package from the Wong Bank tomorrow morning after 10:00.

Larry returned to the kitchen to fix his meal. Being alone was just the thing he needed to calm his mind. He completed his meal and topped it off with a fine rare Port. He decided to watch TV in the den. Taking his drink he walked into the den and sat in his favorite chair, at least he called it his favorite. He really had not used the house enough to have a favorite. CNN world news was on. There was a brief article about the USA sending troops somewhere in the Middle East. *They seem to be trying to solve all the problems in the world.*

He fell asleep watching America's Wheel of Fortune. A loud commercial woke him. The only light in the room was from the TV. He was stiff from sleeping in the chair. He reached over and turned on a lamp. The clock said 23:21. *Wow, that was a long nap.* He got up and headed to his bedroom.

Chapter 11

Queensland's Finest

The break room in police head quarters contained only two people. "Steve, I'm tired of these old stale biscuits, let's go down and get something good to eat."

Steve looked over at his partner Sam. "Yeah, we always get the leftovers. Let's go get some real food."

They went down the lift to the ground floor and out to the car park. Steve got behind the wheel. "Oh crap!"

Sam looked over at Steve. "What's wrong?"

"The seat is hot; I think I burned my bum."

"Yeah, you should have put a towel on the seat when you parked."

Steve just shrugged and off they went towards the Strand. The Strand is a long beach area that has seen some new features added but was still about the same as it was fifty years ago. There was a long jetty that contained several boat docks, various tourist places and at the end the large Sheraton hotel. The Restaurant was in the Sheraton Hotel at the end of the causeway. Steve pulled in to a car park. Sam got out and caught his sleeve on a sharp piece of metal protruding from the car body. "Oh crap!"

"What's wrong?" asked Steve.

"Caught my sleeve on something and ripped my coat. Bummer!" Sam was busy trying to assess the damage. "It looks like my jacket is ruined."

"Look at it this way; you get to buy a new one." Sam looked at his partner for a few seconds.

§

Detectives second grade Sam Granvale and Steve Gibbons, members of the Townsville, Queensland police department were loaned to the Sydney police force to help with an investigation. Their boss was happy for the chance to rid himself of the pair, even if it was only for a few weeks. The two checked out an unmarked police car and headed to Sydney.

Steve had been with the Townsville police for over ten years. Sam had transferred from the Melbourne police when his wife was offered a top job with the Air Force base near Townsville.

Steve had been married but divorced several years ago. He had no children. He and his current girl friend shared an apartment. Both had been born and raised in Townsville.

§

"Dude we have been driving for hours. I need to stretch my legs and use the facilities", said Steve. His head of unruly sandy hair nearly touched the ceiling of the car. Sam, considerably shorter than Steve had a boxers build. He worked out every day in the police gym.

"Okay, I booked us a room near here on the Gold Coast" said Sam. "Hey that looks interesting." Sam pointed to a sign with Tom Watson's picture, Par-Fun driving range and miniature golf course. "That should give us some exercise before we turn in."

"Par-Fun? Dude, the name sounds like some Chinese poofter", said Steve.

"Yeah, well, we can use the exercise before we turn in"

"Dude I've never played golf", said Steve looking over at Sam.

"It's not hard, especially miniature golf."

"Why is it called miniature golf, is the ball tiny or something?" said Steve.

"No, the entire game is played with one club, the putter."

"Oh, okay let's give it a go", said Steve. "I'm stiff as a board. Maybe this game will help my back."

They pulled into the car park and found a space. The entrance to the Par-Fun office building was across a hump back bridge that ran over a large creek running alongside the driving range.

Sam locked the car and the two started across the bridge. A large sign warned not to dive from bridge or swim in the stream to collect golf balls. Danger Crocs present.

"Hey look down below; it's a man in a scuba outfit looking for lost golf balls. He's got a large bag of balls and what's that in his right hand?" asked Steve.

"Looks like a bang stick. It's a pipe with a twelve gauge shotgun shell that has a crude firing pin. It's very dangerous. Could blow your hand off", said Sam.

"Hey mate, I bet he makes a fortune selling those lost balls." Sam looked down and shrugged. They continued to the office.

Steve pushed against the glass door. A bunch of bells were suspended above the door that made enough noise to wake the dead and the nearly dead. The nearly dead appeared to come alive behind the counter as the two walked in and shut the door, which elicited another round of bell ringing.

"May I elp kind gentlemen", said the little Asian, who barely stood tall enough to see over the counter.

"We would like to play mini golf", said Sam. The little man looked up at Sam towering above.

"So solly, time no enough to play."

"Well mate, can we hit a bucket of balls?"

"Close in half hour. Lights turn out. You welcome hit balls", said the little man.

Sam opened his wallet and paid for two buckets of balls. They walked over to an old rain barrel and selected the best of the scarred clubs while the little man filled two baskets with balls.

"You tee number twenty one and twenty two", said the Asian.

Sam picked up his basket and Steve reached and grabbed the other. They went through the sliding door to the raised mound with all the tee boxes. Several people were hitting balls.

"How does this game work? What are those signs with 100, 150 and 250 mean," said Steve. "Do we aim to hit the green areas with flags or the signs?"

"Neither, you aim to hit the range cart."

"The what?"

"You'll see." Sam dumped his bucket of balls on the little green mat. He used the head of his club to move a ball out of the pile and placed the ball on the little white rubber tee, swung and hit the ball past the 150 sign.

Steve watched and copied Sam, except he hit his ball on the toe of the club and it zoomed out past the car park and hit the door to a room at the Samurai motel across the road. Sam and Steve watched as the door opened and a woman clutching a robe peered around; a bald headed man looked over her shoulder. They looked relieved no one was there and slammed the door shut.

"Mate it looks like you disturbed a couple not wanting to be disturbed", said Steve

". I think that's where we're staying tonight". Steve looked at Sam and frowned.

"You're kidding me." Steve hit another ball.

Many of the other patrons were hitting balls in every conceivable direction. One of the hitters shouted the long awaited alarm, "Cart, range cart! Here he comes."

A ball hitting frenzy erupted. Many were way off target, but due to the sheer volume a few hit the target. "I got the tail light", shouted one customer. Balls were bouncing off the wire cage protecting the driver. The young student driving the cart was accustomed to the abuse and concentrated on reading his novel, "Hitchhikers Guide to Ayers Rock" and drinking a Fosters. The range cart weaved back and forth between the range signs scooping up the balls.

Steve teed up a ball and swung the club. A loud twang indicted he had hit the ball in the sweet spot. The ball found its mark. "I got the head light, I got the freaking head light!" shouted Steve with a wide grin.

Sam congratulated Steve and teed up his ball, swung and hit the ball past the 250 sign and into the McDonald's drive through next to the seedy motel. The sound of breaking glass reached them as the lights for the range suddenly went out. Everyone began hitting their remaining balls at the one eyed cart weaving through the range beyond.

The university student driving the cart made a near fatal mistake. He opened the gage door to pitch his empty Fosters can when a ball caught him square in the forehead. He slumped in the seat unconscious. The cart, running slowly on its own, weaved a path across the driving range.

Sam and Steve returned their clubs to the rain barrel and proceeded out to the car park. Just as they started across the hump back bridge, Sam tugged on Steve's sleeve. "I think we should wait a minute or so." Directly in the middle of the bridge, a young couple engaged in a passionate embrace.

A tremendous explosion occurred directly below them. The couple nearly jumped off the bridge. They peered over the edge at a man in a scuba outfit tugging on a large bag of golf balls that were being pulled away from him by a 12 foot croc. The animal had one foot shot off.

Sam and Steve heard the explosion from the 12-gauge bang stick as they observed the couple on the bridge.

"Humm, strange place for making out", said Sam.

The red faced couple continued to look down at the scuba person. The loud chugging of a tractor caught their attention. The range cart went over the steep bank of the stream and landed dead center of the croc. The scuba diver calmly pried open the dead croc's mouth and pulled the bag of balls out of its teeth. He swam away passing the sign that read, No swimming for golf balls. The one headlight of the cart was shining below the water on the dead croc giving an eerie look to the scene.

Sam and Steve looked at one another. "Hey man, I bet he has 200 golf balls in that bag", said Steve. "Dude I don't want to get involved in this scene, let's split."

Detective second grade Sam Grandvale, and detective Steve Gibbons, of Townsville, Queensland, walked to their unmarked police car and drove across the road to the Samurai Motel.

"I don't think we should go McDonalds tonight", said Sam.

"Nope, might get glass in our tyres."

They parked their car and went into the office. The young man behind the counter checked his computer for their reservation. "Ah, here it is. Grandvale and Gibbons?"

"Yes that's us," said Sam.

The young clerk smiled and handed the two registration cards. "Please fill these out and I'll assign you a room."

They filled out the cards and handed them back. "We want a quiet room away from the road," said Steve. The clerk looked up and winked at Steve. He handed them key cards and each a fly swatter. "What this for?" asked Steve.

"You'll find out," said Sam.

They left the office. "Do you think he takes us for two poofters?" asked Steve.

Sam looked at Steve and shrugged.

They removed their bags from the boot of the car and entered the room. Sam turned on the lights. Steve looked around. That's the worst looking wallpaper I've ever seen," said Steve.

"Mate, look carefully."

"Oh crap, those are mosquitoes and other flying things. They are smashed all over the place," said Steve. A loud buzzing sound filled the room.

Sam looked around. "Watch," said Sam. He took aim and swung. A loud slap and one more body decorated the wall.

The night was one of slapping flying bugs and swatting. They did not get much sleep.

Chapter 12

Sam and Steve Arrive

Nigel and Joyce drove to the Sydney office in silence. The case was becoming very complicated and Nigel didn't like the dead ends they were running into. "We need a thorough search of Peter's home, his office and car" said Joyce. They arrived at 08:00 and went directly to their tiny borrowed office.

The phone rang as they entered. "This is Joyce Mathews. Yes sir, send them right up. Well the help has arrived. Two detectives from Queensland have been assigned to us."

"I wonder how the watch commander pulled that off."

"They are on the way up. Let's use the general conference room to brief them" said Joyce. A knock on the door; Joyce reached over and opened the door.

"Gentlemen follow me, we will use the general conference room if it's available" said Nigel. He walked to the watch commander's secretary and inquired about the availability of the general conference room. She told him it was available. Nigel motioned the group to the conference room. "Gentlemen take a seat. I'm

Nigel and this is Joyce."

Mark arrived and was introduced. "Gentlemen we will bring you up to date on what we have so far been able to discover" said Joyce.

Steve and Sam shrugged and sat back to receive the information. Nigel cleared his throat and explained the case from its beginning with the complaint filed by the Jenkins'. When Nigel mentioned the nearly four million dollars missing from the Jenkins' account, the two sat up.

"So, this couple won nearly four million and lost it all in these investments of horses. Did they ever get to ride any of them?" said Steve.

Nigel looked at Joyce who was busy looking at her shoes. "Well no, the horses never left New Zealand" said Nigel.

Sam played with a button on his jacket and looked over at Nigel. "Dude, you are telling me this couple spent nearly four million on horses and have never seen them?" Wow, that's just downright evil." Mark coughed behind his hand hiding a wide grin.

"We have to go away for a few days and will appreciate all the help we can get to dig up as much as possible. We have a list of things we need for you to investigate" said Nigel. We know one of the parties to the conspiracy and possibly one other, but we have nothing to tie them back to the overseas companies and banks where the money was transferred. You are free to use the temp office down the hall until we get back. Hopefully we will not be gone for more than five or six days. We'll check in daily. And this case is confidential to all but us. Any questions?"

Steve looked at Sam. "What about expenses for petrol, food and hotels" asked Sam?

"I suggest you see the watch commander to get answers to those questions" said Joyce.

"If there are no more questions then we have arrangements to make and you have a lot of leg work to get started on" said Nigel.

Mark had listened and watched. He was attempting to assess the two Queensland detectives, but they were very strange and not exactly what he thought of as detectives. *Maybe Nigel and Joyce under-*

stand these two. They remind me of Cheech and Chong.

"Mark, make arrangements for us to fly to Singapore later today. Also, if your boss has gotten the favor from the Singapore AG, maybe he could have one of their detectives meet us at the airport" said Nigel.

"Okay, I'll get right on it" said Mark.

Mark made himself busy with phone calls to Canberra and Qantas Airlines. Joyce began to sort through the various stacks of faxes and documents they had accumulated. "I think I will make copies of these and leave the originals here for safe keeping."

"Great idea" said Nigel. He was not sure how to go about digging out the information in Singapore and hoped the Singapore AG's office would be resourceful. He made a list of things they needed to resolve, beginning with the companies' office and following up the bank accounts. The list was not that impressive. A familiar nagging sensation began to work its way up his spine and he knew he would not be satisfied until he took a personal look at all the evidence no matter how little. Nigel placed his note pad, passport and Federal ID into a pocket in the top of his small brief case.

Mark hung up the phone. "The AG will speak to the Singapore AG's office and request a detective meet us as the airport. I booked us on a Qantas flight at 12:00 arriving at 20:30. I haven't made any hotel reservations. I thought we would wait and ask the Singapore detective our best choice."

Nigel nodded. "Good work Mark. We'll go pack our bags and check out of the Hilton. Mark give Joyce your sister's address and we can pick you up on the way to the airport."

Mark jotted down the address and handed it to Joyce.

"I know where this is and we will pick you up at 10:00. It's only fifteen minutes to the airport from your sister's. That will give us plenty of time to park the car and go through security" said Joyce.

The three left and locked their little office. Joyce noticed the two Queensland detectives still in the watch commander's waiting area. She walked over and handed the office key to Sam. "This is the key to the office. Be sure to lock it up when you are not here.

We don't want any leaks. And please don't discuss the case with anyone outside our group." She waited for their nod of acceptance and turned to leave with Mark and Nigel.

§

"Dude do you think we're going to enjoy this job? Looks like those three are wound up real tight" said Sam.

"I think we have to watch ourselves. This entire bunch is way too serious about stuff. I don't want Rufus coming down on us for some crap this bunch might want to blame us for. I have a feeling we are the preverbal sacrificial lambs."

The watch commander's secretary announced that the commander would see them now. They got up and walked into his roomy office and took seats in front of his desk. The watch commander looked over his glasses at the two. He knew Rufus had screwed him, but at least he had complied with Nigel's request for help.

Chapter 13

The Search Warrant

Sam sat in the passenger's seat as Steve drove down the M1 motorway. The map was confusing to Sam. Some of the roads were not named correctly on the map. He finally found the Botany Bay area. The street Peters lived on was one-way.

"Dude look, it's not a one-way to the left." Steve turned left into a short little street that displayed a two way sign.

"The numbers are right. There is the house. Not much to look at. I hate those red tile roofs" said Sam.

They parked the car in the driveway. The house had no garage. A short foot path led to a small porch. Sam knocked on the door. No answer. "Okay now what?"

"Well let's try some windows and maybe another door is in the back" said Steve.

They tried the two windows in the front. No luck. Steve went to the left and Sam to the right side of the house. No windows were open.

There was a loud bang and a large rubbish can came rolling

around the corner of the house. A furry critter ran for its life. Steve came behind the can with a red face. "Sorry."

They looked around the small back garden area. A grill and a ratty old chair sat on a small square of concrete. "Mate, doesn't look like he uses the grill much" said Steve.

Sam tried the back door, it opened to his surprise.

A curtain fell back from a window in the house next door.

"Okay, let's go in and start the search." They went into a small kitchen with a tiny table for two. Sam opened the fridge. "There's only two Fosters and a stick of butter. Hey, he's not much on cooking either" said Sam. "Maybe we should test the Fosters and see if it's gone bad."

Steve looked at Sam and shook his head no. "This won't take long. There's only the ground floor. I'll take the lounge and you take the first bed room" said Steve.

They were busy opening drawers, looking through cupboards. A loud knock on the front door startled them. "Dude who could that be?" asked Sam.

Steve walked over and opened the front door. Two very large policemen were standing on the tiny porch. "Yes officers, what can I do for you?"

"Who are you and what are you doing in this house?" asked one of the policemen.

"We are police detectives searching a crime suspect's house" said Steve.

"Okay, let me see some ID and a search warrant" said the second policeman.

"Er, Sam show these officers our search warrant."

"Steve, you have the search warrant."

"I don't have it, Nigel gave you the warrant."

"Okay, let me see some ID" said the officer.

Sam and Steve pulled out their official Queensland ID's. The officer looked at them and then passed them to the other officer. "And what are two Queensland dicks doing in Botany Bay?"

"We are on temporary assignment to the Sydney Police. You can call the Sydney office and the watch commander will vouch for us" said Steve.

The officer with the credentials went out to the patrol car. After two or three minutes he returned to the front porch. "They check out, sorry to bother you two, but I'd sure check in with our substation and be sure to find that warrant if any of the evidence you may find will be worth anything in a court of law" said the officer.

"Right, thank you officer." Steve looked at Sam. The two officers went to the house next door, most likely to inform the alert citizen they were not burglars.

"Where is the search warrant?" asked Steve. "I don't have it and I'm sure you took it from Nigel when we left the office."

Sam rummaged through his pockets. "Nothing." He went out to the car and searched through some of their stuff. Steve saw him close the car door and come back with a paper in his hand. "Dude, this is the search warrant. But it has a different street name than this house."

"Oh crap" said Steve.

Chapter 14

Singapore

The plane landed safely at Singapore Changi Airport at 20:15. The three Aussies got off and proceeded through immigration and customs. Nigel saw a sign with his name held by a middle aged man in a printed Hawaiian style shirt.

Nigel walked over and introduced his team. "Hi, I'm Nigel and this is my partner, Joyce Mathews and Mark Young, our legal aid."

"I'm Howard Chong. I have been assigned to assist with your investigation." His English was with a slight local Chinese accent.

"We haven't book rooms, do you have a suggestion?" asked Joyce.

"The Imperial Hotel, it is centrally located and moderately priced. I have a car and can drive you there now."

The four walked to the car park and put their luggage into the boot. The ride into downtown from the airport took twenty minutes. Traffic going into downtown was heavy. They reached the hotel and checked in. Howard waited in the lobby while the trio went to their rooms.

Mark was the first to take the lift back to the lobby. He stepped off and spotted Howard sitting in a small alcove. "We really are appreciative of you assisting us" said Mark.

"It is my pleasure. I have worked with the Australian police before and enjoy your professionalism. I learn something new every time."

The lift doors opened. Nigel and Joyce exited and walked over to join Mark and Howard. "Let's talk about what we need and how to go about getting the information" said Nigel.

"Starting with the Company Registration office, what do you know about their protocols and procedures?" asked Joyce.

"For one thing, they are only open for inquiry two hours per day. Ten till Noon. You must have an appointment. Most of the information is confidential and requires a court order to retrieve" said Howard.

"Can appointments be made anytime during normal business hours?" asked Mark.

"Yes, between nine and five Monday through Saturday. All government offices are open six days per week in Singapore."

Nigel looked at his watch. "It's too late to make an appointment today. How about banking hours?" asked Nigel.

"Banking hours are from nine until four Monday through Saturday. There are a few foreign banks that are closed on Saturday. From my experience, you may need a court order to inquire into details of accounts."

"What are the requirements to get a court order to view accounts?" asked Mark.

"It will depend on several things. If the account is a personal account it's not too hard. Business accounts are protected under a different set of laws. If fraud is suspected with adequate proof, then you will most likely get a court order of examination. This includes the business accounts and the officer's personal accounts. You must have a complete list of officers with addresses. The problem being, getting the officers names and addresses. The Company's office can be very stubborn with information."

"Okay, so we must start with the Company Registration office.

Have you experience with these people?" asked Joyce.

"Yes. Last month I investigated a company that had several complaints lodged by overseas clients. After I showed the judge the complaints, he issued the order. It turned out they were guilty of fraud for not shipping merchandise after collecting from their clients up front. The judge was very pleased with the evidence we assembled. I think I can get an appointment with the same judge."

"Great. We really can't do much more today. Would you like to have dinner with us?" asked Nigel.

"Thank you, I grabbed a bite at the airport while waiting for your flight. What time would you like to get started tomorrow?"

"I think we should be ready to make some phone calls at nine. Give us a call from the lobby about 08:30 and we can setup in my room. I'd prefer if you do the phoning and in Chinese" said Nigel.

"Until tomorrow" said Howard. He turned and walked to the exit.

"Let's talk about how to present a case that will get the judge to issue an order for the Company Registration office" said Joyce. "Let's go sit in the bar." They walked across the massive lobby to the bar and got a corner booth in the back. The place was nearly empty.

"It must be a bit early for the locals" said Mark.

"I don't think this place is popular with locals. I'd say mostly foreign businessmen and tourist" said Joyce.

"I picked up on something when Howard told us about his investigation. He presented written complaints to the judge. If we had a couple of complaints from clients, we may be able to get Howard to get another court order" said Mark.

"We can use the business suite to print out letters of complaint. I think one from New Zealand and one from Australia should do it" said Joyce.

"Hum, I don't know. Wouldn't that be fabricating evidence?" asked Nigel.

"Maybe we won't have to. I will phone the Jenkins' for permission allowing us to file a complaint on their behalf. That would make a true complaint" said Joyce.

"Now that may just work" said Nigel.

Mark sat and listened to their plans. "If I may interject something, I could write a letter on behalf of the AG in Australia to the Singapore authorities that we are looking into a massive fraud possibly involving the Asian Investment company. Nigel and Joyce smiled.

Chapter 15

Surprise Video

Nigel, Joyce and Mark finished breakfast and were in the lobby when Howard arrived. They went up to Nigel's room. When they were seated, Mark presented the letters he had created in the Business Centre.

Howard was quiet and listened to Mark explain the letters. The one from the Jenkins' was the important one. It outlined the suspected fraud and the amount of money involved.

"I think the judge will issue a court order based on this letter. The amount is huge compared to other evidence presented in the past" said Howard.

"Well that is a start. How do we make an appointment with the judge?" asked Joyce.

"I will call now. It may not be necessary for us to actually go before the judge. We can scan and email the documents and his clerk will call us with the decision" said Howard.

"We can use my laptop. I have a digital copy of the complaints," said Mark.

"Great, I'll get the judge's email address" said Howard. He used his cell phone and made the call to the judge's office and wrote the email address down. Mark ready with the document on his laptop typed in the email address and pressed the send button.

"Okay, that's taken care of. While we wait, let's outline the next few steps" said Nigel. He took out his note pad and pencil and wrote Company's Office at the top.

They discussed many different scenarios for an hour and ran out of topics. "After we get a response from the judge, let's hope all the officers and their addresses are listed by the Company's Office" said Joyce. "We can then partition for a search warrant for the bank accounts of Asian Investments.

Mark's laptop dinged with a chime. An email had arrived; it was from the judge's office with the court order attached. Mark copied it to a floppy disk. "I'll be back in a jiffy with the printed copy." Mark hurried out of the room to print the copy down in the Business Centre.

"We have a photo of one suspect in the case" said Nigel. He took the photo out of his case and handed it to Howard.

"Hum, this man looks familiar" said Howard. Nigel looked up.

"Do you know when or where you may have seen him?" asked Nigel.

"I'm not sure, but I may have seen him recently in some airport videos of arriving passengers. We viewed several days of recordings looking for a suspect from Hong Kong. I'm almost sure this is the man I saw. He was pulling a suit case to the taxi ranks. I can ask for that footage to verify if it was him."

"Yes, that would be a real break if you spotted him. We can establish a timeline and will have proof he came to Singapore" said Joyce.

"Give me a few minutes and I will phone the security office at the airport and have the video files emailed to us. I remember it was the very last segment we viewed. It was a recording from last Thursday." He called the security office at the airport and spoke to the person in charge and explained what he needed. Howard gave Mark's email address and hung up. "We should have the videos within the next hour."

"This is moving great. If we can establish Peters' arrival time, we may be able to find the Taxi that transported him to a local address" said Nigel.

"It should not be too hard to find the driver who picked up a foreign business man at a precise time. The Taxi would have recorded the time of the pickup and the destination" said Howard.

Mark came into the room with two copies of the court order. Joyce read over a copy and passed it to Nigel. "Howard can you phone the Company's Office and make us an appointment?" asked Joyce.

Howard phoned the Company's Office and got them an appointment at 11:00. They had over an hour to get to the building. Howard said he had his car parked out front of the hotel. It was only a ten minute drive.

Mark's laptop dinged with another email message. This one was addressed to Inspector Howard Chong. Attached was the video. Mark brought up the video and they watched. Joyce saw Peters. "There he is."

"That is defiantly him" said Nigel. "Look at the time stamp, 19:35. Howard can you find out the Taxi company that picked up a business man at about 19:40 from the airport?"

"No problem, there is only one company that has a license to pick up passengers at the airport. I'll make a phone call to their dispatch office." Howard called a number and spoke Chinese to someone. He waited a few seconds and spoke again. He made notes on a pad and hung up. "It seems our suspect arrived at this hotel at 20:00 last Thursday."

Mark clapped his hands. Nigel and Joyce smiled. "Mark, take this photo down to the front desk and see if you can get anyone to recognize Peters" said Nigel.

Mark returned in less than ten minutes. "No one on duty at the moment was at the front desk at 20:00. They had four check-ins during that time period. One was a single man. We will have to wait until the night crew come in at 18:00."

Joyce looked at her watch. "It's time to head for the Company's

Office. I suggest that only Howard and Nigel go. A large group may cause a delay."

"Good idea" said Howard. "These people seem to think they are the absolute rulers of business in Singapore."

"Mark and I will stay here and wait for your return" said Joyce.

Nigel and Howard left for the Company's office. Joyce and Mark reviewed their documents and worked on a list of items needed to track the funds to and from the bank by Asian Investments.

Chapter 16

Vanished

Nigel and Howard arrived back an hour later. They had re-trieved all of the Company's Office information for Asian Investments. The company was incorporated one week after the Jenkins' check was deposited by Secure Pacific Investments. The capital stock was listed as One Thousand shares with a par value of one Singapore dollar. There were two people listed as share-holders, the managing director and one director. The managing director's name was Lu Phong Chung with one share of stock and the other listed director was an English name, Barry O'Brian with Nine Hundred Ninety Nine shares. Both addresses were local.

"It appears that Mr. Peters is listed as a director using his fake passport alias" said Joyce.

"We do have the Singapore Airlines ticket agent who verified Peters /O'Brian is the same person, but I think we should now pe-tition for a court order to examine the bank records. We have the name of at least one bank they have used to make deposits from Secure Pacific Investments in Australia" said Mark. "Howard, if you will give me the format for the petition, I'll type it and send it to the clerk of the judge."

"I will make a call and have the template for the petition sent to your email address."

"Okay, now we are moving. How far is the bank from here?" asked Joyce.

"About five minutes. We could walk" said Howard. He made the call for the petition format and hung up.

"Let's order up some lunch while we wait for the petition info to arrive" said Nigel. They each looked at the room service menu and made their selections. Mark phoned in the order.

"If we get the petition in before 14:00, I think we can get the court order before closing time" said Howard.

The lunch arrived and they talked about their individual jobs and made small talk. It was apparent to Nigel and Joyce that Mark was not a novice in the workings of the court.

There was a ding from Mark's laptop. The email contained the petition template. Howard assisted Mark in filling out the form and sending it to the judge's office. 13:00 showed in the window of the computer.

At 14:30 the court order arrived in Mark's inbox to examine the bank accounts of Asian Investments, its managing director, Mr. Chong and its only other director a Mr. Barry O'Brian. They had agreed that Joyce and Howard should be the one's going to the bank; Joyce with her skills in accounting and Howard to give a local emphasis.

At 15:00, Howard and Joyce were admitted to the manager's office of South China Sea Bank. Howard spoke English and introduced him and Joyce. The court order was read by the manager. He nodded his approval and punched a button on his phone. A young woman came in and he gave her instructions in Chinese to print out the last two year's transactions of Asian Investments.

Within five minutes the young woman returned with several sheets of printout. "If you will follow me, you may use one of our private rooms to examine the documents. If you have any questions or need additional information, please call this extension" said the young woman in Chinese. She looked at Joyce and smiled.

"Thank you" said Howard in Chinese.

Joyce sat down at the table and began to read the various transactions. It appeared there were very few. All of the deposits were from Australia. There were several checks written to an account in Hong Kong, one very large. There were monthly withdrawals to the managing director's personal account. The latest withdrawal was a check written last Thursday for $50,000 which left the account with a zero balance. A digital picture of the check showed the signature was Barry O'Brian.

"Well, it seems Asian Investments has decided to close up shop" said Joyce.

"Let's show the picture of Peters to the manager" said Howard.

"Good idea."

Howard picked up the phone and called the extension the manager's assistant give him. Howard requested to see the manager again. A knock on the door was the assistant who escorted them to the manager's office.

Howard showed the picture of Peters to the manager. He studied the picture but shook his head no. The assistant looked at the picture but shook her head no also.

Howard thanked the manager and his assistant. Joyce smiled at the young woman and they left the office with the account information.

On the street, Howard said, "We know Asian Investments was wound up on the same day Peters arrived in Singapore. Maybe we should speak to Mr. Chung."

"Good idea. I would like to see his reaction when we show him Peters' picture."

They walked back to the hotel in silence, Joyce thinking of ways to get more information. When they arrived back at the hotel, it was getting close to 16:00. Joyce briefed Mark and Nigel on what she and Howard had discovered. Not much, but the money trail was established from Australia to Singapore and to Hong Kong. The disappointing thing was they were still at a dead end with tying Peters to Asian Investments.

to the time line ?
really no important.

"Maybe when the night crew comes in we can get some ID on Peters being here at this hotel. And maybe confirm him as Barry O'Brian" said Nigel.

At 18:30, Mark took the picture of Peters to the front desk. A male clerk was checking in a couple. A female clerk was busy on a computer terminal. Mark walked to the female's position and waited to be recognized.

The clerk looked up and smiled at Mark. "May I help you?"

"Yes." Mark showed the picture to the young clerk. "Do you recognize this man, he checked in last Thursday at 2000."

The clerk studied the picture. "I'm not sure. We get many European men here, and pardon me but they seem to look the same."

Mark smiled. "Could you show this to your associate?"

"Yes, one moment." She stepped to the male clerk and spoke to him in Chinese. He shook his head no. She returned to her position. "No he does not recognize him either. You might want to check the bell captain's station. Sometimes they spend a lot of time with our guest."

Mark thanked her and walked over to the concierge's desk. "Pardon me but do you recognize this man?" The bell captain studied the picture. "Yes, he was here for one night. He had one bag. I'm not sure when he left."

"Do you know if he took a taxi after leaving the hotel?"

"No, I did not see him leave."

"Thank you. If anything comes to mind, or any other of the employees remember seeing this man, please phone this number. It is a police matter." Mark gave the bell captain Howard's cell number and left a copy of Peters' picture.

Mark returned to Nigel's room and reported his findings. "It appears Mr. Barry O'Brian has hit the wind", said Howard.

"What now" asked Joyce?

"I don't think there is any more to be done here. We have confirmed Peters is Barry O'Brian by his airline ticket and fake passport. We cannot tie him to Asian Investments without positive identification. Howard, do you think you could interview Mr. Chung?" We have his address and he is the only person that can connect Peters as O'Brian to Asian Investments" said Nigel.

"Yes, I will phone in a pickup for questioning with the precinct near this address." Howard used his cell to phone. "We should hear back if they were successful in picking him up in less than an hour."

***

Howard's phone buzzed. It was the precinct captain. Howard's face took on a frown as he listened. "It seems the address of both Mr. Chung and O'Brian is an empty warehouse. I asked the captain to check driver's records for Lou Phong Chung. He will phone me back if he gets a hit."

Joyce looked at the printouts from the bank. "Mr. Chung or Mr. O'Brian do not have personal accounts at this bank. How hard would it be to canvas the local banks for a large deposit of $50,000 to a personal account last Thursday? We do have a court order to examine the personal accounts of the officers of Asian Investments."

Howard thought for a moment. "We could request the AG's office to send out a mass email to all the banks with the request. We may get lucky."

"Do it" said Nigel.

Howard made the call. "The AG's office needs a copy of the court order and a written request. Mark, send the AG's office a copy of the court order for bank examinations of the officers of Asian Investments and a request to query the banks for the deposit" said Howard.

Joyce smiled, "I feel lucky today. So far we have tracked the money directly to Asian Investments and have identified Peters arriving in Singapore and a large payment to Chung which closed the account. Peters is O'Brian and if we find Chung we might prove a tie between Peters/O'Brian and Asian Investments. That will close the loop to fraud and we will have a real crime committed."

"It will be tomorrow before we know the result of the inquiry. I'm starved let's go down and eat" said Nigel. "Howard, are you free to have dinner with us tonight?"

"Yes, but I think I can find us a better restaurant than the hotel restaurant."

They all smiled and left for dinner.

Chapter 17

Lou Phong Chung

Howard arrived at the Imperial hotel at 08:30. He went to the row of house phones and called Nigel's room. "Good morning. I'm in the lobby."

"Come on up, we are all here."

Howard took the lift up to Nigel's floor and knocked on the door. Mark answered the door.

"Looks like a fine day to make some progress. The banks have received the email request from the AG's office. It should not take them long to confirm any deposits of that amount last Thursday or Friday" said Howard.

"Great. Let's talk about how to go about the interview of Mr. Chung. Howard what is the protocol for this type of interview especially where there is no apparent crime but only suspicion?" asked Nigel.

"We normally bring in the suspect, place them in an interview room and let them be alone for some time. They have no idea why they were picked up. We then send in one detective to start the interview, usually just general questions as to job, education, and family. The second interviewer starts with a leading question about some specific point in the case. Like how long have you worked for Peters? Are you aware of the illegal transactions involving Asian Investments?"

"Do you think you can make arrangements for one of us to be in the second interview?" asked Nigel.

"Yes, I spoke to my division captain this morning. He spoke to the AG's office and they confirmed your status. He agreed to allow your team full access to our facilities and procedures. I am sure fraud has been committed by Asian Investments. I think Chung is our link. "

"Yes, I do too. I think Joyce should do the second interview with you. She may be the shock we need to rattle him to talk" said Nigel.

"What should I do during the interview? Most likely he will speak Chinese and I will be useless" said Joyce.

"I will open the interview with English. With his alleged contact with Peters, I am sure he speaks English."

Mark was quiet and observed the three as they strategized the interview. He was thinking of how to shock Chung with legalese. He had an idea and spoke up. "What if we tell Chung the people that invested in Asian Investments are going to sue him personally for fraud? It will add a bit of uncertainty to his situation. He may know the legal penalty of a fraud suit in Singapore."

"That's a good idea. The penalty here is very severe for fraud, especially involving foreigners" said Howard. "If we lead off with implying he is being sued for fraud by one of his investors that will put a lot of doubt in his mind about his legal status. He just may implicate Peters as the principle of the fraud."

"Mark, prepare some documents on behalf of the Jenkins' that indicate they are prepared to sue Chung directly for incompetence, malfeasance and fraud" said Joyce.

"Okay, I'll get right on it."

"Are the interviews recorded?" asked Nigel.

"Yes, we record all interviews."

"Great, if we can get him to implicate Peters/O'Brian, then when we catch up with Peters and show him the recording of Chung giving him up, he may just crack and tell us all."

Howard's cell phone buzzed. "Howard speaking, yes I am with them now. Okay, I'll get right on it. Thanks for the swift reply." Howard smiled and terminated the call. "It seems there is one bank that handled a $50,000 dollar deposit last Friday. They are emailing the details."

"Wonderful news" said Joyce.

A chirp from Marks's laptop indicated an email. It had an attachment. The document showed a deposit receipt for Lou Phong Chung into his personal account at Mali Bank and Trust $50,000 last Friday at 10:00. Also the email gave Chung's address and phone number.

Howard punched in the number for his office. "This is Inspector Chong; I need you to pick up for questioning, Mr. Lou Phong Chung. I am emailing you his address now. Yes, inform me when he has been brought to the office for an interview."

"I suggest we go to the Mali Bank and Trust with Peters' picture and see if maybe he has an account there also" said Joyce.

"The bank is only two blocks from here. We can walk" said Howard.

"Joyce you and Howard go to the bank and Mark and I will make our report to the AG's office in Australia" said Nigel.

Howard and Joyce walked the two blocks to the bank. Joyce felt this was the break they needed to nail Peters and start the close up of the case. "Do you think Chung will cave-in and give us info on Peters?" asked Joyce.

"Unless Chung is secure in his position and knows we are bluffing on the law suit, then yes I think he will eventually give up Peters. The trick is the pace of the questions and how confident we appear in the interview."

"I will follow your lead. I'm in uncharted territory with this type of interview."

"Don't worry, if we go slow and not attempt to badger Chung, he may think we are on his side. I have an idea to gain his trust. We imply that Peters is who we are after and not Chung. We may imply that if he gives up Peters, the law suit against him will go away."

Joyce smiled. *Howard would make a good lawyer.* They arrived at the bank.

Howard went to the receptionist, showed his credentials and asked to speak to the manager. The receptionist made a phone call and told Howard and Joyce to have a seat. Within only a minute a tall European man appeared and introduced himself as the manager for Mali Bank and Trust. Joyce and Howard were surprised a European was the manager.

"My name is Paul Restone, I am the manager. How may I help you Inspector?"

Mr. Restone, my name is Howard Chong and this is my associate Joyce Mathews. We are the ones that requested the information on the $50,000 deposit last Friday. And thank you for coming to our aid. We would like to ask you if you have any business dealings with this man."

Restone looked at the picture of Peters and rubbed his chin. "He seems familiar but I'm not sure. I'll ask my assistant who usually meets most of our business customers" Restone asked the receptionist to call his assistant and have him come to the reception area.

"Mr. Restone, how long have you been manager of this bank?" asked Joyce.

"I have been at this bank for the past fifteen years and as manager for the past three."

A small middle aged man approached. Restone asked him in Chinese if he recognized the man in the picture. The assistant looked a long time at the picture. He spoke in Chinese.

"I'm sorry, but he does not recognize this man."

"Thank you for your time Mr. Restone" said Howard. Howard and Joyce walked back to the hotel.

They were crossing the lobby for the lifts when Howard's phone buzzed. "Inspector Chong" answered Howard. "Yes, we will be there ~~in thirty minutes~~ shortly." He terminated the call. "That was the precinct. They have Chung in an interview room. It will take us about thirty minutes to get there. Call Nigel and update him on the bank and that we are heading to the interview with Chung." Joyce went to a lobby phone and phoned Nigel.

§

They arrived at the police precinct office. Howard introduced Joyce to the watch captain. They were shown to the interview room by a uniformed officer. Chung looked to be in his late forty's. He was sitting with his head hung down. Howard and Joyce sat down on the opposite side of the table.

Howard spoke in English. "I'm inspector Chong and this is my associate Joyce Mathews. Mr. Chung we have reason to believe you and your company, Asian Investments, have been engaged in a massive fraud of investors. I have documents from one investor who may be filing a law suit against you personally for fraud."

Chung looked calm and unconcerned. "I have not committed any crime. Investors are given the standard waver holding the company harmless if their investments turn out bad."

"Mr. Chung, you and your company may be sued by a retired couple for squandering their investments. They claim your company knowingly invested their money in a scheme to lose their money. We are not here to accuse you personally, but are interested in speaking with Mr. Peters or as you may know him as O'Brian."

Joyce watched Chung's reaction to the mentioning of Peters' name. There was none. Howard sat back and waited for a reply. Chung sat straight and said nothing.

"Mr. Chung, we have traced all of the deposits from Secure Pacific Investments to Asian Investments. We know Asian Investment's bank account was closed last Thursday. You received a check signed by Mr. O'Brian/Peters for $50,000 and deposited at the Mali Bank and Trust company on Friday. Is this correct?" said Joyce. She watched his face carefully for any reaction to her using Peters' name.

"I don't know a Mr. Peters" said Chung.

"Do you acknowledge receipt of $50,000 from Asian Investments and depositing the check into your personal account at Mali Bank and Trust on Friday?" asked Howard.

"Yes I received a check for $50,000 as severance pay from Asian Investments."

Joyce took out the picture of Peters and slid it across the table to Chung. "Do you know this man?" asked Joyce.

Chung looked at the picture and shook his head no. "Mr. Chung you do know that if you lie to the police you will be guilty of obstruction of justice with a severe penalty" said Howard.

Chung sat without looking at Howard or Joyce and said nothing. "Mr. Chung can you describe Mr. O'Brian for us?" asked Joyce.

"I have never meet Mr. O'Brian. We did business only on the phone or email."

"Mr. Chung, according to your bank records, Asian Investments made several large investments into a Hong Kong company that purchased race horses. How did you select that particular company for investing your company's money?" asked Joyce.

Chung sat very still and said nothing. Howard motioned for Joyce to join him outside the interview room.

Howard looked very serious. "I am sure he is covering for Peters. I would bet the $50,000 was hush money not severance pay. I am going to ask for a wiretap on his phone. He may try to contact Peters after we release him from the interview."

"Great, I will go back and probe more while you get the wiretap." Joyce returned to the interview room.

"Mr. Chung, you are in serious trouble. You may not know all that is happening. The evidence we have gathered indicates that Asian Investments may have violated many Singapore laws. If I were you, I'd make sure Peters gets his fair share of the blame. It's going to happen and it's only a matter of time before we catch up with Peters. If you cooperate now, I'm sure the courts will take that into consideration when all of this goes to trial."

Chung looked at the table top but said nothing. The door opened and Howard returned.

"Mr. Chung you are free to go. We will be calling on you again shortly, so don't go out of Singapore until we have concluded our investigation. Do you understand?" Chung nodded his understand. "Mr. Chung I must have a verbal confirmation if you understand the conditions of your status."

"Yes I understand."

"Fine, this interview was recorded and your response noted as well. If you think of something you would like to tell us, please call us at this number." Howard gave Chung his business card.

Chung left the room. "The tap is active. We will get recordings of all his conversations or text messages" said Howard.

"That was not what I expected, but at least we now have at least one suspect interviewed even if it was a dead end" said Joyce. "Any ideas?"

"Let's return to the hotel and update Nigel and Mark and plan the next phase."

§

Lu PhongChung hurried out of the police building. He was not happy about having all the pressure on him. *Peters was generous, but his connection to Asian Investments was only verbal and to me.* He took out his cell phone. He looked at his contacts list. Peters was not listed, only Secure Pacific Investments. He knew it was his word against Peters of any involvement in Asian Investments. *Maybe the police were bluffing and had no evidence against Asian Investments. I'll just ride it out and see what happens.* He punched in a number.

Chapter 18

Chung Lied

Nigel and Mark had finished their report to the AG's office when Joyce and Howard returned.

"The interview with Chung was a bust. He did not admit to anything and said he did not recognize Peters and never met O'Brian. It seems to me we have to go on to Hong Kong to follow the money trail" said Joyce.

"Okay, let's review. We know Asian Investments was run by Mr. Chung. Most if not all of the money for Asian Investments came from Secure Pacific Investments. Chung says he never met Peters/O'Brian. Asian Investments only invested in Hong Kong. We know Peters was here in this hotel last Thursday evening as O'Brian. We know he signed a check to Chung. How did the check get to Chung?" asked Nigel.

"Good question. The check was dated the same day Chung deposited it. I think I will call Chung and ask him a couple of questions" said Howard. He pulled out his note pad and retrieved Chung's cell phone number. "Mr. Chung, this is Howard Chong. I have a question for you. Where did you meet O'Brian to receive your severance check?" There was a pause and no response from Chung. "Mr. Chung, you can either answer the question on the phone or back at police headquarters."

"It was left on my desk when I arrived for work."

"How did you know it was a severance check? Did you speak to O'Brian about closing up the business?" Again there was a pause.

"Mr. O'Brian called me the night before and told me the business was closing and I would find the severance check on my desk."

"I see, so Mr. O'Brian had access to your office."

"Yes, he had a key."

"Thank you Mr. Chung." Howard terminated the call and filled the group in on what was said. "So Chung had denied ever meeting Peters or O'Brian" said Joyce.

"Howard, do you think there would be surveillance cameras in Asian Investments building?" asked Mark.

"Hum, I can find out." Howard punched in his office number and spoke to someone about checking out the building where Asian Investments was located and if they have a security system with cameras. "We should know in the next few minutes."

"We know the name of the firm in Hong Kong and the bank where the checks from Asian Investments were deposited. It appears we have to go to Hong Kong" said Nigel.

Howard's phone buzzed. "Inspector Chong speaking. Yes I did. I see. Give me their number and the person's name I should contact. Thank you." Howard punched in the number to the security company. "This is inspector Chong from the Singapore police department. May I speak to Mr. Fong?" Howard raised an eyebrow. "Mr. Fong, this is Howard Chong with the police. I understand you have a recording from last Thursday and Friday of the building housing Asian Investments." Howard listened for a few seconds. "May I come over and view those recordings in the next hour. It is very urgent. Thank your Mr. Fong. I shall see you shortly." Howard terminated the call. "They have recordings of all floors and entrances to tenant offices. We should be able to determine who went in and out of Asian Investments last Thursday and Friday and at what time."

"Great work. Mark you go with Howard and assist in identifying Peters or anyone you recognize on the recording" said Nigel. "Joyce and I will start setting up our trip to Hong Kong."

Chong and Mark rode through the downtown area to the offices of the security company. They were located in a tall building near the court house. Howard parked the police car in an area marked Police Cars Only. "They only speak Chinese here so I will interpret. This should not take too long. It appears that Chung does not spend that much time with Asian Investments."

They took the lift to the 36th floor. Howard introduced himself and Mark to Mr. Fong. They were shown into a viewing room with several large TVs. Mr. Fong started the recording at 07:00 on Thursday. By noon no one had entered or left the offices of Asian Investments. The recording was sped up and stopped by Fong when a man appeared at the door. He used a key and entered the door. It was Mr. Chung. The time stamp said 13:34. The recording resumed in fast forward mode. Fong stopped the recording at the time stamp of 17:15. Mr. Chung appeared at the door and locked the office. The recording was resumed and sped through till 17:00 on Friday. No one entered or left the office.

"Mr. Fong thank you. Can you download those two days on floppy disks?" Mark figured what was asked when Howard handed the floppy disks to Fong. He downloaded the file to the disks and handed them back to Howard.

Howard and Mark shook hands with Fong and returned to the street. Howard had been thinking all the way down the lift. "Mr. Chung has committed a crime when he lied that he retrieved the check from his desk on Friday morning. It is also apparent that Peters/O'Brian did not visit the offices on Thursday or Friday. I'm going to have Chung picked up and charged with obstruction of justice. That may loosen his tongue." Howard called his office and instructed them to issue a warrant for the arrest of Chung on Obstruction Charges.

"I hope he is still in town and not bolted" said Mark. They returned to the hotel and filled in Joyce and Nigel.

"That's great. At least we have something that will stick. His interview recording and the video will be proof positive he lied" said Joyce.

"We have made arrangements for our trip to Hong Kong.

Mark, you will stay here and assist Howard with Chung. We will phone as soon as we arrive in Hong Kong" said Nigel.

Chapter 19

Hong Kong

The plane landed at Hong Kong's airport at 18:10. The train ride into Kowloon took about twenty minutes. They got off the train at the stop near the Holiday Inn on Nathan Road. The Star ferry was within walking distance from the hotel, and the office of Hong Kong Horse Breeders was in an office block on Nathan Road. The bank, South China Trading and Trust was on Hong Kong Island across the bay. The Holiday Inn on Nathan Road was ideal for their purposes.

Joyce and Nigel checked in to the hotel and agreed to meet later in the small bar off the lobby on the ground floor. Joyce arrived at the bar first and while she waited phoned Mark and Howard and gave them an update.

Nigel saw Joyce at a table near the piano and noted she was finishing a call. "How's your room?"

"Fine, I have a great view of the bay. You?"

"I have a view of Nathan Road. Not so great, but if we have any luck tomorrow, we may need only two nights. Let's eat in the hotel dining room tonight. I'm bushed and need to call it a night early."

They went up to the second floor where a large buffet was laid out with foods from all over the world with little flags of the countries protruding above the array and behind each country's offerings stood a chef assisting in selecting the goodies.

"Wow, this is something else" said Joyce.

"I think I will stick to the European variety and save my stomach an ordeal" said Nigel.

They finished up their meal by 20:30 and went to their rooms.

At 07:00 Nigel dressed and was ready for breakfast when his phone rang. "Hello. Good morning to you too. Okay I'll meet you on the second floor."

Breakfast was a series of stations around the dining room with chefs preparing nearly any imaginable concoction. Nigel chose eggs Benedict with hollandaise sauce. Joyce went for eggs over medium with bacon and hash browns.

They finished breakfast. "Let's meet at the coffee shop in thirty minutes" said Nigel.

"Okay. See you then." Joyce got up and went to her room. Nigel finished his coffee and made a phone call home to update his wife.

They showed up at the coffee shop almost at the same time. A few tables were empty and they took one in the back. It was a self-serve bar with the normal collection of coffees from around the world. They selected the brew of their choice and went back to their table.

"I've been thinking about my observation of Chung and his statement." Joyce looked down into her cup. "He may have met Peters at some bar or restaurant to receive the check. I bet he has known Peters for a long time. Based on the length of time when Asian Investments was formed and now, over two years have lapsed. Howard gave me a picture he took of Chung while we were in the interview room. I think we should show his picture to the bank people."

"I hope we will not hit too many obstacles here." Howard

phoned his contact, Lt. Loo Phuong, at the Kowloon police head office and made an appointment. "Phuong's precinct is only a few blocks from here. The walk will do us good," said Nigel. They finished their coffee and headed into Kowloon.

The police precinct was not hard to find. They went to the information desk and asked to speak to Lt. Phuong. The desk clerk phoned Phuong and told them he would be right down.

Lt. Phuong was tall for a Chinese and appeared to be in his mid-forties. "I'm Lt. Phuong, how may I help you?"

Nigel introduced himself and Joyce as who Howard Chong had phoned about. "Lieutenant we have tracked the money in a huge fraud case to a company and bank here in Hong Kong. We did uncover some information in Singapore with Inspector Chong, but we could not tie the main suspect directly to the bank or company that was in contact with the company here. We would like to review the case with you and get any assistance you may be able to provide us."

"Come with me. My office is on the fourth floor and we can talk there." They went over to the bank of lifts and took one to the fourth floor. Nigel was impressed with the efficient way things appeared to be run. The individual detectives had cubicles, not an open bull pen. It was actually quiet. Lt. Phuong's office was located in one corner with windows facing the harbor and the office towers in Kowloon.

"Inspectors have a seat. Now tell me about this case."

Nigel took out his case note book. "Lieutenant the case begins with a retired couple in Australia winning the lottery for four million dollars." He told the entire story in detail.

"The laws here in Hong Kong are similar to those in Singapore. Companies are protected with respect to information about their officers and banking arrangements. We do not take fraud lightly, especially when it involves overseas transactions. We still have most of the British system in place with respect to judges and search warrants. Let me see your evidence of the bank transactions and I will see if our fraud people can make a case for a search warrant. The warrant will include the company's office as well as banks."

"We have all of the transactions on this floppy disk. Joyce has put together a spreadsheet with the transactions and the flow of the funds. I think your people will understand it without a problem."

"Fine, I will take this to our fraud department. We have a committee that determines actions of this type. They will be meeting later this morning. You should hear from me by Noon."

"Lieutenant that is great news, we will need police assistance in executing the warrant in the event we get a positive report."

"I will personally execute the warrant when it is issued. Have a nice morning. Give me your cell phone number so I can reach you with the decision." Nigel gave Phuong his card with his international number. Joyce and Nigel shook hands with Phuong and left his office.

They were silent on the way to the street level. Joyce was pondering how Peters could manage Hong Kong Horse Breeding from Sydney.

"Well, we seem to have an ally in Phuong. We may get lucky with the bank and company's office" said Nigel.

"I've been wondering how Peters would have set up all of these companies. He certainly would have to come here himself or have a very trusted friend to set up bank accounts. I'm not convinced he would trust anyone. He seems to me to be a lone wolf."

"I agree. Peters would want tight control of the bank accounts. If he had an accomplice, that person would also be on the signature of the accounts. That was not the case in Singapore, O'Brian was the only signature. My bet is that he came here with false ID's. I have an idea."

Joyce saw a small park with benches in the next block. "Let's sit in that park over there and talk."

They took a bench facing a large square. "Okay, here's my idea. Let's go in a large bank and pose as business people wanting to open a new account. We should learn most of the procedures and requirements the banks have on business accounts, especially foreign accounts."

"From my experience in Sydney, foreign businesses are very much scrutinized when they apply for any type of business accounts. Transfer accounts are the most popular. These accounts are used as temporary holding accounts. The local money comes in, usually by wire transfer and then sits for the required clearing time and then transferred to an overseas bank via wire transfer. Most of the time checks are not written on the account. The banks charge a transaction fee and get to earn a little interest on the money for a few days while the bank clears the transaction."

Nigel listened carefully. "So, if a foreign company sets up a transfer account, usually checks are not written on the account. Does that mean there are no signatures required? How does the bank verify the transactions?"

"Usually there is a password attached to the account. Only the principal account holder may change the password. The banks are normally not even aware of these transactions. The computer system handles all the transactions. There are exceptions of course and the computer will spit out a notice for someone to check the anomaly. This could be when large amounts are transferred or the limit of transactions is exceeded. These exceptions are predetermined by the account holder and the bank."

"If an exception occurs, the bank contacts the account holder for verification?" asked Nigel.

"Yes. I see where you are going. There must be a name and contact information stored with the account." Joyce sat back and thought about the implication of such information.

Nigel looked around the large square. A large bank was across the square. "Let's go over to that bank and see if we can open a transfer account."

"Okay, but let's talk about the setup. Let's use Asian Investments as our base company. We want an account to collect deposits by investors here in Hong Kong and transfer the money to Singapore. How does that sound?'

Nigel nodded his head. "Sounds good to me. I will use Barry O'Brian as my name. But what if they ask for passports or ID's?"

"Well for now, let's tell the bank we are shopping for a bank and are not ready yet to go through the formality of opening the account. That will get us all the procedure and requirement information without revealing too much" said Joyce.

"Right, let's go and see what happens."

They walked across the square and entered the big bank. The lobby was busy with people. A desk with a sign in English said Information. Nigel pointed out the sign and they walked to the desk.

"Hello, may I help you?" The young woman had observed they were European and spoke perfect English.

"Yes, we are seeking a bank to act as our transfer agents for our business in Singapore. We would like to speak to someone about the procedure and requirements to open a transfer account" said Nigel.

"I see. Please have a seat here and I will make arrangements for you to speak to one of our officers." Nigel and Joyce sat in the comfortable chairs in front of the desk.

A middle aged Asian man approached the desk. He conferred with the young woman in Chinese. The woman turned to Nigel and Joyce. "Mr. Wong will assist you. Please follow him to his office."

Mr. Wong did a shallow bow and led Joyce and Nigel to a small office in the back of the bank. They were seated in front of a modest desk. "I understand you want to open a transfer account."

"Yes, we have a business in Singapore and want to conduct some business here. We are interviewing banks today to find a fit to our requirements", said Nigel.

"What is the nature of your business?"

"We have an investment company. Many of our investors live here in Hong Kong and want to make various investments. Mailing checks takes too long for the transaction to be completed. Many opportunities may be missed because of the length of time for the checks to clear. By having them send their checks to a bank here in Hong Kong and then transferring the proceeds to our bank in Singapore will cut the time by a few days if not weeks."

"What is the name of your company?"

Nigel looked Mr. Wong directly in the eyes. "Asian Investments, Ltd. My Name is Barry O'Brian and this is my assistant Anne Gables."

Wong wrote on a large yellow pad in Chinese. He turned to his computer and typed something. "Your company is listed as a company doing business in Hong Kong. So that part of the procedure is complete. All that is required is for your bank in Singapore to send us an email requesting the transfer account be setup. You may name the account anything you like. We do not need anything from you until we setup the account. We will then need your email address and will send you a temporary password that has registered you in our computer system. You will log on to our system, change the password to anything you desire. Only you and the computer know the password. You can set restrictions such as a cap on the amount of a transfer or the number of transactions per day. That's it."

"You say our company is already registered as doing business in Hong Kong. We are a very private company and I am curious about the amount and type of information that is available about our company."

"Mr. O'Brian, the only thing listed is your company name under registered foreign companies doing business in Hong Kong. It shows you have been registered just over two years. That is all. The company's office will have all the other information as private and confidential."

Nigel and Joyce nodded and thanked Mr. Wong and explained they would be making a decision on the bank in a few days and left the bank for the bench across the square.

"Well, that was interesting. Seems there may be some more information at the company's office, but actually Peters could have had anyone register the company and being here in person was not a requirement to open a transfer account. But remember, Mrs. Thurman has checks written from Hong Kong Breeders, Ltd. That means a regular business account had to be set up" said Joyce.

Nigel's phone buzzed. "Hello this is Nigel." He listened for a few seconds. "That's good news Lieutenant. We will be at your office in a few minutes."

"I gather that was Phuong with a warrant to examine the company's office information."

"Yes and not only that but a warrant for Peters/O'Brian. He did not explain why the warrant for O'Brian but said he had all the paperwork and to come to his office."

They swiftly walked to the police building and went up to Phuong's office. Phuong was busy with several people. Nigel and Joyce sat in the waiting area.

Phuong's office began to clear of people and one of the detectives walked over and told Nigel and Joyce Phuong would see them now.

Phuong motioned for them to have a seat. He closed the door to his office. "I have been busy tracking information on Hong Kong Horse Breeding, Ltd. There seems to be lots of missing information. For one, they are not a legit company. They were never registered in the company's office.

"So the company is bogus" said Joyce.

"Yes. The bank you gave me said they were requested to open an account in the name of Hong Kong Horse Breeding, Ltd. two years ago by a legal firm in Kowloon on behalf of several investors. I phoned the law firm, they have no knowledge of Hong Kong Horse Breeders, Ltd.

"So it appears someone used the law firm's identity to open the account" said Nigel.

"I spoke to the bank people and their records indicate the person representing the law firm had power of attorney from a Mr. B. O'Brian. The account was opened and the signature card was return via post a week later. The checks were printed and sent to a post office box also in Kowloon. We checked the box and it was closed shortly after the account was opened. Mr. B. O'Brian was the name of the box holder. I presented the evidence to our committee and they concurred that further information was needed and a warrant was necessary. The judge issued the warrant."

"I must say I am impressed with the swiftness of your department" said Nigel. "We too have been trying to find out how the bank accounts could have been set up, but it appears your findings trump our findings. So, I conclude that it is possible that B. O'Brian may not have been here at all to set up the accounts."

"Oh, he was here. The banks take photos of all that apply for accounts. The photo sent to us matches the one you gave me. It seems Mr. O'Brian represented a law firm in Kowloon and committed a crime in the process."

"Okay, so the company's office is a dead end, but the warrant we have gives us access to all the checks and transfers from Hong Kong Horse Breeders accounts at the bank" said Joyce.

Phuong smiled, "Yes we should go and speak with the bank officials now."

They left Phuong's office and joined a uniformed officer on the street. He had a car ready and they took the tunnel over to Hong Kong Island. The driver pulled up in front of the bank. Phuong spoke to the driver in Chinese and motioned for Nigel and Joyce to follow him.

Phuong walked up to the information desk and spoke to the receptionist. She nodded and looked at Nigel and Joyce with interest. She spoke on the phone to someone and then spoke a few words to Phuong.

"We are to wait over in the lobby for the bank officer" said Phuong. "It seems that this bank has ties to many overseas banks, including banks in Australia."

A very small man approached and introduced himself to Nigel in English as Wo Ling, Assistant Managing Director of the bank. "Please follow me to our conference room." They walked a short distance and took the lift up to the third floor. The halls were carpeted and gave the entire place a plush appearance. They entered a large conference room and were invited to sit at one end of a five meter table.

Lt. Phuong took out the warrants and passed them to Wo Ling. "As you will see, we are in pursuit of this man." Phuong passed a photo of Peters/O'Brian to Ling. "Do you recognize him?"

"No, but if you will allow me, I will have someone check the files. Do you know the account number?"

"Yes, we have it here," said Nigel. He handed Wo a slip of paper with the account number.

Ling used a phone on the table and spoke to someone. A large TV monitor blinked on and pictures began to slide across. There on the monitor was a picture of Peters/O'Brian.

"Please pull all the information about this account and put the information on this floppy disk" said Phuong.

Wo Ling spoke to the person on the phone. "We will have your information in a few minutes. May I offer you refreshments?"

Joyce said, "Why yes, some hot tea would be lovely." The others declined.

Within a few minutes a young man came into the room and handed a floppy disk to Mr. Ling. "Here is your information. Is there anything else I can do to help you?"

"Not at this time. We appreciate your cooperation" said Phuong. He extended his hand for a handshake and turned. He motioned Nigel and Joyce to follow him out.

They were taken back to the police station. "I have issued an alert. That is about all we can do at the present time" said Phuong.

"We really appreciate your help on this case. It seems you have a case also. With luck we may be able help each other apprehend Peters/O'Brian" said Nigel. "We know he was in Singapore Thursday and Friday. We lost his trail and were left with following the money. It seems that may have also ended. The airline indicated he had an open ticket to Hong Kong and to Bangkok. Maybe we should concentrate on the airport and find out if anyone with his description has come through in the last few days. I'm sure he is not using the name Peters or O'Brian."

"His photo has been sent to all the immigration offices. We may get a hit if he came into the country. The face recognition software is not that good, but we can hope" said Phuong. "I will phone you if anything turns up."

Nigel and Joyce took the lift back to the street level and walked slowly back towards Nathan Road. They were both in deep thought. "We now have a crime committed by Peters. We know he opened the bogus company Hong Kong Horse Breeders' account. This was the account that Asian Investments invested almost all of its money into. We can tie Secure Investments to Asian Investments and to Hong Kong Horse Breeders. A mysterious group in Bangkok bought the horses from New Zealand and sold them to the bogus company. Suddenly the bogus company went belly-up and sold the horses back to a different Bangkok company for a loss of nearly three million dollars. The money ended up in Bangkok. I think we have enough evidence to say we have fraud and money laundering. I think the next stop is Bangkok."

Chapter 20

Bangkok

Nigel called Mark to have the Austrian AG's office contact the Bangkok authorities of their arrival and purpose.

Nigel and Joyce arrived in Bangkok at 11:15 local time. They had rested on the flight and were ready for a full day's work. They made their way through the immigration line and exited to the arrivals hall to claim their bags. Customs was brief and they made their way to the exit and hailed a taxi. Nigel told the driver to take them to the Hilton Hotel on Wireless road. The driver nodded he understood the English destination.

They checked into the hotel and agreed to meet in the dining room for lunch. Joyce phoned home to check on her son. Her mother as usual asked no questions but gave a glowing report of Robby. She thanked her mum and headed toward the dining room.

"We need a plan to follow up as we did in Singapore with the banks."

Nigel shook his head as he ate. "Yes, and we need to find that public fax office too."

"That should be easy. We have the fax numbers, we fax them and ask for their address" said Joyce.

Nigel laughed, "Yes, and what do we expect to find there. It is a public fax office and most likely they keep no records of individual faxes."

"Someone had to receive the instructions to purchase those horses and then refax to New Zealand. I have a feeling that someone in the fax office was paid to facilitate the transactions. They would have had to receive the instructions and then retype those instructions to New Zealand. Not something I would think a public fax office does very often" said Joyce.

After lunch they sent a fax to the public fax office. The reply was almost instant. The office was in the downtown area.

Nigel's phone buzzed. "This is Nigel." He listened. "Yes that would be great. Thanks Mark."

"I gather that was Mark with one of his contacts" said Joyce.

"Yes, it seems the Bangkok AG's office was contacted by our AG's office and they are assigning a task force to assist us."

"A task force! Isn't that overdoing it a bit?" asked Joyce.

"We'll find out shortly. They are on the way here now to meet with us."

Nigel and Joyce went to the lobby to wait for the Bangkok police to arrive. While they waited they outlined a plan to get the bank to cooperate. Mark and Phuong had emailed all the documents involved so far. It was not much but enough to tie the local bank with the accounts used in money laundering from illegal Hong Kong bank accounts. The question still pending was how to find Peters/O'Brian. He did show up in Singapore and possibly Hong Kong. But the trail actually ended in Singapore.

Two very well dressed men came into the lobby area and looked around. They immediately saw Nigel and Joyce and headed towards them. "Hello, my name is Stan Siamone and this is my partner Doug Hstonmi. We are from the Bangkok fraud squad."

"Hi, I'm Nigel Bowman and this is my partner Joyce Mathews. We are with the Australian Federal Fraud Bureau. We are in pursuit of a person of interest that may be involved in a massive fraud.

Sit down and we will bring you up to date." Nigel and Joyce slowly explained all they had uncovered. They especially focused on the public fax office and the local bank where the money appeared to have ended.

"Well, it certainly seems to be very involved. Let's start with the public fax office. I can get us there in about 45 minutes. I will phone them in advance and explain what we are looking for and ask they gather any information that would aid us" said Stan.

"Okay, that is as good as any place to start. But why don't we make it a surprise visit instead of warning them of our interest. Someone at the office may be involved" said Nigel. Stan nodded his approval.

"What are the rules for examining bank accounts in Bangkok?" asked Joyce.

"We will need evidence that a crime has been committed using the bank account. A judge will issue what we call a writ of examination. If we get one, we show it to the bank and they will turn over all of their records for the account" said Doug.

Nigel nodded, "What is considered enough evidence?"

"Sometimes a cancelled cheque or bank statement showing transactions that can be tied back to a situation that constitutes a crime, even if the crime is committed in a foreign country." Stan's partner sat without saying a word. He was watching Nigel and Joyce closely.

"I think we have enough evidence from Hong Kong and Singapore to show probable cause a crime of fraud has been committed. What are the fraud laws in Bangkok?" asked Joyce.

"The courts are harsh to those who are involved in fraud. Foreigners are treated like locals and are not deported until after all sentencing has been completed. Our fraud team was formed to squash fraud and set extreme examples to those who might think about committing a fraud, especially to overseas victims. Doug is a lawyer that specializes in fraud law and our team is lucky to have him sort out the legal areas," said Stan.

Doug nodded. "My job is to assess the evidence from the point of view of the legal system. I draw up partitions for warrants and documents granting account examination. I'm not much of a detective, but have worked on many cases since my appointment" said Doug. "From what I have heard here, we may need more to tie in overseas involvement. The public fax office may be the answer to that. If we can show a judge that instructions were issued from Bangkok to purchase the horses used in the fraud and the money eventually ended up in a bank here, then I am almost certain we can get a writ of examination."

"Okay, that sounds great. Let's get on to the public fax office" said Nigel.

The unmarked police car was waiting at the front door.

Chapter 21

The Public Fax Office

Stan drove the car through the warren of downtown streets. They stopped in front of a very modern looking office complex. "This is the address they sent," said Stan. He placed a large card with the word POLICE on the dash. They went into the lobby.

"There's a directory," said Doug pointing to a large glass display. "The fax office is on the third level."

They entered the lift. There were four offices on the third floor. The fax office was on the back side of the building. Two large glass doors with Public Fax printed in gold led to a lobby with several sofas and chairs. There was a sliding glass window on the wall opposite the entrance. An attractive European woman sat at a desk typing on a computer. A bell button was labeled "Ring for Service" next to the window. Stan pressed the button.

The woman looked up and slid the glass window open. In Tai she ask Stan what he wanted. Stan showed his ID and asked for the manager. The receptionist phoned someone and spoke a few words and motioned for the group to have a seat.

A few minutes later a man entered and introduced himself as the manager. He saw Nigel and Joyce and switched to English. He appeared nervous having the police in his place of business.

"We would like to speak to you in private" said Stan.

"Yes, of course. Follow me." The man did not give his name. He opened the door and allowed the team to enter a large room full of desks and chattering keyboards. Phones were ringing and the usual noise of a busy office filled the air. They were shown into a small conference room.

The man sat down and introduced himself as the managing director. "What is this all about?"

Stan looked at him and slowly took some papers from his inside coat pocket. "We have reason to suspect a serious crime has been committed." Stan let that linger for a few seconds. "We also believe that at least one of your employees may be involved." Sweat broke out on the forehead of the managing director. "We have evidence linking your company to an international fraud scheme." Stan sat back in his chair and stared at the man.

"I have no knowledge of anything like a fraud involving my company. Can you be specific?"

"Your company sent faxes to a company in New Zealand to purchase horses for several nonexistent individuals here is Bangkok. We have copies of these faxes. We also know that someone in your company received faxes with instructions to refax the purchase information to New Zealand," said Stan.

The managing director shook his head. "I knew this was going to get us into trouble. The man said he would pay us to help purchase some horses for his friends who wanted to remain anonymous. It was very straight forward. We received instructions from time to time and we sent faxes to the horse company in New Zealand. That was all we did. That is not a crime."

"Did you meet the man?" asked Nigel.

"No, it was done over the phone. I received a wire transfer for $500 US dollars. That's a lot of money for sending a few faxes. I had no idea there was a fraud being committed."

"Do you have your bank statement showing the wire transfer?" asked Joyce.

"Yes, give me a moment." The man left the conference room and was back in less than two minutes. "These are my statements showing the receipt of the money. It was almost two years ago. I had forgotten all about it until you showed up." The statements showed the transfer. The bank transfer numbers were from a local bank. That surprised Joyce and Nigel.

"This is now becoming a local situation", said Doug who had sat and listened to the conversations. "This is a large local bank."

Stan stood and thanked the managing director. "We will be in touch if we need more information. If you think of anything that may help, please call me." He gave the man a card. They left the office and got into the car.

"Okay, we now know the public fax company was not knowingly involved, but the payment for their services came from a local bank. That is very interesting. I wonder why they used a local account to transfer US$500 to the fax company?" asked Joyce.

"We may have enough evidence now to convince a judge to allow us to examine the bank accounts. The individual accounts of the four men that purchased the horses directly from the horse auction firm in New Zealand and the account where the Hong Kong company sent it's payment for the horses. The account used to receive payment from the Hong Kong company is the same account that paid the fax company and the account used to buy the horses from the defunct Hong Kong company. Give me a few hours and I'll see what I can do" said Doug.

"We'll take you back to your hotel and we will start the process. Doug will call as soon as we have an answer from a judge. Our track record has been good in getting writs and in some cases with a lot less evidence of a crime." said Stan.

Joyce opened her bag and retrieved a photo of O'Brian. "This may help when the time comes, someone may recognize him."

Chapter 22

The Right House

Steve looked at the house numbers. "That's the house over there."

"You sure, I don't want to run into those two police officers again" said Sam.

"Dude, if you hadn't taken a short cut, we would have been on the proper street." Sam's face turned red and sweat broke out on his forehead.

"Okay, double check. Street name, check, house number, check. Now let's do our job and check this out and get out of here. I'm getting bad vibes. I don't think we'll find anything" said Sam.

Sam knocked on the front door, not expecting anyone to answer. Steve peeked into a front window, shrugged and both walked around to the back.

The garden in the back was overgrown and appeared no one really used it. Just as they stepped up on the small stoop, a hedge hog darted across to the other side and disappeared into the deep grass. Steve jumped and knocked into Sam. "Watch out where you going you nearly knocked me over."

"Dude that thing might have bitten me and given me rabies or something" said Steve.

Sam mumbled something, he reached and turned the door knob but the door was locked.

"Look, there's a mat on the stoop. Look under the mat" said Steve.

Sam bent down and raised a corner of the mat. There was a key inside a zip-lock bag. "Well what do you know? Here is a key and I bet it fits that door." Sam removed the key and sure enough it fit the back door.

"Dude, this is spooky. Who leaves the key to their back door under a mat? It's usually the front door" said Steve. Sam looked at Steve and shook his head.

They entered the back door. They were in a sort of hall/mud room with a washer and dryer and cabinets on the opposite wall. The hall connected with the kitchen. "You take the kitchen and I'll go for the lounge" said Sam.

Steve opened one of the drawers. There were old ballpoint pins, batteries, picture hanging stuff, and all sorts of washers and screws. "This looks like the preverbal junk drawer". The other drawers contained knives, pot holders and assorted linens. The cabinets contained dishes and one had enough spices to open complete restaurant. A cockroach crawled out from behind a spice container. Steve jumped back and slammed the door shut. "Holy crap, this place is crawling with vermin."

Finding nothing pertaining to the case, he opened the fridge. "Hey hey, four Steinlagers sat on the top shelf. "Dude must be from New Zealand. Sam you want a beer?"

Sam yelled from a room down the hall, "Yea, I could use something cold." Steve found a bottle opener and popped the top off two of the beers. Sam came down the hall and grabbed one of the beers and returned to his search.

The door of the fridge was well stocked with mustard, pickles, cheese, meats of some kind and most of the items a normal house would have. Nothing looked spoiled.

Still don't care for Steve + Sam!

Steve pulled open the freezer door. There were some packages of meats and other foil wrapped items. He noted that one of the packages was wrapped in brown butcher paper and tied with string. He reached in and pulled it out. At first he thought it was a block of cheese. He untied the string and pulled open the paper. Several bundles of money fell out and spilled onto the kitchen floor. He was holding many bundles of US $100 notes. "Hey, dude, I think I may have found something. Come look."

Sam bounded into the kitchen. "Holy crap must be a fortune in US dollars here. I guess this is what they call cold cash" remarked Sam. Steve was stuffing a few into his pocket. "Take those out of there. You want us to go to jail for stealing evidence?"

"We took two beers, so I thought a few hundred might be okay" said Steve.

"You idiot, don't you know the person who put it there knows exactly how much is in the package. At some point that will come up. You want to explain why it's not all there?" Steve removed the money from his pocket and replaced it in the package.

Sam took his beer and returned to one of the bedrooms. He had searched the closets and all the drawers. He saw a door to a bath. He went in and opened the medicine cabinet. "Wow, look, a whole bottle of Viagra." Steve came to look. Sam opened the bottle and poured a few into his palm. "Here are two for you and one for me."

Steve looked at the two blue pills in this hand. "Why two for me and one for you?"

"I thought your new girl friend would appreciate the enhancements."

"I don't need any enhancements. My girl friend is very pleased with our relationship."

Sam rolled his eyes returned the pills and put the bottle back on the shelf.

"I guess these explain why this case is so hard" said Steve. Sam rolled his eyes.

Sam continued searching the bedrooms while Steve went to a small office near the front of the house. Steve saw evidence of a laptop once occupying a spot on the desk. He moved several items around and opened all the drawers. There were no documents or any items not normally found on a desk. Steve sat in a chair in front of the desk. He looked up at a certificate hung on the wall. "That's strange; the certificate says Peters' was honored for bravery in Iraq. That means we can get his DNA from the Army."

Sam came into the office. "What are we going to do with his DNA?" asked Sam.

"I don't know, but it will look good in our report that we figured out how to get his DNA. We don't have to say why."

"Okay, let's get out of here. We have more places to search" said Sam. "What's that?" Sam pointed at the corner of the leather desk blotter. "There appears to be something stuffed under this corner." He pulled open the leather corner and there was a plastic card about the size of a credit card and a receipt from DHL. "What is this? It looks like one of those key cards to open doors of some kind."

"Dude that may be the key to this case. Just joking. That DHL receipt looks interesting, wonder why he hid it under the keycard?"

They placed the money, DHL receipt and the key card into an evidence bag sealed and labeled it. Sam jotted notes into this notebook documenting what they had found. "Funny thing, the only item that points to Peters is his Certificate of Service from the Army."

"Well, we could follow-up on the DHL receipt. It has a number and they may keep records on these sorts of things" said Steve.

Sam thumbed through the phone book. "Here it is DHL's head office. Let's head over there and see what this receipt leads to."

They backed out of the narrow drive and headed towards the airport area. DHL's huge sign loomed above a two story building. A car park in front made it convenient.

"Look, there's a customer entrance over on the side. I guess they don't get many customers way out here. Most customers phone in their pickups or drop them off in those boxes you see all over the place" said Sam.

The two walked to the customer's entrance end of the building and entered a small room with a counter. A clerk with granny glasses perched on top of her head asked if she could help them.

"Yes, we are police detectives and have an urgent request to trace this package receipt." Sam handed over the small receipt. They showed their ID's and waited for her response. She lowered her granny glasses and looked at the receipt and their ID's while reaching for the phone. She spoke to someone and within a few seconds a huge man appeared. He had tattoos running up one arm and several on his neck.

"How may we be of service detectives?" His voice was rough and carried the tone that he didn't want to be bothered especially by the police.

"We are in pursuit of a person of interest and need to trace this receipt" said Steve. He looked hard at the huge man.

"We will need a search warrant to give out that type of information" said the man.

"I see" said Steve looking at Sam. "It looks like we have a bit of obstruction of an official inquiry here."

"What is your full name and position?" asked Sam.

"Mmm, my name is Marcus Wilstone" stuttered the man. His voice now not so bold.

"Well thank you Milkbone, we are investigating a fugitive on the run and every minute counts. We may have to run a background check on you and all of your employees. It would be a shame if DHL was responsible for this fugitive escaping" said Steve.

"Come on Steve, we need to speak to a judge very quickly and explain that Mr. Milkbone here wants to hold up our investigation for a search warrant."

"Uh, hang on. Its Wilstone! I will ask my boss to allow you access to our database. Please understand, I don't make the rules." Wilstone looked pleading at the two detectives. He picked up the phone and explained to someone what was needed. He nodded his head several time and hung up the phone. "He says okay. You won't do background checks will you?" He wiped sweat from his forehead.

Steve and Sam looked at one another. "Naw, that won't be necessary if you cooperate" said Sam.

Wiltstone went to a computer terminal and typed a few lines then stared at the screen. "This was a prepaid package. It has a foreign address in Bangkok. He pushed a button and printed out the information.

"Mr. Milkbone, thank you very much, you have been very co-operative and we will note that in our report" said Steve.

"Uh, that's Wiltstone."

Sam looked at Steve and nodded. They took the printout and headed to their car.

Outside in the car park, "Dude we may have hit on something here. I think we should inform Nigel and Joyce right away" said Steve.

Chapter 23

Finally a Break

Stan and Doug sat in Stan's office going over their report when the phone rang. Stan picked up the receiver and listened. He smiled and hung up. "We have the green light to see all the financial records of these bank accounts. The Writ came through. Good work Doug.

"This is a very complicated case of money laundering. It reminds me of another case, but I can't put my finger on it. Maybe it will come to me later" said Doug.

"I'll phone Bowman and Mathews and give them the news" said Stan.

§

Joyce was typing on Mark's laptop when her phone buzzed. "This is Joyce." She listened for over five minutes. "No, two beers will not get you in trouble." She almost burst out laughing. "You found some money? How much! Wow! That's a lot of money and you have the address the package was sent to here in Bangkok. Email that to me now. Okay, I'll update Nigel and thanks, you guys did a good job." She sat back and thought about the conversation with the Queensland detective. *Forty five thousand in US currency, a key card to some lock and a DHL receipt.*

Nigel knocked lightly on Joyce's door. She opened and invited him in. He sat on the bed and she sat on the desk chair. "Any news from Stan?" she asked.

"Nope, it's a bit early yet. I expect they have a few hoops to go through before they are issued the warrants."

"I received a call from those two Queensland detectives in Sydney. It seems they found forty five thousand US dollars in the freezer at Peter's house, also a key card to some lock and a DHL receipt. The DHL receipt has an address here in Bangkok. Sam emailed me the address and they are now headed to the Secure Investments office for another look around."

"I guess Peters left in a hurry and forgot he had the money stashed. Maybe the key card is to a gym or club someplace. The Bangkok address will be very interesting" said Nigel. A buzz came from Nigel's pocket. He pulled his phone out and answered. He listened for a few seconds. "That's great news Stan. Okay 09:00 tomorrow. We'll be ready." He hung up. "It seems we have a writ on the accounts in the local bank."

"Fantastic. Let's go over how to piece all of this together" said Joyce. "First, we know the bogus Hong Kong company wire transferred nearly three million to this local bank. We know that cheques were written on four different accounts in the same bank over about a six month period. We know that US $500 was transferred to the public fax company. To me that may be the best clue we have. I think someone slipped up."

"If the person who transferred the five hundred is a local citizen then Stan and Doug can get search warrants for this person. It is most likely that the four individuals that purchased the horses originally don't exist. We know that Napier Horse Auctions are paid fees from one of these accounts to keep the horses. It will be interesting to see if the money is still in the local bank."

At exactly 09:00, Stan and Doug drove up to the front of the Hilton Hotel. Joyce and Nigel saw the car pull up and went through the doors to meet their ride. It was a very hot day.

"Good morning" said Joyce as she climbed into the back seat. Nigel closed her door and walked to the other side of the car and got in.

"Good morning to you" said Doug. He seemed more animated today. "We have the writ for the accounts you gave me. The account that received the money from Hong Kong and transferred the money to the public fax company has not been issued but I should receive it later."

"Great news" said Nigel. "What is the protocol when we go to the bank?"

Stan looked up in the rear view mirror and said, "Let Doug open up the dialogue with the managing director of the bank. They get a bit touchy about the police snooping into their world. I suggest that we remain back until Doug has established what we need and obtain the cooperation of the bank's managing director. We can then either review the documents at the bank or get copies and return to my office."

"I'd prefer to look at the documents away from the bank. That will lessen our impact on their normal business day" said Joyce.

"Okay, I will request copies of all the documents and explain to the bank manager that we need to examine them at police headquarters. I think he will be relieved that we will not be in his bank and taking up his time" said Doug.

The drive took about half an hour. They parked in the bank's car park and entered the lobby. Stan, Nigel and Joyce took seats in the lobby while Doug went to the information desk and requested to see the managing director. Joyce watched Doug as he presented his credentials and explained to the clerk what he wanted. The clerk picked up the phone and in only a few seconds a large man approached Doug. They shook hands and Doug showed his credentials and the Writ. The man read the Writ and motioned for Doug to follow him. They disappeared behind a partition.

"That seemed to go well" said Joyce.

"Yes, and Doug is a professional in every sense of the word. He never bends the rules and is well thought of by the AG's office. He seldom gets turned down for warrants or writs" said Stan.

Nigel nodded. "We have only recently acquired someone with a similar role. He is actually from the AG's office and has saved us loads of time getting the legal things done. We'll miss him after this case is put to bed".

After about thirty minutes, Doug appeared with a large envelope. He patted it gingerly. "Here it is—the works. I didn't have time to review any of it. I showed O'Brian's picture but the officer did not recognize him."

"Let's get to my office and begin the process" said Stan. "We are only a few blocks away."

Stan retrieved the car and met them on the street in front of the bank. They made their way to Stan's office and a conference room. The envelope was emptied on the table.

"I copied all the statements in chronological order along with cancelled cheques. There were not many cheques. It appears the accounts have been open a little over two years. We have a photo of the principal that opened the account. But I don't think it will help much. He is a lawyer I know in a firm downtown. He cannot reveal his client and we may alert the suspects if we attempt to question him" said Doug.

Joyce began to sort through the various statements. There were only a few transactions per statement. The last statement showed a balance of AUD $9,435,000.00. "Wow, that's quite a lot of money. Let's plot where the funds came from."

Doug grabbed a pad and began to write down the various bank

transfers and the amounts. He added up all the inbound transfers. "The total is a bit over ten million. The majority of the transfers came from banks in the Hong Kong and Singapore two years ago. The largest single transfer was from Hong Kong for AUD $3,000,000.

"There are withdrawals of several amounts over the past few years that added up to a little over half a million. AUD $25,000 was transferred to each of the four accounts used to purchase the horses. The cheques written are to the Horse Auction firm. Seems like small amounts on a monthly basis. There is one transfer of AUD $100,000 to another account."

"That would be when the bogus Bangkok company purchased the horses from the defunct Hong Kong company for $100,000," said Joyce.

"Hum, this is getting to look like a well-organized scheme" said Nigel.

The phone rang. "Yes this is Stan. I see. Thank you." He hung up. "That was the AG's office, they are holding back on the other Writ pending a review by another judge. This happens rarely. Doug can you make a few discrete calls and find out what is happening?"

"Right," said Doug. He left the room.

"It appears we have found the money, but who controls it. Is there anything in the paperwork that gives us a hint of who controls this money?" asked Nigel.

"I'll go over all the paperwork and see what I can find if anything" said Joyce. "There does seem to be another bank involved. I don't know who yet but it appears they may have used this account as part of their reserves a couple of years ago. I'll talk to Doug about the banking system here to get a better feel on how these banks share information and accounts."

Stan said, "I'm going to send a picture of O'Brian to the immigration people at the airport to screen all incoming for a match. Who knows, maybe we'll get lucky."

Chapter 24

Sutton Arrives in Bangkok

Larry Sutton/O'Brian/Peters sat back in his first class seat and pondered the future. He had a lot of money. His Sutton identity was not known by anyone outside of his mistress. He felt good about his situation. He would execute his exit strategy as soon as he had all the money transferred to its final bank.

The plane landed and taxied to the passenger terminal. Sutton removed his carry-on from the bin above his seat and quickly walked off the plane. He entered the arrivals hall and opened his brief case. There were two passports. One in the name of O'Brian and one in the name of Sutton.

He chose Sutton. His USA passport was shown to the officer and stamped without comment. A small flash occurred as his picture was taken. He pondered if he should have used his Singapore passport. *Too late now.*

Sutton went to the carrousel and retrieved his bag and walked calmly to the exit marked "Nothing to Declare" He handed the officer his declaration document and was waved through without incident.

In an office deep in the building, a computer was analyzing hundreds of photos in a database with photos of arriving passengers. One picture stopped the computer. A message with a printout was sent to the airport police headquarters. It was a match of Barry O'Brian to Mr. Larry Sutton; a USA citizen just arrived in Bangkok. The BOLO said to apprehend and hold for questioning.

§

Sutton saw the sign indicating the ground transportation area and briskly walked to the automatic doors and signaled for a taxi. He gave the driver a card with the address in Thai and sat back in air conditioned comfort as he was sped through the police check point towards the central business area. Behind the taxi a gate was lowered to stop all exit traffic.

All cars and buses were stopped at the airport exit. The police held up pictures of someone and looked at all the faces, only seconds ago the face they wanted had passed them unknowingly. They continued to stop all traffic for two hours.

§

Doug's phone buzzed. "This is Doug. Yes I did issue a BOLO on someone. I see. The match is to a Mr. Larry Sutton with a USA passport. Okay, better luck next time". Doug switched off the call. He nodded at Stan, "Mr. O'Brian is now Mr. Sutton. Someone matching his photo has just arrived at the airport, but they missed apprehending him before he left the airport area. I'll notify Bowman and Mathews that O'Brian is now Larry Sutton and he is here."

Stan looked down at the news that Sutton had slipped through the net. "It will be near about impossible to find a taxi service that picked up O'Brian/Sutton. He is in the wind for sure."

§

A phone chirped in a desk drawer. A key was inserted into the lock and the phone retrieved. "Yes. I see. When? Okay you know where to pick up the envelope; it will be available in two hours." The phone was switched off and replaced into the drawer. The key was turned in the lock. *Humm, looks like I've got to clean up this mess before the police get nosy and start asking questions.*

The man picked up the phone on his desk and punched in a number. It rang several times before the click of connection was heard. "We have a cleaning problem. Seems our client has been exposed somehow and the police know he is in Bangkok. We need to get him a new passport and other documents as soon as possible. Have them delivered to me when they are ready." He put the phone down and terminated the call. He consulted a little red book lying on the desk top. *The police will not be a problem but there is no reason to take any chances. Sutton was careless to use the Sutton passport. There will be a hefty fee for this mess up. As for the writ for the account at the bank, I'll have to pull some strings for that to be squashed.*

§

Sutton arrived at his hotel and checked in. The desk clerk handed him an envelope with a message. Sutton smiled and thanked him. He walked across the lobby and went up to his room. He tore open the envelope and read the short message.

[The police know Sutton is in Bangkok. Call me.]

He was shocked. He had taken every precaution he could think of. How did they know I was here? Oh crap, it's the Sutton passport.

He stripped and showered and dressed in light casual clothing. He knew he had to be very careful until he spoke with his contact. He took his new mobile phone out of his brief case. He punched in the number. It rang three times and was answered. The voice was flat and asked for his code. "8710", he said.

"You have been compromised. I have new documents for you. You must move out of the hotel as soon as you have the new papers. Do not check out. Just leave. I have a courier on the way with the papers. There will be a prepaid reservation to another hotel under your new name in the package, along with my invoice for services." The call disconnected.

Sutton sat on the edge of the bed thinking how stupid he had been using the wrong passport. He took out his phone and punched in a number to Singapore. Chung answered on the second ring.

"This is Chung how may I help you?"

"Have you spoken to anyone about what we talked about?"

"The police picked me up and tried to tie you to Asian Investments. I told them nothing. There were Australian policemen with the local police. They know your real name and the one you use in Singapore. They also know all about the Hong Kong company and the horse deals. They said I was going to be sued personally by a couple in Sydney by the name of Jenkins. I never heard of them before. What am I to do?"

Sutton/O'Brian sat on the edge of the bed contemplating what was happening. He hesitated only a few seconds. "Okay, sit tight. The $50,000 will be followed up with another $25,000 if nothing more comes from the police." He switched off the phone. *Bloody Hell!* There was a soft knock on his door. A uniformed courier presented him with an envelope and left.

The new passport, credit cards and drivers license along with the reservation receipt for his hotel. The invoice for the service was high but under the circumstances he had no choice.

He was still disturbed over his stupidity in using the Sutton passport. Chung said they know my O'Brian name. They did not know Sutton. If they matched my photo to the arrivals then they would have known I was using the name Sutton. Crap, I was too careless.

He had never heard of the hotel on the reservation, but that may be a good thing. He took his old passport and anything with Sutton's name on it and flushed them down the toilet. He was now

Mr. Gerald R. Patterson from Surry County, England. He closed his bag and rolled it to the service elevator and punched in the ground floor.

The service door to the hotel was in the center of the block behind the hotel. He could see traffic ahead to the right. He rolled his suit case to the left. Just has he rounded the corner behind the hotel, a taxi slowly cruised down the nearly deserted street. He raised his hand and waved at the driver. The car pulled to the curb in front of him. He handed the taxi driver the reservation sheet with the name and address of the hotel. The driver nodded he knew where the address was. He loaded in the suit case and got in the back seat. Thank goodness the car was air conditioned. He was still in shock. *Maybe Bangkok is not the place I should be.*

The taxi pulled up to the passenger loading area for the nondescript hotel. It was not in the best section of Bangkok, but maybe that was a good thing. Sutton/Patterson got out of the taxi, paid the driver and pulled his bag into the lobby. He presented his reservation sheet to the desk clerk. It took only a moment to register. The clerk never asked to see his passport or any ID. His room was on the fifth floor.

He pulled his bag to the two lifts in a small alcove off the main lobby. One was arriving as he stepped to press the up button. He waited for a couple to step out of the lift. They hesitated and looked him over carefully then exited to the lobby.

Patterson was getting jumpy. Why did they stare at him? Maybe he had something on his face, or maybe his fly was open. He pushed his bag onto the lift and pressed the fifth floor button.

His room was standard with a king size bed, mini bar, a working desk and TV. He opened his bag and hung up his dress outfits and placed all the remainder into the drawers of the large dresser. He got to thinking about all the plans he had carefully made to escape and now the police were here waiting for him. His stupidity was driving him crazy. He had to think about his next few moves. One of the first things was to move the money out of the current bank. His account in Vanuatu had only a minimum balance to keep it active. He would move the money to Vanuatu. He took out his computer and logged into the bank. He put in the numbers for the account to transfer the funds. He halted. *Maybe they are tracing the money.* He closed the page and shut down his computer. He would consult with his contact before doing anything else.

Chapter 25

Dead End

Morning coffee was poured as the group sat in Stan's office silent. Each thinking thoughts about the twist and turns the case had taken.

"We have the local address the Australian DHL office says Peters addressed a package. Let's check that out and then we meet to decide how to proceed," said Stan.

Doug nodded and got up. He turned and said, "I'll get a search warrant for the address."

Nigel and Joyce were not happy with all the dead ends. "Why would Peters send a package to a local address if he was coming here himself anyway?" said Joyce.

"We could speculate for hours, but until we examine the local address we will be spinning our wheels", said Nigel. "Stan, why don't you fill us in on all the evidence you have in the cold case that is similar to this case."

"Good place to start today", said Joyce.

Stan looked at Joyce and nodded. "This case was the highest

profile case I've ever encountered. There are people in very high positions that seemed interested in the case. They never interfered but were constantly interested in the progress by the police. I was told to keep all evidence and interviews confidential until the evidence was good enough to get a conviction in court. My boss was bypassed by the AG's office."

"Wow, that is exactly what we are up against in this case" said Joyce.

"The evidence was never convincing enough to issue arrest warrants. The AG was not happy with the result of our investigation. He ordered all the notes, evidence and recordings confined to our files and sealed. This folder is an outline of all the procedures and evidence we collected. We spent nearly four months on the case."

Nigel listened carefully to all that Stan said. "Let's look at what you've got" said Nigel.

Stan made copies of the documents in the folder and handed them to Nigel and Joyce. "This information is confidential. You will note there are no names and the dates have been coded. The bank names are also coded. We took every step to keep the information confidential." I have included a copy of the code sheet so you can decode the names of the banks and the dates. The copies of the warrants have the same codes. As you can see, we were not able to get to see the bank accounts. The judge said we didn't have enough evidence to issue a writ."

Joyce sorted the various forms and pages into three piles. Faxes, internal memos and interviews. Nigel leaned in to read a fax. "This fax from Hong Kong seems to be a transfer of funds for a large amount of oil."

Doug returned from the judge's chambers and sat down.

Stan looked at the document. "Yes, the oil was stored in Iraq. It never left the storage facility. A company in Bangkok purchased the original oil for the going rate at that time. A year later the Bangkok company sold the oil to a Hong Kong company for a profit of several million dollars. The Hong Kong company waited about four months and sold the oil to another Bangkok company for a loss of several million dollars. Sounds just like your horse trading scheme. We were not successful in actually finding the oil due to poor co-operation with the Iraqi authorities. We came up with a dead end in Bangkok due to the lack of hard evidence. There were some mysterious characters involved but we could never get names. One in particular was thought to be an Australian living here in Bangkok. We never got a name."

"That certainly sounds like the scheme in our case. It would be interesting if there is a connection. Let's start with the DHL address of the package Peters sent from Sydney." They all nodded yes.

Stan closed up his office and escorted the group to the police garage to retrieve his car. He had a map of Bangkok in the console of the police car. Doug spread out the map and found the street. "It looks like about a forty five minute drive from here. It's on the far north side of the city, a middle class area. Mostly professionals and small business owners live in the area."

Stan turned into a tree lined avenue with neat homes and lawns. The house they were seeking was about half way down the second block.

"That's the house" said Doug. "There's no car in the drive and the yard needs attention."

Stan parked the car in the empty drive. He got out and walked to the front door and rang the bell. No one came to the door. Doug walked to the house next door and knocked on the front door. A small middle aged woman came to the door. Doug and the lady spoke a few moments and Doug returned to the car. "The next door neighbor says there has been no one living here for several years. A lawn care company comes once or twice a month and cuts and prunes the lawn. She also said she has seen a man in a white van come several time in the past few months and enter the house. His last visit was a day or so ago. He didn't stay long and as far as she could see didn't leave with anything."

Nigel sat thinking. "Maybe he came to retrieve the package Peters send to that address."

"That is my thinking too" said Doug.

Joyce was not a happy camper. "That leaves us with nothing, just another dead end."

Doug said, "Let's go inside, I have a search warrant."

Stan tried the door. It was locked. The back door was also locked. There was a patio door on one side of the front that opened onto a small wooden deck. Stan went to the police car and returned with a small plastic case. He opened the case and took out what looked like a large metal brick. He placed the brick onto the glass near the latch. With a short tug, the latch began to lift and cleared the mechanism that kept the door secure. He pushed the door open and replaced the brick into the plastic case.

"Now that is what I call neat", said Joyce.

"We have thousands of these type doors in Bangkok and the department decided to equip each patrol car with a magnetic kit to allow officers entrance in the event of an emergency", said Doug.

They entered the door and were standing in a very neat den with one wall of all books. A small desk with an old style computer terminal sat in front of the book shelves and several comfortable looking chairs facing the desk. Three two drawer file cabinets sat next to the desk.

Stan pulled one of the file drawers open. It appeared to be full of hanging files. "Doug, you and Joyce sort through this stuff and Nigel and I will examine the other rooms in the house."

Joyce pulled several of the folders from the drawer. On first glance she raised an eyebrow. "Wow, this is very interesting. It appears to be invoices for many different products."

Doug had another batch of the documents. "Yes and look at these. There are copies of cheques from various banks attached to each of the files."

Doug fell face first onto the desk with a loud thud, scattering papers into the floor. The breaking of glass was the only sound.

Joyce ran around the small desk and felt for a pulse. He was alive but bleeding badly. She yelled for Nigel and Stan to come. She saw the bullet entrance near his right shoulder. Not too close to the heart but it may have punctured a lung. She placed her hand over the wound. There was no exit wound so the bullet was lodged within Doug's upper chest.

Nigel and Stan came running into the room and saw Doug lying across the desk. "Let's get him off the desk and over on that sofa. Stan and Nigel each slid an arm under Doug's chest and lifted him to the sofa. He was coming around and moaned with the pain. "Doug, be still, you've been shot and we are calling for an ambulance", said Stan. "Joyce, keep pressure on the wound."

Nigel went to the window that had a large spider web of cracks surrounding a small hole. He saw a dark SUV backing out of the drive and speeding down the street. "It looks like there were two of them in a dark SUV. Maybe a BOLO would be in order."

Stan punched in a number and requested an ambulance for an officer down with a gunshot wound. He then called into headquarters and reported what had happened. He gave the location and info about the two suspects in the dark SUV.

The wobbling sound of the ambulance could be heard. Within minutes Doug was in the ambulance and on his way to the nearby hospital.

Joyce stayed with Doug keeping pressure on the wound. The ambulance assistant relieved Joyce and placed a large bandage over the wound. The driver announced that the hospital was dead ahead.

The ambulance came to a halt and several people in scrubs opened the back door of the vehicle and removed the stretcher with Doug. They wheeled him into the first ER room available. Several doctors attended Doug, who was again unconscious. One of the nurses pulled the curtain around the area. Joyce could not see what was happening.

Joyce sat on one of the plastic chairs outside of the ER. She noticed all the blood on her hands and some on her trousers. A small woman in scrubs approached her. She spoke in broken English. "You saved life. You want clean up? Follow."

Joyce nodded and followed the nurse to the restroom where she washed her hands and dabbed some water on the blood splashed on her trousers. The nurse handed her a dark bottle. "Hydrogen Peroxide, remove blood," said the nurse.

Joyce took the bottle and with a paper towel removed most of the blood stains from her trousers. "Thank you very much. I must return to check on the officer's condition" said Joyce.

The nurse nodded and led Joyce back to the waiting area. She had just sat down when one of the attending doctors came from behind the curtain and approached her.

"Are you a relative?" asked the doctor.

"No I'm a colleague. We are police officers" said Joyce.

The doctor looked puzzled. "You are a police officer?"

"Yes, I'm from Australia working with the local police on a case, which just got very interesting."

"Your officer is doing fine. The bullet missed his lung and lodged into muscle tissue. I removed the bullet. It's in this container for the police. I had no idea he was a policeman. He should be good to go in a few days. He will not have the use of his right arm for a few weeks, but otherwise he should recover with minimum problems. He is in the recovery room and should be moved to a room in a few hours."

"Thank you doctor. I am most appreciative of your service."

Joyce punched up Nigel's number. Nigel answered immediately.

"He's doing fine. I'm still at the hospital. It will be several hours before he is out of the recovery room. There were no vital organs hit and the doctor gave me the bullet."

"That's great news. We're still at the house. The forensic team is here doing their thing. I don't hold out much hope on them finding anything. The shooter was in the SUV and shot though the window in the den facing the front. It was almost a perfect shot—too perfect to be a pistol. A silenced long gun of some sort would be my guess. The bullet should tell us more. The fact that the window was not shattered means it was a high velocity. I'll have Stan send a car for you to come back here. The documents you and Doug were examining are very interesting."

"Okay, I'll wait down stairs for the car. Any news on the BOLO?"

"No news. I don't think we'll hear much. According to Stan, these SUV's are common in Bangkok. See you back here."

~~They disconnect the call~~. Joyce headed to the front of the hospital to wait for the car. She was thinking why the assailants would risk a shot in broad daylight. It didn't make sense. Why Doug? I was standing closer to the window. The information we were looking at could not have been known to the shooter. Maybe it was a warning—But from who? We're at a dead end.

Chapter 26

Clean up

The dark SUV traveled along the main road at normal speed. The two occupants were silent. They had taken out the policeman as instructed. They had no idea who their employer was and didn't care. The money was good. The risk was worth it.

The passenger's cell phone buzzed. He looked at the caller-id and recognized the number. It was the same as the one that hired them. He answered in Thai. "Yes!" He listened for a few seconds. "Yes sir, we did exactly as your instructions. The tall one was in the room with the woman. We took him out. It appears he was taken to the hospital. I'm not sure if he is alive. Does it matter?"

The voice on the other end said, "No, the warning was made. They'll get the message. Your fee will be deposited to your account today." The connection was broken.

The two occupants of the SUV turned down a dusty road that led to an abandoned chemical plant. The car pulled up to a closed overhead door. The driver removed a small device from the console and pressed the button. The overhead door never opened.

The SUV exploded into hundreds of pieces.

Fifty miles away, high up in one of the tallest buildings in Bangkok, a beep was made on a computer. A man walked over and pressed several keys. He turned and spoke to the other occupant in the room. "It is done. The cleanup has been completed."

"Good, now make sure that all the documents removed from the house are secured and destroyed. It was a mistake leaving them there. You should never have given out the address to Peters. What's done is done. We learn from mistakes."

"Yes sir, I will consider it a lesson learned."

The other ocupant left the room. He arrived at the ground floor and went through the front entrance where a car was waiting. The car, with official government license plates, pulled into traffic and disappeared into the mid day rush.

Chapter 27

Discovery

The two Queensland detectives parked their police car in a no parking red zone. They headed for the door to the building housing Secure Pacific Investments. Steve pushed the lift call button and they waited for the lift to take them to the eighth floor.

"Do you think we will find anything? It seems the locals have searched this place and came up with nothing" said Sam

"This is on our to-do list so we have to give it a go."

"Okay, let's get this over with. I think we are wasting time. We did find some stuff at the home, but that had not been searched. This place has few hiding places" said Sam.

They reached the smoked glass door to the Secure Pacific Investments office. Steve had the key the police locksmith gave them. The crime scene tape was across the door. They signed the entrance log posted on the door and removed the tape.

"Steve, you take the cubicles on the left and I'll take the ones on the right."

"Hey, you only have one and I have two."

"Okay, I'll take your two you take my one", said Sam.

They began their search. Each opened drawers, pulled furniture away from the walls and peeked under carpet.

"Hey I think I found something", said Sam.

Steve looked over the partition. "What?"

"Behind this file cabinet is a metal plate covering something. Give me hand to slide this cabinet away."

Steve went around the cubical to assist Sam in moving the heavy file cabinet away from the wall. Sure enough, a square metal plate covered something in the wall. Sam examined the plate carefully. "We are going to need some tools to get this off. It appears to be attached with bolts. Run down and get the kit from the back of the car. It has a lot of neat stuff we can use."

Steve looked at Sam and started to protest, but turned and started for the door. He went down and out on the street towards their car. A traffic cop was examining their car.

"Hey officer is there a problem?" asked Steve.

The cop turned and gave Steve a good look over. "This your car?"

"Yes."

"Show me some ID" said the traffic officer.

Steve reached into his pocket and produced his official ID. He opened it and handed it to the officer.

"What is a Queensland detective doing in North Sidney?"

"Officer that is a long story. But if you check with the Sidney watch commander's office you will find we're on official business."

The officer looked at Steve for a few seconds. Handed him back his ID and turn and walked back to his motorbike. Steve opened the boot and removed the tool kit and headed back to the building. The officer stood next to his bike talking on his radio.

"Okay, you check out," said the officer with a frown on his face.

Steve looked at the officer as he mounted his bike and went on down Clark Street. Stupid cops, all he had to do was radio the license number for a check out and would have found it to be a police car. Oh well, this is New South Wales.

Sam was down on his knees looking at the metal plate. *Maybe it's a plumbing thing or an electrical box.*

Steve returned and handed the tool kit to Sam. "Some cop was nosing around our car and made me show him my ID. He didn't checkout the car's registration as a police car. Where do they get these guys?"

"Did he write you a ticket?"

"No, but he was sure rude. After he checked the car out, he just got on his bike and just buggered off."

Sam selected a spanner from the kit and began to remove the bolts. There were six bolts holding the plate in place. Steve watched as Sam removed each bolt. After the last bolt was removed, Sam took a screw driver and pried the plate off the wall.

"Holy crap house mouse" said Steve.

Behind the metal plate was a large metal box similar to an electric switch panel. It contained two mobile phones and many bundles of Australian $100 notes stacked to the top of the box.

Sam took his time responding. "This guy hides money like squirrels do nuts. This looks like an emergency get away depository just like the bundle of cash we found in his freezer." Sam pulled a pair of latex gloves from his pocket and stuffed his hands into the gloves with a loud snap. He turned to Steve and said, "I think you should wear a pair also. This is beginning to look serious." He reached in and carefully removed one of the phones. "This is brand new, one of those non-traceable throw-away kinds most likely."

"Let's count the money", said Steve.

Steve and Sam removed the bundles of money and placed them on the desk. After several minutes of counting, they added their totals.

"$230,000! Wow, that's some get-away", said Sam.

Steve reached into his inside jacket pocket and removed two plastic evidence bags. They put all the money in one bag and the phones in another.

"This does not tell us who owns this money or phones. I think Nigel will be interested. Hey look a folded piece of paper on the bottom of the wall box" said Steve.

Sam removed the folded paper that was actually several pages. He carefully opened the paper. It was a typed letter of three pages. He read all three pages. "Good grief, if this doesn't shake up the powers to be, nothing will."

"What does it say", asked Steve.

"Here, you read it."

Steve took his time reading the three pages. "Crap, you really think this is for real?" asked Steve.

"We have to assume so. Nigel and Joyce are going to go ballistic when they read this. Let's go back to the office and fax it to them. Let the feathers hit the fan as they say or something like that."

When Sam and Steve arrived back in the office, the watch commander had left a message for them to come to his office. They looked at the message and shook their heads. "Now what", remarked Steve?

"Well first we'll send a fax to Nigel with an update and this letter. Then we'll go to the watch commander's office and find out what we did this time. You don't think it's about us drinking those two beers?" Steve shrugged.

They knocked lightly on the watch commander's office door. A ruff voice said, "Come in."

Steve turned the knob and opened the door. The watch commander was seated at his desk. He looked up and motioned for them to enter.

"You two have a seat." He motioned to the two chairs in front of his desk. "I received a call from Canberra this morning with a query into the progress on something called the Jenkins case. What's the Jenkins Case?"

Sam started to answer, but Steve cut in. "Sir we are not privy to the details. We were given a list of things to check into by Nigel. He didn't share any details." Sam heaved the two evidence bags up on the watch commander's desk.

"What the hell is this?" asked the watch commander.

"Sir, this is evidence we found at the Secure Pacific Investments office in North Sydney this morning. It's two burner phones and $230,000 Australian" said Sam. He didn't mention the letter.

The watch commander's eyes bulged. He looked hungrily at the cash. "What are you going to do with this?" asked the commander.

"We are waiting for instructions from Nigel. I sent him a fax with some information. We should hear any moment now" said Steve.

Sam's phone buzzed almost on cue. "This is Sam. Yes, we are in the watch commander's office at the moment. No. Yes, we carefully put everything in evidence bags. I'll ask if he can process them as soon as possible. Yes, we are very well aware of that. I'll do that." The connection was broken.

"Just what is going on?" asked the commander.

"Just routine stuff" said Sam. "Nigel requested that your lab guys check the phones and money for finger prints." Sam opened the money bag and retrieved a bundle marked $10,000. He left the phones on the desk in the evidence bags.

"We'll be down the hall in the office if you need us" said Steve.

They gathered up the evidence bag with the money and started towards the commander's door.

"Hold on you two", shouted the watch commander. "Where are you going with that evidence bag?"

"Our instructions are to place them in the office you gave Nigel and Joyce to use" said Sam.

"You are going to leave $230,000 in cash in an office?" asked the commander.

"Yes sir" said Sam. "Only you and we know it's in there. After all it is in the middle of the police building. Don't you trust your people?" The watch commander stared at the bag of money and then at Sam with a twisted frown.

With that, they continued through the door and down the hall to the temporary office. They unlocked the door and went in. They locked the door behind them and placed the evidence bag on the small table.

"What did Nigel tell you to do?" asked Steve.

"He told me not to trust anyone, not to tell anyone about the Letter and not to let the evidence out of our sight. We are to place the document into an evidence bag. There will be a special courier coming soon to take possession of all the evidence and to get a receipt from the courier. Nigel said to leave the office as soon as the courier left and not to return" said Sam.

"What do you make of that?" asked Steve.

"Dude, I have no clue. This is the strangest case I've ever worked. No one trusts anyone. The stuff in the letter is explosive. It appears as though this has the making of some kind of political fallout. I think I want to get back to Townsville before the crap hits the fan", said Sam.

"Okay, but let's not stop at that same motel on the way back. Too much going on around there for me."

Chapter 28

Sharing the Evidence

Nigel received a three page fax from Sydney. He read it twice and handed it to Joyce. She whistled at its contents. "Wow, this is going to open up a can of worms. If this is proven legit, at least two governments are going to have some real fallout."

"Yes, I know. We have to be very careful to verify this document before it is put into evidence", said Nigel. "It certainly has the potential to end the careers of two Australians and who knows how many here. This may be more far reaching that we know."

Stan sat quietly as Joyce and Nigel read and discussed the fax received from Sam and Steve. He did not ask to see it and was very still and waited until Joyce spoke.

"Stan, it appears that our case has just turned up some evidence that involves some people in Bangkok. If we can verify this document, then we have a direct lead that should result in an arrest warrant, both here and in Australia. It may also shed light on why the shooting of Doug occurred when it did and why he was the target."

Stan looked surprised at the news. "If I may, what has happened that makes you sure someone locally is related to your case?"

Nigel nodded at Joyce. Joyce cleared her throat. "This document was discovered at the offices of our prime suspect and reveals a huge blackmail of several of your top government and police officials. It also implicates your partner Doug as a target due to information he may have and not even know.

"There must be a leak in the police system that allowed the parties to know we were investigating the residence where the shooting occurred. It is obvious to me that they targeted Doug specifically because of his past association with the Justice Department. If this document is verified, then you have some real issues with the entire Justice Department, the Judges and the top brass of the police department," said Joyce.

Stan stood and leaned against his desk. "If what you say is verified, then how can I proceed when the information will certainly be available to the very people you say I should be investigating?'

Nigel sat back in his chair. "Stan, I think this document should be kept secret until we have a strategy to move on all the parties. If this is leaked, then you and Doug will be targets by some very powerful people. We have taken steps in Australia to put all the collected evidence into the hands of someone that will not know its contents and will safe keep the evidence until it is ready to be presented to a jury."

Joyce stood and went to Stan's desk and looked over at Nigel. "I think we should share this document with Stan and with the understanding that no copies are made and that he keeps its contents confidential to only us."

Nigel nodded his approval. Joyce handed the document to Stan. He took his time reading the fax. He looked up at Joyce and Nigel and reread the document again. "This is unbelievable. How could this have happened? It may bring down the entire Justice Department. This is a disaster. I don't know the people in Australia, but I assume they are high up in your government."

"Yes," said Joyce. One of the names is purported to be our next Prime Minster. One is not in the government but is a national celebrity known by almost everyone in the country. We had suspected him of being involved, but could not tie him to the scam until this document was discovered. Peters was blackmailing your group here in Bangkok. How he obtained information about the group is not stated. He made sure the parties knew he had the goods on them and was willing to expose them should they not play along with his game. The Australian parties were not being blackmailed most likely because the scam was still in progress.

Nigel said, "Should he be arrested or end up in the morgue, all would be revealed with hard evidence. As you read in the letter, there are tapes of transactions and copies of documents on file at a secure place near Singapore. It seems he had squirreled away nearly a quarter million to insure he had funds to finance his doomsday scheme. As you can see, the instructions to the recipient of this letter were explicit on how to get to the funds and what to do with the evidence in the event of his death or incarceration. I don't know the individual the letter was address to, but I intend to find out. I would venture a guess that his is a copy and the letter has been mailed."

Stan moved back behind his desk and sat down. He rubbed his chin and shook his head several times as if to get some pesky insect out of his hair. "Okay, it looks like you or we will have to go to Singapore and try to find the evidence Peters has stashed. We know he is somewhere here in Bangkok. We can make sure he does not leave by air. That is really the only way he can get out of the country. If we can get that cache of evidence then we have to determine how to use it to arrest all the parties."

Joyce looked through her note pad. "The tracking of the cheque to the public fax may not be important in light of this new evidence. Let's take a break and meet again in an hour to come up with a plan to unravel all this detail."

Nigel and Stan nodded approval and they each gathered up their papers and departed Stan's office. Nigel leaned over to speak into Joyce's ear. "I saw a small café on the street near here. Let's go there".

"Okay, I'm confused on one issue. I'll wait until we are at the café to discuss it with you. We may need to bring Mark into this also" said Joyce.

Chapter 29

The Café

J oyce and Nigel entered the small café and chose a table near the back. A waitress approached their table and placed menus in front of them. "May I get you a beverage?"

"Bottle water for me" said Joyce.

"Same for me."

The waitress went to get their water. Neither Joyce nor Nigel spoke until the waitress returned. They ordered a rice dish and opened their water.

"What are you concerned about?" asked Nigel.

"With the revelations of the fax, I'm concerned that we may be blocked by the AG's office. How are we going to get arrest warrants?"

"You mentioned that you thought Mark should join us. Why?"

"Mark seems empowered to do a lot on his own. Arrest warrants for one. My feeling is that Mark should begin working on getting at least two warrants and have them in hand to execute. The two Queensland detectives know about the contents of the letter. I'm worried this may leak and become a political football," said Joyce.

Nigel thought for a moment. "I don't think bringing Mark here will help. I think we meet him in Singapore and bring him up-to-date and get his help in finding the location of the evidence. As for the two Queensland detectives, I don't think they'll leak anything. I suspect they are happy to get back to Townsville."

The waitress brought their order and placed the dishes on the table. "Anything else?"

"No, just the bill please" said Nigel.

Joyce's face was showing her concern about the latest developments. "If we cannot locate the evidence, then we will never be able to prove any of this."

"There is still one other way. If we find Peters and make a deal, then his testimony will be enough to issue warrants. It'll be weak if he is not willing to turn over the hard evidence. It'll be his word against some of the most powerful people in Australia and Thailand."

Joyce put her chopsticks down. "I suggest we send Mark out to find the person the letter is addressed to now. That will save us days of work. He can ask for help if needed from Howard."

Nigel looked up. "Good idea. I'll call Mark now. I will not reveal any of the parties with the exception of Peters. We know that Peters used the name Sutton. My guess is that will be a start."

Joyce made a note in her note pad. "In the fax, it stated how to open the secret safe and where to find the mobile phone. I assume the person the letter is addressed to knows the physical location since the address was not given. It stands to reason, if we can find that person, then we can find the physical location" said Joyce.

"Right, I think Howard Chong will be of great assistance in helping Mark find this person." Nigel took out his mobile and punched in Mark's number. The phone rang several times before Mark answered. "Mark, Nigel here. We have a hot lead and it's near you. Do you think you can check out a person and get back to me"?

"Yes, I've completed most of my paperwork and got it off to

the AG's office" said Mark.

"Uh, Mark, in this instance, you cannot report anything about this to anyone. If we are correct it will have ramifications all through the government. It is absolute essential that what I'm instructing you to do is kept confidential. You will need Howard Chong's help. You are to attempt to locate Gwen Leong, she's a close friend of Peters. We think she has some very sensitive information and will be a key player in unraveling this case. Do not speak to her. Get me her phone number and physical address. Peters is using the name Larry Sutton. Call me as soon as you have located her. Joyce and I will take it from there."

"Yes sir. But, if I'm asked by the AG's office about the investigation, what should I tell them?"

"Tell them all is going well and a request for an arrest warrant may be forthcoming in the next few days."

"Yes sir, I'll get right on it", Mark disconnected the call.

"Well, that should get some interesting results. I wonder how many Gwen Leong's there are in Singapore. I don't think Larry Sutton will be in the phone book." said Joyce.

"Maybe Sutton owns some property and it's listed. Let's get back to Stan's office."

Chapter 30

The Search

Mark put down his mobile phone and made some notes on a pad. He was puzzled as to why Nigel was concerned about anyone knowing about the investigation. He looked up Howard Chong's number and made a call. Chong's number rang but went to voice mail. Mark left him a message to ring him as soon as he got the message.

Howard Chong returned from a departmental meeting and checked his email and voice mail. He immediately called Mark.

"This is Mark Young, may I help you?"

"Mark, this is Howard Chong. You needed to speak with me?"

"Yes, it's about the case. We have uncovered someone that may have critical information. I need your help. I have two names. One a female and the other is a name Peters is using in Bangkok."

Howard sat down at his desk. "Tell me the two names and I will run them through the system and see what turns up."

"The first name is Gwen Leong. The second name is Larry Sutton. I just received them from Nigel. He indicated that the woman may be a close friend of Peters/Sutton. I'm not to interview her, but to get her number and physical address."

"Fine, I'll phone you as soon as there's a hit on the names."

"Thanks Howard." Mark disconnected the call. He made notes of the time and what was asked of Howard Chong. It was past his lunch time, so he decided to explore a local restaurant he had seen earlier. He packed up his notes and left the hotel room. The walk to the restaurant was only a few minutes. It was not crowded in that it was past the normal lunch hour. He was seated at a table near the bar area.

"May I help you?" A very attractive young waitress had approached him from behind and startled him with the question.

"Yes, I'll have a pot of hot tea and what do you recommend?"

"The seafood medley is a favorite. It is really good. I had some myself for lunch."

"That sounds good; I'll have the seafood medley." The waitress took the order and returned to the kitchen. Mark's phone buzzed in his pocket. He pulled it out of his pocket and answered. He listened carefully.

"Can we be certain that the property belongs to Peters/Sutton? I see. Okay I'll come to your office in about an hour. I just sat down to lunch. Thanks for the help." Mark pulled his notepad from his pocket and made notes just as his lunch arrived.

Mark finished his lunch and went out on the footpath in front of the restaurant. He hailed a passing taxi. He gave the police department address to the driver on a printed card. The driver turned and looked at Mark for a long time. "You in trouble?" asked the driver in very halting English.

"No, I work with the police and need to attend a meeting." With that the driver looked puzzled but pulled into the afternoon traffic to take Mark to the police headquarters.

Mark checked in with the information desk and explained he was there to see Detective Howard Chong. The officer phoned Chong's office and got permission to send Mark up. He handed Mark a visitor's badge.

Mark knocked on the door to Chong's office and heard a polite "Please Enter". Howard stood when Mark entered. He smiled and offered Mark a chair in front of his desk and he took other companion chair.

Howard took a file from his desk and opened several pages. "We have narrowed down Gwen Leong to two possibilities and have found a property registered to a Larry Sutton." Howard looked at Mark. "Now tell me why these two people are important. I understand Sutton but the Leong name is very prominent on the Malay side. The family is into banking and has been for several generations. Gwen Leong is married to a Mr. Wu who has a large export business, but Gwen Leong still uses her maiden name. I suggest we be very careful with talking to Gwen Leong. The property of Mr. Larry Sutton is in an exclusive area on the Malay side and out of my jurisdiction. I do have the address. I suggest you and I take a ride to view the property before we speak to anyone. You will need your passport."

"I have my passport with me. I agree that we should not speak to anyone at this time. My instruction from Nigel is to only obtain a phone number and the physical addresses if possible."

"Fine, let's go. I'll take us about 45 minutes. The causeway is crowded at this time of day with workers crossing at shift change time."

The two left the police headquarters and started the journey to the community where the property registered to Larry Sutton was located. The traffic was bumper to bumper. Soon the road widened with several lanes leading up to a check point. Howard handed the guard both passports. The guard leaned down to view Mark, but handed back the passports without comment. He waved them through. From the check point the drive was about fifteen minutes.

Howard turned off the main road and after several hundred yards of turns a huge gate with a guard standing beside a small guardhouse came into view. Howard pulled up and told the guard they were there to visit Larry Sutton. The guard went to the guard house and used a phone to presumably phone the Sutton house to get permission. The guard spoke to someone on the phone and hung up. "I'm sorry sir; Mr. Sutton is not in residence at this time."

"I see. Okay thank you", said Howard. The guard motioned how to turn in the small turn area and return to the road. Howard maneuvered the car around the guard house and slowly motored toward the main road. After he was around the bend and out of sight of the guard, he pulled over to the side of the road.

"Well I guess that's the end of that", said Mark.

"Not yet it isn't. I have a friend on the local force. We do each other favors from time to time to save a lot of legal hassle. I'm going to give him a call. Maybe he can get in somehow. He's very resourceful." Howard pulled out his mobile phone and made a call. He spoke in Chinese and finally hung up.

"My friend says to wait; he will be here in twenty minutes."

"Do you think he meant that we could actually see the house?"

"Not only see it, but go inside. Malay law is different than Singapore or most any place else. The police have far reaching powers. They need no search warrants", said Howard.

While they waited, Howard made several calls. Mark sat quietly not understanding any of the conversations.

A small SUV came slowly down the road towards them. It was the only traffic they had seen on the road. Howard put the window down and the other car pulled alongside his car. The two men spoke in Chinese for several minutes. Finally Howard turned. "He says we can get in his car and he will take us to the house. We may not be admitted but it's worth a try."

Mark and Howard got in the policeman's Chinese made SUV. It was small but comfortable. When they approached the guardhouse, the policeman spoke to Howard in Chinese. Howard nodded. The policeman produced his credentials and the guard never even looked at the passengers. He opened the huge gate. They drove through.

They passed several streets branching off the main road, but the one that was the address of the Sutton property was not one of them. When it appeared there may not be any more streets, Howard pointed to a sign with the name of the street for Sutton.

The SUV turned into a lovely lane. At the very end was a modest home set back into the trees. There was a car in the drive and a man washing it.

The Malay policeman pulled up and got out. He walked down the drive and spoke to the man washing the car. He showed the man his credentials. The policeman turned and motioned for Howard and Mark to come. They went to the front door and entered the house.

Mark was impressed with the décor and expensive furniture. The small office was just off the foyer. Mark examined the desk and the bookcase behind the desk. He was careful not to touch anything. Howard stood with the policeman and observed. "I will take a few pictures" said Mark. He took out his small camera and snapped several pictures.

They wandered through the house but did not open any drawers or doors. Mark saw something on a small table that interested him. He walked over and looked at a framed picture. It was of Peters and a large man. "Well this certainly is Peters/Sutton's house. That is Peters in this photo." Mark took a picture of the framed photo.

Howard confirmed that it was indeed Peters. "I think that's all we can do for now. I'm certain the man washing the car will contact Peters and informed him the police were here at his house. I think we have proof that this is his residence."

As the small SUV pulled away from the house, Howard looked back and saw the man speaking into a mobile phone.

Chapter 31

On the Road Again

Sam drove while Steve sat very quiet. That in itself was very unusual. Sam looked over at his partner. "What the hell is wrong with you? The cat got your tongue?"

Steve didn't say anything at first. He just stared out of the windscreen. "This case we've been assigned, do you think we will have to testify at any hearings or trials?"

"We might. Why do you ask?"

"Well, we did go to the wrong house, and then we drank two beers at the house. We did intimidate that poor manager at the DHL office and we didn't take pictures of the stash in the wall of the Secure Pacific Investments office. We gave $10,000 to the watch commander without getting a receipt. They could fire us."

"We did document in our report where we found the phones and the money. The watch commander was told and he witnessed the evidence bags. We have a receipt from the courier that picked up the evidence bags. If we can't trust the watch commander then who?" said Sam.

Steve sat still for a few minutes. Sam was not sure what Steve's problem was. This was not like Steve.

"I need this job. If we screwed up somehow, we may face charges" said Steve.

"Hey man, we didn't screw up. Relax!"

"But why pull us off the case send us packing?" asked Steve.

Sam sat for a few seconds thinking. "I don't think we were pulled off because of something we did, but because of what we saw. The letter we found. It was a political nightmare for a lot of people" said Sam.

Suddenly there was a loud bang. Steve nearly jumped out of his seat. "Holy crap, what was that?" said Steve.

"I think a tyre just blew out." Sam slowed and pulled the car over to the side of the road. They got out and examined the tyre. The rear tyre on the passenger's side was flat. "Steve, get the jack and spanner out of the boot."

"Give me the key to unlock the boot." Sam handed the keys to Steve. He went around to the boot and opened the lid. "The spare looks OK, but I don't see a jack or spanner."

"Look under the mat, there is a cavity that houses the tools" said Sam.

"Yep, here they are. I've never changed a tyre before" said Steve.

Sam looked at Steve as if he was making a joke. The look on Steve's face showed it was no joke. "I'll do it, just get the jack out and insert it here in this little hole. It's the place the jack goes to raise the wheel off the ground."

"Dude that's neat. I never noticed those little holes before" said Steve.

Sam cranked the handle of the jack. The tyre began to rise. He stopped and took the spanner and loosened the lugs holding the tyre onto the wheel.

"Dude the tyre is not off the ground. Won't the tyre slide off?" said Steve.

"No, this is the way you do it. If you raise the tyre off the ground before you loosen the lugs, then the tyre will turn and you can't loosen the lugs."

Sam cranked the jack handle until the tyre was completely off the ground. He turned the lugs with the spanner until all were removed. He tugged the tyre until it came loose and off the wheel.

"Dude that was easy. Now what?" asked Steve.

"Roll that spare over here and place it on the studs." Steve placed the spare on the wheel. Sam reapplied the lugs and gave them a quick jerk with the spanner to tighten them slightly. He lowered the wheel until the tyre touched the ground.

"Here, take this spanner and give each lug a turn until you can't turn them anymore" said Sam. Steve took the spanner and grunted several times giving each lug a turn until he could not turn them anymore.

Sam placed the flat in the boot along with the tools. Steve watched until Sam closed the lid. "Dude, what happens when we get another flat? We don't have another spare." Sam looked at Steve and shook his head.

"If we get another flat, then you walk to the nearest garage for help."

"Why me?" Steve got in and slammed the door.

Sam started the car and pulled back onto the road. They drove in silence for several miles.

"I've been thinking about that letter we faxed to Nigel. If it is on the level, then several very high ranking people are going to jail. I don't know the Chinese names, but I'm sure they are in another country. Nigel and Joyce may be in the middle of a huge mess" said Sam.

"Yep, my thoughts exactly. What can we do to help?" asked Steve.

"I don't think we should do anything until Nigel asks. If we even utter one word about what we found, I think some very important people will be interested in our health" said Sam.

"Why would they be interested in our health?" asked Steve.

"Because if we are still breathing, then we know too much."

"Oh crap house mouse. What should we do?"

Sam looked over at Steve with a steely look. **"WE KNOW**

NOTHING" shouted Sam.

Steve jumped. "Okay, I got the picture. But I really like one of the people mentioned in the letter. He was my idol when I was in high school. Do you really think he is involved in this fraud case?"

"I think we should forget what we saw in that letter. If we are asked, we say, What Letter?"

Steve sat and nodded. "My mum told me there would be days like this. I really hate this job sometimes."

Chapter 32

Gwen Leong

Gwen Leong sat in the back of her Bentley as the driver navigated though traffic. She was late to a monthly board meeting at the bank her family had owned and managed for more than a hundred years. Even with the various wars and occupations, the bank survived and thrived.

The car pulled into an underground garage and up to a guarded entrance. The guard opened the door and Gwen Leong stepped out onto a plush red carpet. She inserted her key card and the lift doors opened. She rode the lift up to the top floor of the bank building where all the executive offices were located. One was her private office even though she rarely occupied it.

A uniformed guard stood outside two huge ornate doors that opened into the board room. He opened the doors and Gwen took her seat at the head of the table. Since she was the owner of the bank, being late was not an issue. Each of the board members stood. She acknowledged the gesture with a nod. They all sat down.

Gwen's husband was also a board member as matter of family

courtesy. He never really got involved in the bank's business and knew little of the decisions his wife made. He was content to go through the motions as her husband.

Gwen brought the meeting to order. The agenda was passed around by a clerk who departed as soon as all had their copies. Gwen nodded at the bank's managing director to begin the meeting. He stood and began to go over each of the agenda items. Most were financial reports by various officers of the bank. After all the reports were read, the managing director closed the general meeting. All but three of the directors left the room.

Gwen looked at those remaining. Her husband was not one of them. "I have some rather disturbing news. Our business with Bangkok is in jeopardy. One of my sources told me the police have paid a visit to Peters' home and examined several rooms in his house. At this time I do not know to what extent they are investigating."

Each of the three remaining directors looked at each other. One spoke. "Are you saying that we may come under investigation?"

"No, but we should be prepared if there is an inquiry. Peters was not aware of our other business with Bangkok. I don't think there is any threat to us. But to make sure, I'll take steps to clean up the loose ends."

The three directors nodded in agreement. They each gathered up their documents and departed the room, leaving Gwen alone. She took out her mobile and made a call.

The call was answered on the second ring. "Hello, I wasn't expecting your call. What can I do for you?"

"I'm afraid that we have a problem that needs a solution. I've just learned that the police paid a visit to Peters' house. It appears that something has gone wrong and I think it's time we closed the connection. I'm sure you have the resources to make this as clean as possible." She pressed the disconnect button to close the call.

Wo Jun Fat sat back and thought about the call from Gwen. He enjoyed the income from their association and was concerned about the possibility of it drying up. He pressed a button on his desk. A young man entered almost immediately. "Yes sir."

Wo Jun Fat motioned for him to sit. The young man was dressed in a business suit that would have been fashionable in any law firm in the world. "I have an assignment for you. There is an Australian going by the name of Sutton staying at this address." He handed a folded piece of paper to the young man. "I want you to have him brought to the warehouse. Do not harm him but place him in a secure room. He is not to make any calls. Be sure to collect all of his belongings and scrub the hotel room of any trace that he had ever been there."

The young man opened the paper and read the address. He looked up. "Consider it done." He left the office of Wo Jun Fat, Chief Justice of the Thailand Supreme Court.

Wo Jun Fat knew that if all was exposed, he would be facing some very serious charges. Peters had made threats to expose certain details. The payments made to him had been within reason and was not a burden. Gwen had handled all of the transactions without Peters knowing where the money came from. The warning given the nosey detective may have been a mistake. But it was done, so they would have to live with that. This Peters problem should be easy to solve.

Chapter 33

The Warehouse

Peters had checked into the hotel recommended by his contact. He was rattled by the fact that the police knew who he was and had traced him to Bangkok. His contact had helped save his hide. He knew that things were getting close to him having to go to plan B.

Peters typed on his laptop. The email was to Gwen Leong. He needed her assistance. He only knew of her official email. He had never emailed her, only phone calls from his home. He was desperate and needed to know how exposed he was. Plan B was dangerous and full of pitfalls. He knew she had the letter with all the names and the instructions on how to get the evidence. He typed, **Get the information from my home and hold it for me.**

A knock on the door startled him. He peeped through the little eyepiece. A well dressed young man was standing in the hall. He opened the door. "May I help you?"

The young man smiled. "Are you Larry Sutton?"

"Yes, what's this all about?"

"I'm from a mutual friend. The one that helped you relocate. He would like to meet with you and make some very important plans." The young man was very formal and addressed Peters with very polite manners.

"I see. When does he want to meet?" *Hum, I've actually never met the man. Only phone calls.*

"Now. I have a car waiting to take us to his location." The young man motioned for Peters to follow him."

"Just a moment I want to shut down my computer." Peters turned to walk back to his laptop and clicked the send button.

§

That was the last thing he remembered before waking up in a modest size room with no windows and little in the way of furnishings. He felt a large lump beginning to form on the back of his head. He had been kidnapped. He had no clue as to who snatched him or where he was. He sat on the edge of a bed that had clean sheets and was made up. He could tell he had been laying on it for some time. The covers were warm to the touch. It was obvious that the young man that came to his hotel room had mugged him from behind.

The room had a toilet, wash basin, and two chairs. There was no carpet, only tile floors. He thought at first that this may be a modest hotel, but he doubted it was a hotel. He walked over to the door and tried the knob. To his surprise the door was not locked. He gently pulled open the door. Standing outside were two men with large automatic weapons. They motioned for him to close the door.

As far as he could ascertain, he was defiantly not here as a guest. I'm someone's prisoner, but why? Who would know I'm in Bangkok and would want to kidnap me? My contact is well paid and certainly would not want to harm me. He sat back down on the edge of the bed. His head was hurting like hell.

The door to the room opened. The well dressed young man that had come to his hotel was standing with the one of the guards.

He entered and took a seat in one of the chairs. He said nothing. He just waited.

"Why am I here?" asked Peters.

"I'm sorry for the lump on your head. I had my orders. You were not to communicate with anyone. I had to stop you from writing your email."

"Orders from whom? What do you want?" *He doesn't know I sent the email.*

"You will find out shortly. Please remain calm. No harm will come to you." The young man nodded at the guard with the large weapon. The guard left the room.

Peters sat looking at the man. His mind was in turmoil. *What is going on? They are not the authorities.*

The young man got up and walked around the room. "You have some information about the business of certain individuals that you claim will expose them somehow. What is that information and where is it?"

Peters sat stunned. *So this is what this is all about.* "I have no idea what you are referring to."

"We know you have made certain arrangements to release damaging information of certain persons if you should be arrested, or disappear—shall we say. You have been paid a great sum of money for a long time to keep this information from being circulated. Is there more than one copy of the information? The parties you have been blackmailing are now ready to conclude their business with you. If you want to walk out of this room, then you will comply with my request."

Peters sat and stared at the man. He was speechless. He never thought they would put it to a test. His concern had been with the authorities. He looked down at the floor. "I don't have the information with me. There is only one copy. It is in another country. It is safe and will not be released unless I do not report in on a scheduled basis."

"I see. So you have someone who will retrieve the information and release it to the public."

"That information my young friend will remain my secret." He was bluffing but what else was he to do.

The young man got up and walked to within a few inches of Peters. "That was a grave mistake. Goodbye Mr. Peters or Mr. Sutton or whatever your current name is." He looked directly into Peters' eyes, turned and left the room.

Sweat was running down Peters' face. Those eyes were as cold as ice. His stomach felt queasy as if he was about to throw-up. No one knew he was here. He had no way to call his contact for help. For the first time in his career, he was afraid for his life. His only hope was that Gwen would go to his home and retrieve the package and hold it for him.

Wo Jun Fat saw it all on his monitor. He smiled at Peters' obvious distress. Gwen had phoned him the moment she got Peters' email.

Peters is a loose cannon. He could cause a lot of unpleasant events. I could make it appear he was saved by his unknown contact. Killing Peters would not serve any purpose. It would only raise questions from the authorities. He may or may not have others ready to expose his information. But if he thought he was safe, then all would be quiet. I'll give him a day or so to mull over his situation.

Chapter 34

Nigel's Plan

Nigel received the phone call he had been expecting from Mark. He was not ready for the surprise he got. Mark not only had found Peters' home, but had the phone number and address of Gwen Leong.

Nigel and Joyce sat in the bar of the Hilton Hotel on Wireless road. Joyce said, "Now what?"

Nigel was thumping his fingers on the table. "I think we have to plan very carefully how to approach Gwen Leong. If we are not careful, this could just go away and we will be left with nothing but circumstantial evidence."

"My first thought on this is to come up with a story that will force Gwen Leong to make a move. If we can get her to go to Peters' home and remove the evidence, then we have a chance of getting our hands on the hard evidence he hid away."

"I think you have something there. If we can get Howard Chong to put video cameras in the home to record everything and then arrest her in the act of removing the evidence we will have at least some hard evidence to present to a jury."

Joyce was smiling. "I have a feeling that Peters and Leong were more than just business contacts. I think she and Peters were having an affair and Leong was using the affair to gain Peters' trust. That's why he designated her to get the evidence and expose all. She must know what that evidence is and where it is located and I think she has the letter. That was a copy he kept in North Sydney. Let's phone Mark and explain what we want and see if he and Howard can pull this off."

Nigel nodded. "What I haven't put together yet is what the blackmailed group gained by their association with Peters. It appears that all the money went to Peters and he had control of the accounts."

Nigel phoned Mark and explained what he wanted. Mark assured him it would be done.

Joyce said, "Maybe there is some other way to control the accounts and Peters has no idea it exists."

Nigel looked puzzled. "I don't follow. How could there be any unknown control of the account?"

"When Doug explained the banking laws, I found a reference to something that we should check out. It appears that the local bank where most of these deposits ended up is really a branch of a foreign bank. Even if the board appears to be local, the ownership is foreign. I'll get Doug's expertise on the procedure to find out who owns the bank."

"If this bank is owned by a foreign bank, then how would that make a difference?"

Joyce thought for a moment. "Let's speculate until we get proof. If a bank in Hong Kong owned this bank then their systems and accounts would be exposed to the parent bank. That means that the foreign bank could control all of the accounts from afar and certain transactions would be nonexistent locally, since the information is actually on the servers of the foreign bank. Statements could be made to show anything. This would give whoever is controlling the accounts an advantage of hiding all the transactions with minimum exposure. We need to speak to Doug."

Nigel was not quite following the logic but accepted Joyce's knowledge of banking systems. "If that is true, then this case is much larger than we imagined. I'll call Mark and ask him to get a complete file on Gwen Leong."

Joyce said, "I think that would be interesting. What do we know about her other than she and Peters were involved and he trusted her with the evidence associated with the blackmail."

Nigel placed his call to Mark and requested a complete work-up on Gwen Leong. Mark said he would get Howard to help and would get back as soon as he had all the information.

"I'll go over the accounts again. I may have missed something. The incoming transactions are the ones I'm interested in. We know that according to the statements, very few withdrawals were made or at least show up on the statements", said Joyce.

Nigel placed a call to Stan's office. "Stan, this is Nigel. Is Doug back at work?" He listened for a few seconds. "Great, we have some theories that he may be able to help us with. We will be at your office in about an hour. Joyce would like a list of all the directors of the local bank and all the corporate information available on its charter."

"If what I suspect becomes fact, then we may have to contact Interpol. This may be far reaching and much more involved than the Jenkins case" said Joyce.

§

They finished breakfast and took a taxi to the Police headquarters building. When they arrived, Stan and Doug were sitting having coffee. They stood when Nigel and Joyce came into the office.

"Good morning", said Stan. "Would you like coffee?"

"No thank you, we have just had breakfast", said Nigel. "Doug it's great to see you back and recovering."

"Thanks Nigel. It is a bit uncomfortable and hurts if I move to fast, but I'm on the mend."

"Please have a seat" said Stan. "It appears that Doug was able to get some information on the bank. Doug you explain."

Doug took out a pad with hand written notes. "It was surprising to us that it is owned by a bank in Malay. The parent bank established this branch over fifty years ago. The directors are mostly local politicos. This is more of a courtesy than actual administration. Most of the local board members receive modest fees for attending the meetings and are given certain perks. The shock is two of the names on Sutton's letter are on the board and the owner of the bank is where the surprise comes in. The Leong Family owns the local bank. They have been in the banking business for several generations in Malay. Why they are keeping the branch a secret is puzzling."

Nigel smiled and said, "Joyce and I have a theory about that. We think the local bank is used as a master depository for several overseas groups that want to launder money. We think the group has laundered hundreds of millions through their system. They take a percentage as their fee. Some, they take all. We are just beginning to put together a theory. We may have to consult with Interpol. Peters is not aware of the fact that he may not have any money in the bank. It is all on paper to make it look as if his funds are safe and sound. He thought his boss was an Australian, but in fact we believe it to be someone else."

Doug sat taking in all that Nigel had said. "That is a very interesting theory. I became interested in following a similar theory a few years ago on a case, but my boss at the time told me it was nothing and to drop it. My boss was a district judge at the time, and now is the Chief Justice of the Supreme Court. He is also on the board of the bank and one of the names on the letter."

Joyce looked up at Doug. "Wow that is interesting. Why do you think he stopped you from investigating the case?"

"At the time, I had very little evidence and was not aware of all the players. I did make a report to him that I suspected that the bank may have had a part in the cover-up. All of my evidence pointed to the bank, but I was unable to find the accounts. I think I may have been too close to the real evidence."

Joyce said, "I think you may have been right all along. Of course we think that the accounts were wiped clean when you went probing. It seems that if that is the case, the only person that knew you were getting close was the judge."

"I didn't know he was associated with the bank until you requested a list of all their board members. It makes sense to me now. With most of the administration of the police force reporting to him, he is in a position to squash any investigation" said Doug.

Stan was listening very carefully. He got up and closed the door to his office. "People, I think we must involve Interpol. If this theory leaks, we are in for some very bad consequences. Interpol will have the authority to investigate without revealing anything to the local government. Our country signed the agreement with most of all the world's countries to abide by international law. If a crime is committed in one country and impinges on another country then Interpol has the authority to investigate and arrest anyone involved."

Nigel nodded and said, "I know several contacts within Interpol. If you agree, I will phone them now and start the process."

Each nodded approval.

Stan said, "Nigel you take the lead on this and work directly with Interpol. I suggest you limit your personal exposure as much as possible. We should not meet here again. I will make a report that you have concluded your investigation. Doug and I will concur that there is no evidence of a crime being committed in this country. We will meet at your hotel when necessary. I also suggest we limit phone conversations to only mobile units."

Joyce looked at Doug. "I'm truly sorry you got injured because of our investigation."

"Hey, this started long before you arrived. I'm hoping that whoever tried to take me out was not associated with my previous boss, but it's not looking good for him."

"I suggest that both of you appear to have no more interest in this case. You can help by pointing Joyce and me in the right direction when Interpol arrives" said Nigel.

Stan said, "I will write an email to my superior now and explain that we are open for a new assignment in that you have concluded your investigation and no longer need our assistance. I am sure that will get back to your country also."

Nigel looked at Joyce, "We know."

Chapter 35

Interpol

Nigel phoned his Interpol contact in London and filled him in on the situation. To his surprise he was told that Interpol had three agents already in Bangkok. They were just winding up a case and were available to help.

Nigel filled Joyce in on the good luck. They were to meet at a hotel in the business district at 5 PM.

At exactly 5 PM, Nigel and Joyce entered the lobby of the hotel. They were told to go to the concierge's desk and ask for the guest conference room. They were led to a suite of rooms marked Business Centre. The concierge tapped lightly on the door. It was opened by a very attractive woman.

"Yes may I help you?" Her accent was French.

"These two asked to be brought here per your request" said the Concierge.

She looked pass him and smiled. "Please come in."

Nigel and Joyce entered the small conference room. They were introduced to the other two, a short man, named Granville Watson, who appeared to be in his late fifty's or early sixties. The other man was much younger and was obvious very fit. His name was Hans Frehoffer. The attractive woman introduced herself as Rose Bloomingthal. She smiled and offered them a seat at the conference table.

Granville Watson had a very pronounced English accent. "We received a communication that you have a case we should consider."

Nigel took the lead. "Yes. We have been investigating what appeared to be purely an Australian case until recently. We now believe the case to be very wide in scope and involve multiple countries. We have a theory but have little evidence to back it up. There are very important and high ranking people from at least three countries involved."

Nigel gave the Interpol agents the full story from the beginning of the Jenkins case to the discovery of the names of two that are on the bank's board and the Malaysian bank controlling the local bank. Nigel explained their theory of money laundering on a grand scale.

Joyce said, "We believe a bank in Malay is the center of the laundering scheme. We discovered they own a bank here and kept that knowledge very low key. We found out that our principal suspect may have had an affair with the owner of the bank. We think she manipulated our suspect into moving most of his ill gotten funds to their branch bank here. We have copies of the account statements, but believe they are bogus in order to hide the fact that the money is actually not in the bank. There are other indications of funds coming from several other countries over the past seven to eight years."

Nigel picked up the conversation. "The local police administration is very much in the pocket of one of the major players. There are two detectives that we trust. One of the detectives was shot and injured while assisting us in searching for evidence. It became obvious that someone within the police department reported our intention on searching a certain home. He may or may not have been targeted to kill. We speculate that it was meant as a warning to us. It seems he was working on a case several years ago and was unaware until this week that his boss at the time is involved in our case. It began to come together. We think we can get some damaging evidence that is most likely in Malay, but we are going to need your help in formulating a plan that will not involve any of the local law enforcement."

Watson sat very still with his eyes closed. The room was silent. He opened his eyes and looked at Joyce. "We need to diagram the evidence you do have and put in chronological order your investigation. We will need a place to setup and hash the results."

Bloomingthal leaned forward and said, "I will make arrangements with the hotel for a large suite for our working room."

Watson nodded. "Do you think anyone other than your two detectives is aware of your theories?"

Nigel said, "No, we only came to this theory this morning. We have an associate working with us in Singapore. He works with a local detective who has been very helpful in researching clues. He is not aware of anything other than the original Jenkins case."

Watson made a note on his pad. "We should meet again at 8 AM in the suite.

Frehoffer had not uttered a word. He made several notes on his pad, but never asked a question. Joyce wondered if he spoke English.

Nigel and Joyce left the conference room and hailed a taxi back to their hotel on Wireless road. They spoke little on the ride.

Nigel paid the driver and they entered the Hilton. "It's early, want a drink before dinner?" asked Nigel.

"Yeah, I think I need one after today's revelations. "

They headed for the bar. There was only one table left in the very back. They each ordered a drink.

"You know, I feel like there will be a huge fallout over this case. I'm not sure where we will land in that fallout. It seems that if the names on that letter are in fact true, then we should not be involved in the arrest. Let's let Interpol make all the moves," said Nigel.

"How will we be disconnected? We will have to turn over all

our information. We will certainly be named in the evidence chain. I don't see how we can escape not being involved."

Nigel took a sip from his drink. "This is very complicated. It will have to be done in a very precise manner and timing must be exact. At least we have the full resources of Interpol."

Chapter 36

First Interpol Meeting

Nigel and Joyce stepped off the lift on the seventh floor. The Suite was at the end of the hall. Nigel knocked. The door was opened by Watson.

"Good morning. Coffee is on the side table, help yourself", said Watson.

"Thank you", Nigel walked over to the side table. Joyce was right behind him.

Bloomingthal was busy typing on a laptop. Frehoffer was not in the room.

Watson watched the two carefully while they made their coffee. "I contacted my office early this morning and had you two checked out. It seems you are celebrities within the police community. Not to worry, we did not contact your government. We in Interpol do keep tabs on possible contacts in each of the member countries. Your work is well thought of by our people. I thought you should know we always vet our associates before beginning an investigation, especially one that has the high profile this case seems to have."

Nigel raised an eyebrow. "I'm flattered. I didn't know how Interpol worked with regards to teaming up with police from other countries."

"We are the servants of our member countries" said Watson. "We respect each country's laws and attempt to stay within our charter and guidelines. One of the hardest things to do is gain the trust of local law enforcement. Sometimes they think we are there to take over their jobs. Sometimes they feel so threatened that it makes our work very difficult. Often we never let them know we are in the country unless we need to make an arrest. The local police have no idea we are here. The case we just worked did not involve arrest or apprehension of any suspects. It did not need the intervention of local authorities. I think it best that you not reveal that to your two detective friends. "

Joyce sat a listened to Watson. "I understand your need to get your job done, but on foreign soil, don't the rules require an invitation? We have to go through a contact procedure to make the locals aware we are on their soil investigating a possible crime?"

"We always try to evaluate each case as to the need to make the member country aware we are on their soil. In most of the cases we are invited by the member country to assist in following leads in other countries. When those cases are purely investigative, we rarely involve the locals. We gather our information and leave."

Nigel put his cup down. "When an arrest is made of a high ranking member of the government, how do you handle the political side of the problem?"

Bloomingthal looked up from her laptop. "We usually go right to the top, the Prime Minister, President or whoever is in charge and present our evidence and get their blessing on the arrest. Sometimes the military is involved to assure safety. Most of our member countries have a protocol already in place for such an event. We have the authority to arrest even the Prime Minister of a member country. This has never happened but if necessary the procedure is in place."

The door to one of the bedrooms opened and Frehoffer came

into the room. He nodded at Nigel and Joyce and placed some documents in front of Watson. He exited the room without a word. Watson read the documents.

Watson reached into his pocket and retrieved a small recorder and placed it on the table. "We will record all of our meetings. This is required according to our procedure. It assures no misunderstandings."

Nigel nodded. "Where shall we start today?"

Bloomingthal said, "I have a large white board that we can use to put as much of the evidence as possible." She reached over and removed a cover from the white board. It had several headings and information already entered under some. "I have begun with what you told us yesterday. We can fill in more as we go down each thread."

Watson took a long time digesting the various threads. He got up and wrote a new heading, USA. "According to your bank statements, some of the deposits were made from USA banks. We need to trace those transfers and find out the source of the deposits. Joyce did you bring all the bank records?"

"Yes I have them here." She produced the fat envelope from her briefcase. She removed the documents. They were grouped into years and months. "But I doubt their authenticity now that we know they could have been manipulated by the Malay bank."

Bloomingthal nodded. "Yes that is entirely possible. Maybe we should hear your ideas on how to proceed." Bloomingthal got up and took the documents and opened the bedroom door. She handed them to Frehoffer without a word.

Nigel looked up and said, "I think one of the things we need to determine is the type of enterprises that are behind each of the groups laundering the funds. We know the Australian firm is ripping off lottery winners with phony investments."

Watson made a note on his pad. "Let's look into the oil scam that was the local case. What was the structure of that scam?"

"We are not quite sure" said Joyce. "Doug and Stan, the local detectives, never went into detail as it was old history. They did say it resembled the horse purchasing scam. I think if you approve, we ask Doug and Stan to come meet with us. They are aware that I was going to contact Interpol. We can simply say you were nearby and came in last night."

Bloomingthal looked over at Watson. Watson nodded his head. "Okay, contact your detectives and have them bring all the information on the cold case", said Bloomingthal.

Nigel got up and walked to the window. He dialed Stan's number. Stan answered on the first ring. "Stan this is Nigel. We are in luck. Our friends at Interpol were nearby and are here. They would like to see all the information you have on the cold case Doug mentioned." Nigel gave Stan the hotel name and the suite number and terminated the call. "Stan says he and Doug will be here in about an hour with the cold case documentation."

The four began to flesh out what they had discussed. The white board was full of names, places and theories. There was a knock on the door. Bloomingthal placed the cover over the white board. Watson answered the door. He was presented with two ID's. "Welcome gentlemen. I'm Grandville Watson; this is Fife Bloomingthal and I think you know Nigel and Joyce."

Stan and Doug came in with Stan carrying a large cardboard box. "I'm Stan and this is my partner Doug. We have the documents you requested."

Watson indicated a place around the table for them to sit. "Put the box over there on the floor. We will bring you up-to-date on where we are." He looked at Doug with his arm in a sling. "I've heard of your incident with a gunman. I'm sorry you were wounded." Doug nodded.

Watson gave a brief up-date as he walked over to the white board and removed the cover. He pointed out that it seemed obvious that the money was being controlled from the Malay bank.

Doug raised his hand. Watson nodded. "My original investigation indicated that most of the money came from US banks and a good portion from Hong Kong and the UK. How are we going to check out these leads?"

Bloomingthal stood and walked to the whiteboard. She pointed at two banks in the UK. "First the transfer numbers and local account numbers were on the documents Joyce got from the bank. We have a method of obtaining ownerships of the accounts and statements. There are transfer numbers. If these are real, then we can track the transfers back to an account. We are already on that path as we speak."

Joyce now thought she knew the job of Frehoffer. He was their online research person. "Doug give us a detailed account of your investigation into the oil scam a few years ago," said Bloomingthal.

"We were contacted by an individual that claimed he and his investors were embezzled out of a great deal of money. Many of our investment groups are small. They usually are members of a family or some social organization. The man told me they had lost over one million US. He explained that a man he had dealt with on several occasions in small real estate purchases had a deal to good to pass up. It involved the purchase of shares in an oil distribution company." Doug cleared his throat. "May I have a glass of water please?"

Watson got up and brought a bottle of water from the side table.

"Thank you. The deal was that if the group invested one million US dollars, they would be returned two million US dollars. The group gave the man the money. Months went by but they were not given any information on their investment. On several occasions, they met with the man but he explained that because of the war going on in the Middle East things were not good. Their shipment of oil was delayed. That was when the group came to me. I looked into the deal. The oil was purchased by a group in Bangkok. They sold the oil for a huge profit to a group in Hong Kong. Then several months later the Bangkok company sold their interest in the oil to a company in Singapore for a loss of over one million US dollars. The money ended here in Bangkok. I was able to track the money to the same bank as Nigel and Joyce discovered. I was unable to track the actual location of the oil. Iraqi authorities were not cooperating. I pursued checking who owned the Hong Kong and Singapore accounts. When I took this evidence to my boss, I was told to shut the case down due to the lack of evidence. I informed the investor group that they had lost their money and there was no case against the man they named that took their money. I later found out that the man they named worked as an employee of my boss. I was never able to tie my boss directly to any wrong doing. I assumed the employee was working on his own.

Watson listened very carefully. He went to the white board and wrote the locations of the transfers for the oil. "In both cases the money actually ended in the local bank owned by the Malay bank. If your theory is correct then the Malay bank could easily control the software to make it appear the money was actually in the local bank, when most likely it was in a bank in some other country."

"Wouldn't the money end up in the parent bank in Malay?" asked Joyce.

"It's possible, but highly unlikely. In schemes like these, most of the money ends up in a bank that has secrecy laws protecting the account holders, similar to the laws in Switzerland. There are many locations that have these laws," said Watson.

Bloomingthal moved to the white board and began to trace lines from bank to bank. "It appears to me that there were many different players unaware of each other. The scheme was basically the same which leads me to think someone in the parent bank gave the players the scheme to immolate. In the oil scheme, the investors lost all of their money and the police were called off the case. In the Australian horse scheme, the investors lost their money and the scam artist was following the same scheme but was unaware that all of the ill gotten money was actually hidden in another bank."

"Is there a way to trace the funds from these accounts to the other foreign bank?" asked Joyce.

"We may have a problem. Malay is not one of our member nations. Therefore we will not have authority to ask for warrants and writs," said Watson. "If the parent bank in Malay simply moved the funds from Bangkok accounts, which were on their server anyway, to a clearing account and then wired it to a safe haven bank, we would have no trail. Without access to the data files, there would be no way to trace. If we knew the receiving bank, then we may stand a chance of tracking the ownership of the account, but that would be a long shot."

Bloomingthal said, "It's almost lunch time and we are getting a bit stale on ideas. Let's take a break and meet back here at 15:00." They all were relieved to take a break. Nigel and Joyce left and went to the lobby coffee shop. Stan and Doug left and took their car back to Stan's office.

"I'm getting bad vibes from all of this. These people are pros and have covered their tracks very well. I hope Mark comes through with the supposed hard evidence."

They ordered lunch.

215

Chapter 36

First Interpol Meeting

Nigel and Joyce stepped off the lift on the seventh floor. The Suite was at the end of the hall. Nigel knocked. The door was opened by Watson.

"Good morning. Coffee is on the side table, help yourself", said Watson.

"Thank you", Nigel walked over to the side table. Joyce was right behind him.

Bloomingthal was busy typing on a laptop. Frehoffer was not in the room.

Watson watched the two carefully while they made their coffee. "I contacted my office early this morning and had you two checked out. It seems you are celebrities within the police community. Not to worry, we did not contact your government. We in Interpol do keep tabs on possible contacts in each of the member countries. Your work is well thought of by our people. I thought you should know we always vet our associates before beginning an investigation, especially one that has the high profile this case seems to have."

Nigel raised an eyebrow. "I'm flattered. I didn't know how Interpol worked with regards to teaming up with police from other countries."

"We are the servants of our member countries" said Watson. "We respect each country's laws and attempt to stay within our charter and guidelines. One of the hardest things to do is gain the trust of local law enforcement. Sometimes they think we are there to take over their jobs. Sometimes they feel so threatened that it makes our work very difficult. Often we never let them know we are in the country unless we need to make an arrest. The local police have no idea we are here. The case we just worked did not involve arrest or apprehension of any suspects. It did not need the intervention of local authorities. I think it best that you not reveal that to your two detective friends. "

Joyce sat a listened to Watson. "I understand your need to get your job done, but on foreign soil, don't the rules require an invitation? We have to go through a contact procedure to make the locals aware we are on their soil investigating a possible crime?"

"We always try to evaluate each case as to the need to make the member country aware we are on their soil. In most of the cases we are invited by the member country to assist in following leads in other countries. When those cases are purely investigative, we rarely involve the locals. We gather our information and leave."

Nigel put his cup down. "When an arrest is made of a high ranking member of the government, how do you handle the political side of the problem?"

Bloomingthal looked up from her laptop. "We usually go right to the top, the Prime Minister, President or whoever is in charge and present our evidence and get their blessing on the arrest. Sometimes the military is involved to assure safety. Most of our member countries have a protocol already in place for such an event. We have the authority to arrest even the Prime Minister of a member country. This has never happened but if necessary the procedure is in place."

The door to one of the bedrooms opened and Frehoffer came

into the room. He nodded at Nigel and Joyce and placed some documents in front of Watson. He exited the room without a word. Watson read the documents.

Watson reached into his pocket and retrieved a small recorder and placed it on the table. "We will record all of our meetings. This is required according to our procedure. It assures no misunderstandings."

Nigel nodded. "Where shall we start today?"

Bloomingthal said, "I have a large white board that we can use to put as much of the evidence as possible." She reached over and removed a cover from the white board. It had several headings and information already entered under some. "I have begun with what you told us yesterday. We can fill in more as we go down each thread."

Watson took a long time digesting the various threads. He got up and wrote a new heading, USA. "According to your bank statements, some of the deposits were made from USA banks. We need to trace those transfers and find out the source of the deposits. Joyce did you bring all the bank records?"

"Yes I have them here." She produced the fat envelope from her briefcase. She removed the documents. They were grouped into years and months. "But I doubt their authenticity now that we know they could have been manipulated by the Malay bank."

Bloomingthal nodded. "Yes that is entirely possible. Maybe we should hear your ideas on how to proceed." Bloomingthal got up and took the documents and opened the bedroom door. She handed them to Frehoffer without a word.

Nigel looked up and said, "I think one of the things we need to determine is the type of enterprises that are behind each of the groups laundering the funds. We know the Australian firm is ripping off lottery winners with phony investments."

Watson made a note on his pad. "Let's look into the oil scam that was the local case. What was the structure of that scam?"

"We are not quite sure" said Joyce. "Doug and Stan, the local detectives, never went into detail as it was old history. They did say it resembled the horse purchasing scam. I think if you approve, we ask Doug and Stan to come meet with us. They are aware that I was going to contact Interpol. We can simply say you were nearby and came in last night."

Bloomingthal looked over at Watson. Watson nodded his head. "Okay, contact your detectives and have them bring all the information on the cold case", said Bloomingthal.

Nigel got up and walked to the window. He dialed Stan's number. Stan answered on the first ring. "Stan this is Nigel. We are in luck. Our friends at Interpol were nearby and are here. They would like to see all the information you have on the cold case Doug mentioned." Nigel gave Stan the hotel name and the suite number and terminated the call. "Stan says he and Doug will be here in about an hour with the cold case documentation."

The four began to flesh out what they had discussed. The white board was full of names, places and theories. There was a knock on the door. Bloomingthal placed the cover over the white board. Watson answered the door. He was presented with two ID's. "Welcome gentlemen. I'm Grandville Watson; this is Fife Bloomingthal and I think you know Nigel and Joyce."

Stan and Doug came in with Stan carrying a large cardboard box. "I'm Stan and this is my partner Doug. We have the documents you requested."

Watson indicated a place around the table for them to sit. "Put the box over there on the floor. We will bring you up-to-date on where we are." He looked at Doug with his arm in a sling. "I've heard of your incident with a gunman. I'm sorry you were wounded." Doug nodded.

Watson gave a brief up-date as he walked over to the white board and removed the cover. He pointed out that it seemed obvious that the money was being controlled from the Malay bank.

Doug raised his hand. Watson nodded. "My original investigation indicated that most of the money came from US banks and a good portion from Hong Kong and the UK. How are we going to check out these leads?"

Bloomingthal stood and walked to the whiteboard. She pointed at two banks in the UK. "First the transfer numbers and local account numbers were on the documents Joyce got from the bank. We have a method of obtaining ownerships of the accounts and statements. There are transfer numbers. If these are real, then we can track the transfers back to an account. We are already on that path as we speak."

Joyce now thought she knew the job of Frehoffer. He was their online research person. "Doug give us a detailed account of your investigation into the oil scam a few years ago," said Bloomingthal.

"We were contacted by an individual that claimed he and his investors were embezzled out of a great deal of money. Many of our investment groups are small. They usually are members of a family or some social organization. The man told me they had lost over one million US. He explained that a man he had dealt with on several occasions in small real estate purchases had a deal to good to pass up. It involved the purchase of shares in an oil distribution company." Doug cleared his throat. "May I have a glass of water please?"

Watson got up and brought a bottle of water from the side table.

"Thank you. The deal was that if the group invested one million US dollars, they would be returned two million US dollars. The group gave the man the money. Months went by but they were not given any information on their investment. On several occasions, they met with the man but he explained that because of the war going on in the Middle East things were not good. Their shipment of oil was delayed. That was when the group came to me. I looked into the deal. The oil was purchased by a group in Bangkok. They sold the oil for a huge profit to a group in Hong Kong. Then several months later the Bangkok company sold their interest in the oil to a company in Singapore for a loss of over one million US dollars. The money ended here in Bangkok. I was able to track the money to the same bank as Nigel and Joyce discovered. I was unable to track the actual location of the oil. Iraqi authorities were not cooperating. I pursued checking who owned the Hong Kong and Singapore accounts. When I took this evidence to my boss, I was told to shut the case down due to the lack of evidence. I informed the investor group that they had lost their money and there was no case against the man they named that took their money. I later found out that the man they named worked as an employee of my boss. I was never able to tie my boss directly to any wrong doing. I assumed the employee was working on his own.

Watson listened very carefully. He went to the white board and wrote the locations of the transfers for the oil. "In both cases the money actually ended in the local bank owned by the Malay bank. If your theory is correct then the Malay bank could easily control the software to make it appear the money was actually in the local bank, when most likely it was in a bank in some other country."

"Wouldn't the money end up in the parent bank in Malay?" asked Joyce.

"It's possible, but highly unlikely. In schemes like these, most of the money ends up in a bank that has secrecy laws protecting the account holders, similar to the laws in Switzerland. There are many locations that have these laws," said Watson.

Bloomingthal moved to the white board and began to trace lines from bank to bank. "It appears to me that there were many different players unaware of each other. The scheme was basically the same which leads me to think someone in the parent bank gave the players the scheme to immolate. In the oil scheme, the investors lost all of their money and the police were called off the case. In the Australian horse scheme, the investors lost their money and the scam artist was following the same scheme but was unaware that all of the ill gotten money was actually hidden in another bank."

"Is there a way to trace the funds from these accounts to the other foreign bank?" asked Joyce.

"We may have a problem. Malay is not one of our member nations. Therefore we will not have authority to ask for warrants and writs," said Watson. "If the parent bank in Malay simply moved the funds from Bangkok accounts, which were on their server anyway, to a clearing account and then wired it to a safe haven bank, we would have no trail. Without access to the data files, there would be no way to trace. If we knew the receiving bank, then we may stand a chance of tracking the ownership of the account, but that would be a long shot."

Bloomingthal said, "It's almost lunch time and we are getting a bit stale on ideas. Let's take a break and meet back here at 15:00." They all were relieved to take a break. Nigel and Joyce left and went to the lobby coffee shop. Stan and Doug left and took their car back to Stan's office.

"I'm getting bad vibes from all of this. These people are pros and have covered their tracks very well. I hope Mark comes through with the supposed hard evidence."

They ordered lunch.

Chapter 37

The Evidence Package

Howard Chong and Mark met with Howard's Malay police contact Hue Sun Yatt. They discussed how to go about planting the cameras and equipment without getting observed.

"All the cameras are the latest wireless versions and needed simply to be put in position. Each camera is equipped with infrared LED lamps and batteries that last for several days. It will take about six to eight minutes to get into the house and place the four cameras. The broadcast range is not far, so the receivers will have to be very close to the house."

Hue Sun said, "I can have a power company utility van parked near the house with us dressed as employees. That should take care of the recording of the event. How are we going to plant the cameras?"

"I observed an alarm system when we went through the house. If we try to go in at night the alarm will trip. I suggest we go in the middle of the day. We can explain to any one on the property that there is an electrical problem and we need to get to the mains inside the house. We can put the cameras in our tool kits," said Mark.

"That's a great idea. Let's to it," said Howard.

"I'll get the uniforms and the van and we can meet tomorrow morning at police headquarters. We can change into the uniforms and start out from there and should be done by noon. I'll have one of the clerks phone the guard house and explain that there is a power problem and some workers are due to arrive to fix the problem," said Hue Sun Yatt.

"Good plan," said Howard. "We'll be here by 09:00 tomorrow."

On the trip back to Singapore, Howard and Mark planned how to get Gwen Leong to take the bait.

"The man we saw washing the car may be the full time caretaker and may even live there," said Mark. "If we can make him think we will be doing something in the home/office that required moving the bookcase and desk, he may call someone and alert them to what we intend to do. I have a feeling it may be Sutton or Gwen Leong."

"Good idea. We may have to stake out the place for a couple of days. We can explain our truck by making sure the caretaker over-hears us complain about it taking several days to make the repairs."

§

Mark showered and was in the lobby of his hotel only a few minutes before he saw Howard's car pull up to the door. He got in the car and greeted Howard with a cheery "Good morning."

Howard smiled and said, "And a good morning to you. The traffic will be light this morning going out so we should make very good time.

Howard pulled into the car park at the Malay police building. He noticed a large van with Malay Electric Company painted on its side. He pulled alongside and parked. He and Mark got out and looked around for the Hue Sun. Not seeing anyone, they headed towards the building.

The back doors of the van opened and a voice said, "Hey, come on in. We can change into our uniforms here and head out. The clerk has phoned the guard house of the compound and informed them we will be arriving shortly. I took the liberty of getting our lunch packed."

"Good, this is great. I have all the equipment in the car. Mark and I can load it up and we can get underway," said Howard. He translated for Mark.

Mark opened the boot of their car. There were three tool kits. He pulled out all three and handed each one to Howard who was standing in the back of the van. There were three tool belts with various tools hanging on the belt. Mark pulled the van doors close and the vehicle started up. They discussed the plan for how to approach the caretaker.

Howard said, "I suggest we go to the house next door first. Let's spend about fifteen minutes there and then I go over and explain we are upgrading some of the equipment and need access to the house. The caretaker will probably have noticed the van and us walking around the house next door. I don't think he got a good look at me on our last visit."

"That sounds very good," said Hue Sun. "We do all the talking and Mark can be our grunt man getting tools and stuff from the van. We'll take it slow and make it appear we are in no hurry. This is the Malay normal workers way."

Mark had no idea what was said, but the way the other two laughed it must have been a joke.

Howard smiled and looked back at Mark. "You have been designated as our go-for person. No talking. Just fetch tools and stuff needed for the job. There's plenty of stuff here to be used as props."

"Okay, I can do that. You yell something in Chinese and I'll bring you a thingy from the van. Just make it vague in case someone knows what some of this stuff is used for."

The trip to the compound went without any an incident. They pulled up to the guard station. The guard stepped out and raised the gate without even speaking. They pulled through to gate and drove to the street with Sutton's house. The house next door was not set as far back as the Sutton house. They parked the van on the street almost between the two houses completely visible from both houses.

Howard went up to the front door of the house and knocked. A maid came to the door. Howard told the maid that they were from the power company and had to examine the equipment in the house. She nodded and stepped back to let Howard enter. Mark pulled his cap down over his eyes as he and Hue Sun walked looking up at the power line and following it to the box on the side of the house.

Mark heard Howard's voice yelling something from the front of the house. Howard's voice was loud enough to hear at last half a block away. He took this as his signal and walked to the van looking around. He found a meter with several wires hanging from the back and picked it up. He closed the doors to the van with a loud bang and headed back to the house. Howard was waiting at the front. Howard nodded and took the item. Mark returned to the box in the back where Hue Sun was examining the box.

They had consumed about twenty minutes. Howard came back and told them in Chinese that they had to order something and would have to come back tomorrow. It was loud enough to be heard by anyone trying to eavesdrop.

Mark nodded towards the Sutton house. The three walked down the drive and before they got to the front door. The man who they had observed washing the car and assumed was the caretaker, came to meet them. Howard explained in Chinese what they were doing and needed access to the house. The man hesitated but nodded and opened the front door. Mark kept his head down and walked toward the back of the house tracing the power line to the junction box.

Howard went to the closet in the kitchen with the electrical equipment. He rummaged around for three or four minutes. The caretaker stayed very close and observed what Howard was doing. Howard came out of the closet. "I'm going to need to get into a junction in the office." He began walking to the small office.

The caretaker jumped in front and blocked the way. "I must get permission before you can go into the office."

"Okay, but make it fast we have four more houses to check."

The caretaker took out a mobile phone. "What exactly are you going to do?" he asked.

"We are going to need to pull the bookcase away from the wall and get to some equipment in the wall," said Howard.

The caretaker made his call. Howard overheard him explaining what was needed to be done by the power company employee. The caretaker listened for a moment and punched off the call.

"Do you have other things that need to be done before moving the bookcase? My employer says that many valuable items in the bookcase must be carefully removed before you move it. You must wait. Maybe tomorrow."

Howard looked into the eyes of the caretaker. "Okay, we have to comeback for next door anyway. We have some small things that can be done today."

The caretaker looked relieved that they would come back tomorrow. It was about lunch time and three power company men went to the van to eat their lunch.

"The bait has been set. The caretaker called someone and they don't want us to do anything until tomorrow. That means they will come here before tomorrow and get the evidence package," said Howard.

They finished their lunches and sat around like most workers talking before returning to work. They were closely observed by the caretaker.

Howard and Hue Sun each grabbed one of the special cases Howard had brought. They walked very slowly towards the front door. The caretaker again meets them before they were on the front stoop.

Howard said, "We have some clean up to do before we come back tomorrow. We need to install some devices to monitor the power."

The caretaker hesitated but stood to the side to allow them entry. Howard went directly to the closet in the kitchen followed by the caretaker.

Hue Sun watched as they went down the hall. He opened the case and removed two cameras and mounted them within some books and picture frames on the table opposite the bookcase. He closed the case and proceeded to the closet where Howard was working.

The caretaker sat on a chair in the kitchen but couldn't see into the closet. Howard came out and Hue Sun went in. Howard took his case and walked down the hall. He stopped and put his case down. He was far enough down the hall that the caretaker could not see what he was doing. He removed two cameras and placed them behind two tall statues.

Hue Sun finished his work in the closet and picked up his case. He closed the closet door and nodded at the caretaker. They walked down the hall to the front door. Howard had already left for the van. Hue Sun thanked the caretaker and said they would be back early tomorrow. "Will it be OK to leave the van parked out front between the two houses? We have several houses yet to go." The caretaker nodded his approval.

Hue Sun climbed into the back of the van. Howard was busy setting up the monitor and recorder. He turned on the receivers. The four cameras came on with perfect views of the bookcase and the hallway.

"I can stay here and monitor what's happening in the house, you two can go to the other houses and do your thing," said Mark. Howard translated for Hue Sun.

"Fine, I don't think anything will happen until someone comes to get the package. The time is 15:00, we'll give it three hours and then think of something else," said Howard. "If you see someone opening that bookcase call us on the radio." Howard took a radio and tucked it in his uniform pocket. He opened the door and Hue Sun and he stepped out to go to the next house. The house was further down the street and almost out of sight.

Mark kept an eye on the monitors. Nothing was happening. The caretaker had left the viewing area. An hour went by then two.

A large car came slowly down the street and pulled into the

drive. A woman got out of the back and went directly to the front door. She used a key to enter. She showed up immediately on the monitor. Mark pressed the record button. He pressed the talk button on the radio. "We have a female in the office," said Mark.

"Okay we're on our way. Give us a few minutes."

The woman paused at the entrance to the office and looked around. She continued to the kitchen and out of range of the camera. She was gone about a minute and returned to the office. She sat down in the chair behind the desk and took a bundle of keys from her purse. She began to try several keys into the center drawer of the desk.

The van door opened and Howard and Hue Sun entered and closed the door.

"All that has happened so far is she went into the kitchen for about a minute and returned to the office. She started testing the keys just as you arrived," said Mark.

They observed the woman trying to find the right key to open the drawer. She finally found the key. She pulled open the drawer and took out a mobile phone and consulted a piece of paper that she took from her purse. She punched in a few numbers. A door sprung open in the bookcase. A large wall safe was clearly seen on the camera. She consulted the paper again and turned the combination lock, then turned the handle and opened the safe. The woman removed several envelopes, and two boxes of floppy disks. She took a laptop computer from the safe and closed everything back the way it was. She opened the computer and removed one of the floppies and inserted it into the computer.

"Let's go, she may try to destroy the evidence," said Howard.

The three jumped from the back of the van and rush to the house. They found the front door open and were in the office in less than thirty seconds.

"What is the meaning of this?" said a shocked Gwen Leong.

"You are under arrest," said Hue Sun

The front door banged against the wall as a large man came barreling into the room. Howard stopped him by pointing a large automatic pistol at him. "I don't think you should do anything rash," said Howard. "Please put your hands behind your back." Howard place handcuffs on the man's wrists.

"Do you know who I am?" asked Gwen. "You will be sorry you ever heard of me after this display."

"Oh we know who you are Ms. Leong and we know your connection to Peters," said Howard.

Mark was helpless. He had no idea what was being said. He could only stand and observe.

Gwen Leong stood and spoke and nodded at the bound man. Howard nodded and removed the handcuffs from the man. The man turned and left the room.

Hue Sun Yatt called his office and requested a car be delivered to the compound. He picked up the house phone and pressed the button that said gate. He told the guard that an unmarked police car would be there in twenty minutes and to allow them entrance.

Gwen Leong stared ahead and was silent.

Wong heard and saw everything from the kitchen. He quietly went into the garage and punched in numbers on his mobile. The phone buzzed as the call was put through. A voice answered, "Yes?"

"Ms. Leong has been arrested by the police. The package she came for is in the hands of the police," said Wong. He didn't wait for a reply. He punched off the call and put the phone in his pocket. He walked out of the garage and ran into Mark standing in the open doorway.

"May I have your phone?" said Mark. Wong was startled. He was unaware that he was being observed and did not understand what Mark wanted.

"I not understand. Little English," said Wong.

Mark stood in front of Wong. They were both about the same size. Mark had no weapon and was hopeful it would not come to a hand to hand fight. Mark held his hand up to the side of his head as if it were a phone. He motioned with his other hand to give him the mobile. Wong held up his hands and slowly reached into his pocket and removed the phone. He handed it over to Mark. Not a word was spoken. Mark motioned to move into the house. Wong turned and walked to the open front door. Howard and Hue Sun were standing in the hall with Gwen Leong. They turned as Mark and Wong entered.

"This man made a mobile call. I have his phone. He speaks very poor English. I think we should determine who he called and why."

Howard started speaking Chinese to Wong. "What is your name?"

"I am Wong. I work for Mr. Sutton. I drive him and look after the house."

"Who did you call on your mobile?" Howard stared directly into Wong's eyes.

"My wife," said Wong.

Howard took the phone from Mark. He scrolled through the recent calls. "Your wife lives in Bangkok?" Gwen jerked her head up and looked at Wong.

Howard motioned for Mark to follow him out to the front of the house near the van. "Wong said he worked for Sutton, but this number may be to his real employer. Call Nigel and inform him of what has happened and give him this number to checkout. I have a feeling it is very important to your case."

Chapter 38

Evidence Collection

Nigel's mobile rang. "This is Nigel." He listened. He pulled his note pad out of his jacket and wrote down a phone number. "Were there any problems?" He smiled. "Great. Take the package and place it evidence bags and give to Howard. Be sure the floppies are labeled and any documents are numbered."

Joyce listened to Nigel's side of the conversation and concluded that Mark had been successful in finding Sutton's hidden evidence stash.

Nigel punched off the call. "Mark has the evidence and Gwen Leong is in custody. Sutton's caretaker made a call to Bangkok when they arrested Gwen Leong. I have the local number. I don't think we should try to call the number but leave that up to the Interpol agents."

"What is happening to the Sutton Evidence?"

"Mark is bagging it and giving it to Howard to take to Singapore. I'm going to call Howard find out what the proper procedure is for handling the evidence," said Nigel. He took out his mobile and punched in Howard's number.

"This is Inspector Chong. Hello Nigel. We have made some progress on our end. What can I do for you?"

"Howard, what will happen to the evidence bags?"

"They will be processed and put into our evidence locker."

"Interpol is now taking over the case. Is it possible to have the evidence released to Interpol?"

"That is possible. We will need a release document from Interpol to release the evidence. They can fax or email the request to the Singapore AG's office," said Howard.

"That's great. I'll get right on it. What time do you expect to arrive back in Singapore?"

"We are on our way as we speak. I think in about thirty minutes. Traffic is increasing but not as bad as usual."

"I will inform Interpol of the developments. I will send you an email when they request the evidence. They are going to request that Mark accept the package on their behalf. Do you see any problems with that?"

Howard hesitated for a moment. "No I think as long as Mark is indicated in the release that he is working on behalf of Interpol, the AG will release all to Mark. He has done a great job by the way."

Nigel smiled. "Yes, he is a rare find." Nigel disconnected the call. "The Singapore AG's office will release the evidence to Mark so long as Interpol names him in the release as their agent."

Joyce smiled. "We are getting very close to the connections we need to have Interpol issue arrest warrants."

They finished lunch and returned to the Interpol hotel suite. Watson and Bloomingthal were busy working on paperwork. The German was not in the room.

Bloomingthal put her papers aside. "What have you heard from Singapore?"

"They have the Sutton blackmail evidence. None has been viewed yet. They are on the way to Singapore now. I spoke to Howard Chong, one of their detectives who assisted us. He says you must make a release request to the Singapore AG's office naming our Mark Young as your agent to receive the physical evidence."

Bloomingthal looked over at Watson. "Since this started out as your case, I see no problem with Mark Young receiving the evidence on our behalf. I'll have the release prepared." She got up and went to the room next door.

"There is one other item. The caretaker for Sutton made a call to Bangkok as Leong was being arrested. Here is the number," said Nigel. He took the page from his note pad and handed it to Watson.

"We need to find out who is on the end of this number. I would like to involve the local police in tracking this down. It will save us time and show cooperation," said Watson.

There was a knock on the door just as Bloomingthal returned to the room. She answered the door. Stan and Doug entered and took their seats.

Watson stood and went over to the white board. "Most of the evidence so far only points to methods but no conclusive evidence tying any individuals directly to the case. We have received word that Sutton's blackmail evidence has been obtained. The letter found at Secure Pacific Investments names several people in at least three different countries but until we examine the evidence package, we will not know if there is sufficient information to issue warrants. We received a local phone number that was made by the caretaker at Sutton's home when Gwen Leong was arrested. I would like for you gentlemen track it down."

"I will be my pleasure to assist," said Stan.

Watson handed Stan the note paper with the number. "Because time is of the essence, I suggest you get the information on this number as quickly as possible."

Stan nodded. He and Doug left the suite immediately.

The door opened to the other room and Frehoffer emerged with a document. He handed it to Watson and left without a word spoken.

Watson read the document and nodded to Nigel. "Here is the release request to the Singapore AG's office. It will be sent from our Paris headquarters. It names Mark Young as our agent authorized to receive the evidence on our behalf." He handed the document to Joyce.

"This is the break we hope will tie all these cases together. I think we should bring Mark here with the evidence," said Joyce.

Nigel nodded yes. Bloomingthal shook her head yes. Watson made no sign of agreeing or disagreeing.

"Transporting the evidence is always a risky business," said Watson. "But, it will expedite our efforts and save us a trip to Singapore."

"I'll call Mark and inform him. I think it would be wise to email him a copy of this document in the event someone challenges his authority," said Joyce.

They all nodded agreement. Bloomingthal took the document back to the room next door.

The group spent the next hour speculating the various threads the case could take. Nigel and Joyce were only concerned about the Jenkins case but were equally curious about all the other cases that were popping up. Nigel's phone rang.

"Yes, this is Nigel." He listened and wrote several things on his note pad. "Thanks, we'll see you at the Hilton tonight." He disconnected the call. "That was Mark. He has the evidence bag and has booked a flight to Bangkok arriving tonight."

"We will meet Mark at the airport and take possession of the evidence bag. It is protocol for the chain of evidence. We will copy everything that can be copied. The original bag will be placed in the vault here at the hotel. We have used this method many times and will document every step with pictures and written narration," said Bloomingthal.

"Will we be able to view the evidence tomorrow?" asked Nigel.

"Yes, all the copies will be here in this room for us to digest and discuss," said Watson.

"I will phone Stan and Doug and give them an update on the evidence," said Nigel.

"I don't think that is a good idea. We don't know if their phones are bugged. I think we should wait until tomorrow morning after the evidence is safely copied and in the vault. After the shooting of Doug, we know there are desperate parties in this case," said Bloomingthal.

"Right, I'll phone Mark and inform him you will be meeting him at the airport and you will show him your credentials to take possession of the bag," said Nigel. He immediately phoned Mark and informed him of the protocol concerning the evidence bag.

With nothing more to be done before tomorrow's arrival of the evidence bag, the meeting was closed. Joyce and Nigel took a taxi to the Hilton on Wireless road.

Chapter 39

Bank Accounts

Nigel and Joyce were met by Stan and Doug in the lobby of the Hilton Hotel. Nigel informed Stan and Doug of the break on finding the blackmail evidence of Sutton's and the protocol Interpol used in safeguarding the evidence.

Doug spoke. "If this blackmail evidence points to the same people in the letter with damning ties, then we will ask Interpol to make several arrests. I fear this will not be easy. We may have to ask for the military to assist."

"We are going to be in the same position. If what we suspect is true, then the network can communicate to all parties that something has gone wrong. The phone call made by the caretaker may have triggered action from some of the parties. If the information is confined to Bangkok, then we stand a chance of making our arrest a surprise. Were you able to track the number?" asked Nigel.

"Yes and it was to the Chief Justice of the Supreme Court. We were able to get the phone records of that phone without going through the AG's office. Doug has a friend with Telecom and they got us the records late last night. It is very interesting. We haven't tracked all the incoming numbers, but some of the outgoing numbers are very interesting. Several were to a warehouse that we thought was abandoned. The latest was only two days ago."

"Let's go to the Interpol Suite and take a look at the evidence," said Nigel.

They arrived at the Interpol hotel at 09:20. Frehoffer answered the door and motioned for them to come in.

Bloomingthal and Watson were viewing something on a computer screen when the group entered the suite.

"We have viewed several of the floppy disks. There are many bank statements. We have yet to find anything that ties the individuals in the blackmail letter to any of the information," said Watson.

"That's disappointing," said Joyce.

They gathered around the computer and watched as the information was displayed.

Frehoffer was hooking up another computer on the coffee table. This computer had a tape drive attached. He inserted the tape and pressed several keys. After several minutes, he pressed another key. "Fife come look."

The entire room stopped and looked at Frehoffer. Bloomingthal rushed over and looked over the German's shoulder. "This may be what we are looking for," said Bloomingthal. The others came over to view the screen.

On the screen a spread sheet with bank account numbers, dates and amounts was displayed. At the top of each account was a name. The bank was in Hong Kong. All of the incoming funds were from one bank, the Malay bank. The right hand column showed amounts transferred to other accounts. Some of these accounts were in Bangkok. There were several to banks in Sydney, Melbourne and Brisbane, London, Chicago and one bank in Vanuatu.

"The funds transferred to these accounts all came from the same account in Malay to the bank in Hong Kong. The Hong Kong bank immediately transferred the funds to each of the individual accounts in other banks. The Hong Kong bank was simply a transfer bank. But we have to confirm that the names associated with the accounts are in fact the persons named," said Watson.

Joyce was reading one of the documents. "That may not be so hard. This document is an application to open one of the accounts. There is a signature on the form. The name is the same as the name on the account. We now have hard evidence that the person named on the account opened the account. We should be able to get writs to examine the accounts and find out where the money finally ended. This one is for Doug and Stan. It's their suspect. There appears to be an application for each account signed by the owner."

Doug viewed the spread sheet and wrote down the number, the date it was opened and several dates of deposits. "If I go to the AG's office with this, I think he will stop any investigation."

"We have a protocol that allows us to examine any bank account that may be implicated in a crime committed in a foreign country. Let us get the account information for you," said Watson.

"We will certainly appreciate you helping us put these people behind bars," said Doug.

Watson spoke to Frehoffer about getting the proper authority to examine the bank account issued to the Chief Justice of the Supreme Court.

Joyce spoke up. "If you remember when we first briefed you, we have evidence that looking at the accounts in the local bank may be a waste of time. They are controlled by the server at the Malay bank."

"Yes, we are aware of that. We will be approaching this using other means," said Watson.

Watson nodded at Frehoffer who immediately left the room and closed the door.

§

Frehoffer used a Satellite phone to make a call. He spoke briefly in Russian. He read from a note pad. He terminated the call and returned to the other room.

When Frehoffer entered and took his seat, he nodded at Watson and Bloomingthal.

"We should know more about those accounts within a few hours," said Watson.

The group continued to examine all the documents and data on the floppies and tapes. It became late in the afternoon and all were exhausted from the work of reading and note taking. Watson's phone beeped. "Yes. Hold I will get Hans." Watson handed the phone to Frehoffer.

Frehoffer spoke in a foreign language and listened. He wrote down several lines of information in German. "Spasiba." He disconnected. Everyone was looking at Frehoffer.

"The information available. I connect our server and print out," said Frehoffer. He keyed a number of strokes on the keyboard. The printer started up and printed several pages. He retrieved the pages from the printer and handed them to Watson, who handed them to Nigel. Surprising to Nigel, they were in English. Joyce looked over Nigel's shoulder.

"Wow, this is amazing. Every detail of each account is here, even the hidden information not available on the local accounts. It matches the stuff that Sutton put on the tapes. How did you get this?" asked Joyce.

Bloomingthal looked at Watson. He nodded yes. "We have friends in Kiev who have special skills. We only use on non-member nations. In this case, we feel justified in using any means possible. There will be no trace we were in their server."

"But will this information hold up in court," asked Doug.

"I don't think it will be needed in court. With what we know about the banking relationship with the local bank and the Malay bank, the local bank will be hard pressed to explain why some of their accounts are missing various transactions," said Watson. "If we can bypass the local AG's office with most of our information, then we can proceed. We must speak to our superiors in Paris before we take any action."

Nigel had been reading some of the printed sheets. "This shows that some of the transactions transferred funds to regular bank accounts, like the Judge's personal account. If the receiving bank tried to track it back, they would only see a clearing account at the Malay bank. The connection would break at that point. With this hidden information, we have proof positive of the connection. What's the next step?"

Bloomingthal went to the white board and drew several lines from the Malay bank to the local bank. "We must document each account and identify who owns the account. As far as the Bangkok and Australian cases, we concentrate on those first. Once we are sure we have solid evidence, we plan on a simultaneous arrest raid. It may be better for Doug and Stan to be unavailable at that time. Nigel, you and your team should be in Australia to assist our people there. We should convene again tomorrow morning and strategize on the coordinated raid."

"I will be speaking to our superior tonight and get their assistance to make all the raids at the same time. That should bring down all the major players at the same time," said Watson.

.

Chapter 40

Strategy

Couldn't you say - the next morning - instead of a time?

The group met at 09:00 in the Interpol hotel suite. Mark Young had met Watson and Bloomingthal at the airport last evening. Watson looked a bit tired and sat without saying much more than good morning. Bloomingthal was typing like mad on her computer. Hans Frehoffer was not in the room.

Stan and Doug arrived about ten minutes after the hour. They and took their seats around the dining table. "We have a plan, we hope, that will take us out of Bangkok for a few days. Our boss was thrilled that we have good leads on a case that is in a small village about two-hundred kilometers from here," said Stan.

Watson smiled. "Well done. I suggest you get on your way.

Stan and Doug shook hands with all and exited the room. left

Watson again stood and began. "We have agents on their way to Australia, UK, USA, and Canada. These countries are all members of Interpol. None of the countries will be notified of our agents or what is likely to take place. Our superior has made contact with the head of the military here in Thailand. He has offered his assistance. That should make it safer for all concerned. We did not get through to the head of the military in Australia, but I'm told they will make contact in a few hours." Watson sat down and was visibly relieved.

The door to the other room opened and Frehoffer came in bearing several documents. He handed them to Bloomingthal and returned to the other room. Bloomingthal went to the white board. The board had been cleaned of all the scribbles from before. She wrote the initials of all the countries involved across the top. She listed the names of the suspects in each country below the country's name. She drew a line and under Thailand and Australia she wrote the name of the general in charge of the military. She drew another line and wrote the names of the Interpol agents under each country. She included Nigel, Joyce and Mark under Australia. She wrote Howard Chong under Singapore.

"We will know in a few hours the arrival of all the agents in their designated locations. With the exception of Thailand, Singapore and Australia, we will not be discussing the plans in other countries," said Bloomingthal.

Watson got up. It was apparent to all that he must have worked all night and was very fatigued. "Our plan is to make one sweep in each country at the same hour. Until we have met with the general here in Bangkok and talk with the general in Australia, we cannot set a time for the arrests. All the warrants have been prepared under international law."

"Sir, how exactly does the international law describe the arrest of a citizen of a sovereign country?" asked Mark.

Watson did not hesitate, he handed Mark one of the arrest warrants. "If you read the first paragraph, it says that in accordance with the membership agreement, each country has given Interpol full arrest authority to its citizenry when evidence is sufficient to stand up in the international court. Note the international court, not local courts, is referenced. This is very important, especially here in Bangkok. Since the court system is compromised, it is imperative that international law is used to make the arrest. In your own country, you cannot be certain if the criminal justice system is compromised or not. We will not take that chance."

"Where will the arrested parties be kept?" asked Joyce.

"For Thailand and Australia, the military prison has been designated. These will be temporary arrangements until each government is reasonably sure they have the situation under their total control," said Watson.

Frehoffer came into the room and handed Bloomingthal a document. He quickly exited the room. She read the document. "General Wu is on his way up. I suggest we cover the board. Please do not mention any other country. I think Nigel, Joyce and Mark should wait in the next room."

Nigel, Joyce and Mark went through the door into the room. Mark was amazed at the equipment installed. There were at least three computers, several printers, a high speed scanner, and several pieces of unidentifiable equipment.

"Wow," said Mark.

Frehoffer turned and motioned for them to take seats in the two chairs. Mark sat on the bed. "What is this for?" asked Mark, pointing at a rather large electronic device that had many led lights and switches. There was a large cable running through the slightly opened window.

Frehoffer looked at Mark with a smile. "It transmitter. Satellite. Latest model." Nigel and Joyce looked at the equipment and were impressed even if they had no clue what it was.

They spent most of the next hour talking among themselves while Frehoffer went about his business typing on various keyboards and removing documents from the printers.

The door opened and Bloomingthal entered. "The general is on board and will supply all the assistance needed. Hans, can you try the Australian Military again."

Frehoffer pressed several buttons and handed the phone to Bloomingthal. She listened for a few seconds. "This is agent Bloomingthal with Interpol. May I speak to General Ashton please, he is expecting my call."

She waited a few seconds. "General this is Agent Bloomingthal with Interpol. You may have received a communication from Paris a short time ago." She paused. "Good. I'm here to discuss the details." She listened again for a few seconds. "I see. We have warrants for two of your country's citizens. Each is accused of committing crimes involving several of our member nations. Two of your federal police are assisting in this investigation. They and our agents will be contacting you tomorrow to coordinate the execution of the warrants. You will be receiving shortly all the details pertaining to the scope of your assistance. Because of the sensitivity of the case, you will be briefed in person by Mr. Nigel Bowman of the Australian Federal Fraud Bureau with details concerning the warrants. They will be arriving back in Australia tomorrow afternoon." [Pause] "Yes sir, thank you sir." She handed the phone back to Frehoffer. "Did you get all of that?" Frehoffer nodded and pointed to the digital recorder.

Nigel was impressed and concerned at the same time. He looked at Joyce and Mark. "Any thoughts before we get on a plane to home?"

"We have no evidence of anyone in the AG's office involved. We only know that the AG is a personal friend of one of our suspects. How are we to approach the AG concerning his not being told of what is happening?" asked Mark.

"I think we use the time on the plane to plan how to find out if there is any involvement. We still do not know where Peters is located. We have solid evidence involving the other two. It sure would be nice to grab Peters before we leave," said Mark.

"We think we may have a clue as to his location. It seems there is a warehouse used by the justice department to entertain certain guest. We have that on our raid schedule. If we find Peters you will be notified immediately. I don't think extradition will be a problem after our arrests.

"When your flight arrives in Sydney, our agents will contact you. Good luck."

Joyce smiled. "Thank you for all you have done. I've learned a lot and hope we meet again."

Mark called the airline and made reservations on the next flight out to Sydney. The flight would leave at 19:00 that evening.

Nigel, Joyce and Mark left the suite after thanking Watson and Frehoffer. The hailed a taxi to the Hilton.

"We have an hour or so before we leave, let's have a drink. It's been an exhausting day," said Joyce.

They found a table near the back of the bar. "Nigel, why so down?" asked Mark.

"I'm thinking about what will happen after the raid. If the AG is in on this, then all hell is going to break loose. There may be blame thrown against the PM. Some idiot may even call for a vote of confidence."

"I think the AG is straight," said Mark. "He has always played it by the book. I think his odd behavior is due to the impending election. He is under a lot of pressure to clean up crime. A lot has been done, but for the most part it is petty stuff. He needs a really high profile case. I think this may just be what he needs to secure the election. I hope it plays out that way."

"What is happening with Gwen Leong?" asked Joyce.

"The last time I spoke to Howard, she is mum. She thinks she will get away with all of it because she was arrested in Malay."

"Well it will come as a big surprise when she is arrested by Interpol and tried in an international court on money laundering in more than five countries. She will certainly face several years in jail," said Nigel. The plane departed right on time. It was sparsely occupied. One of the uniformed cabin attendants came back and offered to upgrade the three to first class. They grabbed their overhead stuff and moved into the first class section. There were only three other passengers in first class. Mark had never been in first class. He was examining all the amenities. "Now this is the way to travel," said Mark.

Nigel smiled, "Yeah, as long as someone else is paying." They all laughed. Dinner was served immediately. Rare steak cooked to perfection, two red wines, and bananas Fosters for dessert. This was a totally unknown dessert to the three. The cabin attendant explained it was a New Orleans delight. This plane normally was on the transpacific route with loads of Americans.

The flight was a long one, nearly 10 hours. After dinner and dessert, Nigel suggested they get some sleep and first thing the next morning they begin their plans. "Even though we don't know what Interpol has planned, we will have to deal with the small stuff. We need to have a plan for any turn of events. Think about all the things that can go wrong or come up. Have a nice sleep."

They each grabbed a blanket and pillow. They were asleep within moments.

Chapter 41

Plans

Mark was the first to wake. He looked all around. The cabin was still dark. One of the first class cabin attendants came immediately to offer juice and coffee. Mark took both. He had bad dreams but could not recall any details. The menu for breakfast was on his tray. He selected scrambled eggs, bangers, chips and toast. His breakfast arrived just as Nigel and Joyce awoke. "Hey sleepy heads. Good morning."

Nigel yawned and stretched his arms. Joyce removed her blanket and got up for the loo. The cabin attendant quickly brought juice and coffee. Joyce returned to her seat and perused the menu as she enjoyed her juice.

"How long until we land?" asked Nigel.

The pretty young attendant checked her watch and said, "About three hours."

Nigel and Joyce ordered breakfast.

"I've been thinking about how the Interpol agents will serve the warrants. It seems to me it should be done with dignity and quietly. No press. Just us and the military police. No more than two maybe three officers," said Nigel.

"Where do you think we will find our suspects?" asked Joyce.

"I know one will be in his office. The other one may be hard to locate, he only has duties on the weekend," said Nigel. "Mark you take on the responsibility of locating him. I will make sure our other one is in his office.

"Got it," said Mark. "Are we going to split up?"

"Yes, we each will be stationed with one of the Interpol agents to make the arrests. Joyce will go to Canberra and standby for any indication the AG should also be arrested."

"Will I have an arrest warrant for the AG?" asked Joyce.

"I would think so. We will not know until we interview our suspects if the AG is involved, but we may not learn enough to execute the warrant. If that happens, it is important that every move made by the AG is monitored," said Nigel. "After we land, you take the first flight to Canberra. Maybe the flight can be booked from here."

Nigel got up and walked to the area of the plane where the attendants were working. "Excuse me, can we book another flight from the plane?"

One of the attendants looked up. "Yes. Give me the flight details and we can radio ahead and book your flight."

"That's great. We need Joyce Mathews booked on the first available flight from Sydney to Canberra, one way."

"Yes sir, I will notify you when it's done. How shall we offer to pay for the flight?"

"Tell them she will pay by credit card upon picking up the tickets."

The flight attendant smiled and went up the stairs to the cockpit area.

Mark made notes on a pad. "You know, I'll most likely be fired for holding back this information from the AG."

Nigel wrinkled his forehead. "If the AG is innocent, I would think he would give you a raise for the work you've done giving him his high profile case."

"Hum, haven't thought about that," said Mark.

The flight attendant came back with a piece of paper. "Here is your reservation for Joyce Mathews." She handed the paper to Nigel. He looked it over and handed it to Joyce.

She frowned, "Damn, I'll not leave Sydney until near noon. What will I do until then? I hope the raid is not scheduled during that time."

They discussed several scenarios. They made notes and argued why one would work over the other. In the end they concluded that they had backup plans to each scenario.

The cabin attendants came through the cabin collecting cups and putting away blankets and pillows. The captain came on the PA system and announced they would be landing shortly in Sydney. One of the attendants made another announcement, "Please put away your personal items in the overhead bins and store your trays and return the seats in a full upright position."

Nigel raised the curtain on the window. There was a slight light in the far left side of the plane. He couldn't see any light of cities below. To him the world looked asleep. He thought about what the Jenkins' would make of what they sparked. The engines changed pitch and Nigel felt the first lowering of the flaps. They were preparing to land.

The wheels were jarring when they were extended. The lights of Sydney were now visible. The plane was making a westward approach. The plane banked and Nigel could see most of downtown Sydney. In a minute the wheels touched the tarmac and the engines begin to roar in reverse thrust.

The immigration line was short. They presented their passports and claimed their luggage. The customs area was crowded from an earlier flight. When they exited the customs hall, Nigel spotted three men holding a sign with his name. He walked over and showed his credentials to the men. They shook hands. The lead man was obviously from Ireland. His accent, red hair and freckled face gave him away immediately.

"I'm Inspector O'Hurley and these two fine gentlemen are Kosic and Bergeron. They nodded at each other.

"Gentlemen, let's go to the airport security office. They have a conference room we may use," said Nigel. He led the way up the stairs to the departure hall and across to the administration offices.

They entered the main door and Nigel stopped at the desk to identify himself and the others. He requested the conference room. At that time of day, the room would most likely not being used. The officer pointed to a door down the hall. Nigel led the group to the conference room.

"Inspector O'Hurley, you tell us what you have planned. We are here to assist." said Nigel.

O'Hurley pulled from his inside coat pocket a packet of documents. Referring to them, he read the protocol that was in place. "Due to the time in some of the other locations, the raids are scheduled for 17:00 hours today. We have spoken to the Australian general and five of his military police are on standby at the local barracks and three in Canberra. We have made two surveillance trips to the offices of the first suspect. The second suspect is in his residence. We have two teams to arrest both at the same time. While there is always a risk of violence, in this case I think the probability is very low. We plan to present the warrants with as low a profile as possible. The military police will not come into the buildings unless asked."

"What will happen after the warrants are presented to each of the suspects?" asked Joyce.

"We will take them to the military facilities and interview them. You are to be part of the interview. We have not been made aware of the details of their crimes, so that is your job."

"I suggest that when executing the warrants we answer no questions from the suspects until we have them in the interview room," said Nigel.

O'Hurley agreed. "I suggest you get a hotel room to rest up before this begins. I am sure it will last well into the evening."

"Good idea. I'll phone and make reservations at the Hilton for Mark and myself. We were just there a few days ago. Joyce will be going to Canberra with your man and won't need a room. She lives in Canberra. May we get a ride to the hotel?"

"No problem. What about Joyce, what are you going to do until late this afternoon?"

"I'll rest here in the terminal. I have a flight out at noon and will go home first and freshen up. Is your man already in Canberra?"

"No, Inspector Bergeron here is also taking the noon flight. You will be met by the military police. I understand that the warrant issued for the AG may not be executed at this time."

Nigel spoke up, "Yes, well we are going to make a hard try at determining that during the interview sessions. If it turns out the AG is named as being involved, then the arrest can be made at his home. Stan and Doug will be doing the interviewing in Bangkok. We will be in contact with them and coordinate any information that is related to our case as well as theirs."

Chapter 42

The Raids

The military police were ready and had vehicles to transport all to their destinations. One group would go to the Olympic Park area and one to an apartment complex at Darlington Pont. Nigel decided Mark would go to the apartment complex and he would go to the Olympic Park.

"Sir, here are the Interpol warrants," said O'Hurley. He handed a packet of documents to Nigel.

"They look in order to me," said Nigel. He gave one of the documents to Mark.

The Interpol officer gave the driver instructions and off they went. The drive was slow because of the going home traffic. "We have a man on site at all three locations to observe if the suspects are still in the locations. We can speak to them via radio," said O'Hurley.

They drove in silence for about thirty minutes. The radio squawked and a voice reported that all was secure at the Olympic park. Another voice said all was secure at Darlington Point. Nigel was surprised when another voice reported all was secure in Canberra. "Wow, that is some communications system," said Nigel.

"Yes, we use the latest equipment. The Canberra officer is using a mobile phone to report through to our headquarters here in Sydney and then the transmission is routed to the radios."

Nigel saw the large building housing the Lottery Board's offices. A man stood in the front and waved as the vehicle stopped. Nigel and O'Hurley were the only ones that got out. "That's officer Smothers who kept watch," said O'Hurley.

The two walked up and Nigel was introduced. They entered the door to the building. Nigel walked to the information desk and requested to see Sir Rodney Stonebridge. He showed the clerk his credentials. The young clerk raised an eyebrow and made a call. He spoke to someone and nodded his head several times. "I'm sorry sir, but Sir Rodney is engaged at the moment and cannot be disturbed."

Nigel was prepared for this response. "Young man, I have official business with Sir Rodney. Please show us to his office."

The young man started reaching for the phone. "No, please put the phone down and come with us. Do not attempt to obstruct our official business," said Nigel.

The young clerk got up from his desk with a shocked look on his face. He led them to the lifts and pressed the call button. The lift doors opened and the four men entered. The clerk pressed the button for Sir Rodney's floor. The lift began its ascent slowly. It stopped at the level with the offices of the Lottery Board.

The clerk led them down the hall to an office suite. The name on the door was Sir. Rodney Stonebridge, Chairman. "Thank you, you may return to the lobby," said Nigel.

The two Interpol agents and Nigel went into the office suite. Sir Rodney's secretary sat at a desk with a computer terminal. She looked up when they arrived. "I'm sorry Sir Rodney is in conference." Nigel went directly to the door that opened into Sir Rodney's office. The secretary bolted out of her seat and tried to intervene. Nigel was already in the office which contained several individuals seated around a small conference table.

"What's the meaning of this?" said Sir Rodney. He looked perplexed.

"Sir Rodney, I am Inspector Nigel Bowman and these two gentlemen are with Interpol. We need you to conclude your conference and speak with us."

Sir Rodney's jaw dropped. He quickly told the individuals around the table to please leave. "It seems these gentlemen have urgent business with me." The people at the table gathered their papers and stood. They looked questionably at Sir Rodney and left the office.

"What is this all about?" questioned Sir Rodney.

"Please come with us. We have a warrant for your arrest," said O'Hurley. "You may not make any phone calls or speak to anyone."

Sir. Rodney Stonebridge was speechless. He got up from the table and was presented with the warrant. He held it in shaking hands as he read the details. He looked up at the three officers and nodded his head. He quietly walked with the officers out of the building and was transported to the military barracks.

§

Mark rode in the passenger's seat of the jeep. The driver must have been briefed on the address because he drove directly there with no instructions. Mark was a bit nervous because this was his first police action to arrest someone. The Interpol agent Kosic was quiet in the back seat. Another jeep followed with three military policemen. The jeeps pulled up in front of the building. A man got out of a car across the street and approached Mark's jeep. "Mark this is officer Murtry. He has been on stakeout for most of the day."

"The suspect left briefly and I followed him to a convenience store. He bought a newspaper and returned about an hour ago," said Murtry.

"Let's get on with this," said Kosic. The three walked to the lobby of the apartment complex. There was a uniformed doorman seated at a desk.

"May I help you gentlemen?" asked the doorman. He eyed the three men carefully.

Kosic explained to the doorman who they were there to see. "We do not want to be announced. This is official government business. Please show us to his door," said Kosic. All three showed their credentials.

The doorman got up and escorted the three to the lift. They entered and the doorman pressed the button to the penthouse level. There were two apartments on each level. The door opened on the top level and the doorman walked to the door marked B. He rang the bell. The door opened and there stood one of Australia's most popular rugby and TV personalities.

"Yes, George?" said the man.

"These gentlemen would like a word with you sir."

Kosic stepped forward and presented the warrant to the man. "Please come with us."

The man did not look shocked. "I must tell my wife before we go." He turned to go back into the apartment. Kosic was right behind him. "Please sir, may I have a private moment with my wife?"

"Sir, you may not. I will accompany you to your wife. You are to make no phone calls or any contact with anyone at this time."

They went to the kitchen. He told his wife he had to leave with these gentlemen on business and would be back shortly. His wife looked at Kosic. "Who is this man?"

"I am officer Kosic with Intropol. Your husband is being asked to help us with an investigation."

The TV celebrity said nothing. He didn't show his wife the arrest warrant. They turned and exited the apartment. The man asked many questions on the way to the street. No one answered his questions. They reached the street. He was surprised to see military police standing next to the two jeeps.

"Sir, you will please get into the first jeep. We will not put restraints on you unless you become uncooperative," said Mark.

He nodded and got into the back with Kosic. Mark got into the front. The jeeps pulled away from the building and headed towards the military barracks.

Chapter 43

Interviews

Sir Rodney Stonebridge was fuming and spouting all sorts of threats all the way to the barracks. He was so engrossed in yelling at Nigel that he never noticed they had entered the military barracks compound. The jeeps pulled up in front of a building used for incarcerating individuals. The windows had bars and the door was steel plated.

"What is this place?" yelled Sir Rodney. No one answered.

"Please come with me," said Nigel. He held the jeep door open. Sir Rodney sat in the jeep with a look of total disorientation. Nigel reached in and took Stonebridge by the arm and helped him exit from the jeep.

O'Hurley walked around and spoke to one of the military policemen. The policeman walked up to the door and pressed a button. The door opened and the policeman handed the guard a document. The guard carefully read the document and stepped back to allow O'Hurley, Nigel and Stonebridge entry.

The military policeman led the way along a stone hallway to

a room. He opened the door and stood aside. The room had one table and two chairs. Nigel entered the room and motioned for Stonebridge to take a seat without a word spoken. Nigel stepped out of the room and closed the door. The military policeman escorted O'Hurley and Nigel to a room down the hall. It contained several video screens and several men occupying various pieces of equipment. Nigel looked at one of the screens. Stonebridge was seated at the table with his head hanging down.

"How long are you going to wait until you question him?" asked O'Hurley.

"Let's check with Mark and find out how he made out with Zellman."

O'Hurley took out his phone and spoke several seconds. "Your other suspect is arriving now. We will put him in a room upstairs."

Nigel and O'Hurley sat down at a long counter that contained various screens and devices unknown to either. They watched Stonebridge sitting staring at the wall. Another screen came on and showed Mark followed by a large man with grey hair. Mark motioned for the man to sit.

Nigel told O'Hurley that he would start the interview with Mark's man first. They saw Mark leave the room and close the door. The man sat looking at the floor. The door opened to the operations center and Mark came in with one of the military policemen.

"Any problems?" asked Nigel.

"No. He never said a word. His wife was there and he told her he was going to be back soon. That was it."

"I want you to be with me when we interview each man. The goal is to try to find out if the AG was associated with any of this mess as soon as possible. We will then update Joyce," said Nigel.

"Should we let her know we have the other two?" asked Mark.

"Good idea," said Nigel. He took out his mobile and pressed the speed dial for Joyce's mobile. It rang twice.

Joyce looked at the caller ID. "Hi, I've been wondering how things were going on your end."

"We have our two in custody and are about to begin to interview. I will call you back as soon as we know with some certainly if the AG is in on this mess."

"Okay, good luck. I'll be waiting," said Joyce.

Nigel put his mobile into his coat pocket. "Mark, I think it's time we begin the interviews."

Nigel, Mark and O'Hurley followed a military policeman to the first floor. The hall looked the same as the one below. The policeman opened the door with a key and ushered the three into the room. Mark stood with O'Hurley against the wall. Nigel took the other chair. The man looked at Nigel with contempt.

"You bloody fools have nothing on me. What is this about?"

"As you can read from the warrant, you are charged with fraud, specifically regarding Marty and Denise Jenkins. It seems Mr. Peters has given you up and will testify in court as to your participation in the scheme." Nigel watched his face for any signs. Nothing was detected.

"I have no idea what you are talking about. I never heard of a Mr. Peters."

"Well that's sort of hard to believe. I have records showing you received calls from Mr. Peters and made calls to his mobile. I phoned the number Peters used and you answered the phone. I recognized your voice. We have traced funds from an account in Bangkok to your personal account in Vanuatu." He looked up when Nigel mentioned the Vanuatu account.

"I have no personal account in Vanuatu. You can't prove anything."

"We shall see about that. Your association with Sir Rodney Stonebridge will no doubt reveal a great deal. The AG has been very interested in this case, and I think I know why."

"Why would the AG be concerned?" He looked very puzzled.

"I don't know. Why don't you tell me," said Nigel.

The man sat looking at Nigel. "I know the AG. He is a personal friend. We socialize together. I have no idea why he would be interested in this matter."

Nigel turned and motioned for the other two to follow him out into the hall. "I think the AG may be clear. He may only be interested in the case from the high profile it may have."

Mark shook his head in agreement. "I feel the same way. None of the money seems to be connected to the AG in anyway. I think it's the high profile this case will generate that has his interest."

"Okay, I'll call Joyce and call off the arrest of the AG." Nigel took out his mobile and called Joyce.

The three went back into the interview room. The man appeared to be in distress. Sweat had broken out on his forehead. He was dabbing his face with a handkerchief.

"Sir, when did you and Stonebridge dream up this scheme?"

He sat and said nothing. He wiped sweat from his brow.

"Stonebridge has given you up as the one that headed up this whole thing. You hired Peters to front as an investment company. Peters cleaned out all of the money and ran off to Bangkok. He was caught. He has a very elaborate estate in Malay. He has passports from Singapore and the USA. He left you high and dry as they say."

The man sat and stared at the wall. He started to say something but stopped. He sat back in his chair.

"Mark Young is from the AG's office. He knows the various charges facing you. Interpol arrested you because the crime extended to other countries. When we are finished with you, you will be extradited to each of those countries. Mark outline to him what he is facing."

Mark moved toward the table. He looked down at the sweating man. "Sir, you are in very serious trouble. You have committed fraud by setting up a phony investment company to steal the winnings of the lottery winners. Your bogus company laundered money in New Zealand, Singapore, Hong Kong and Bangkok. Your employee, Fredric Peters decided to go into business for himself and moved all the funds to Bangkok so you would never find the money. The Queens Council will ask the court to give you the maximum of twenty-five years for each charge of fraud. If you live long enough, Singapore, Hong Kong and Thailand will have their go. You will never be a free man again." Mark saw a break in his face. The situation was sinking in.

Nigel's phone rang. It was an international call. "This is Nigel Bowman." He listened for several moments. He made some notes on his pad. He handed the pad to Mark who read it and handed it to O'Hurley. The three left the room with the suspect looking like death warmed over.

"It seems Stan discovered Peters' whereabouts at a special place for the Judge's prisoners. Stan and Doug rescued Peters and arrested the Judge. If what the judge has said holds up, then they will be arresting most of the police administration and several bank board members and a host of the judge's employees."

"Do you think our suspect knows about the Judge?" asked Mark. O'Hurley listened very carefully to what Mark and Nigel were discussing.

"I don't know, but I'm about to find out," said Nigel.

They returned to the room. The man looked up when they reentered. "I want a barrister." O'Hurley stepped forward. "I'm afraid that won't happen. This is an international case and the rules are different. You will not contact a lawyer. The court will appoint one for you. You will be tried under international law." The man looked blank.

"Sir, can you tell us about your association with a certain judge in Bangkok." The suspect had a genuine look of terror on his face. Something had triggered extreme fear. He was visibly shaken.

"I don't have to answer any of your questions. You have nothing on me. I am innocent."

"For your information, the judge has given us a list of names. Yours and Peters' are on the list. Peters was being held as a prisoner of the judge. A young man working for the judge was killed in an exchange of gunfire during the rescue of Peters. It seems the judge has men working for him in many countries. We may be the safest place for you at present."

The man had turned pale. His face was red and sweat was pouring from his scalp. He opened his mouth to speak but hesitated. "What if I cooperate, will that make a difference?"

O'Hurley looked him in the eye, "Maybe we should just turn you over to the Judge's men. That would save the tax payers of several countries a lot of money."

The suspect jerked at what O'Hurley said. His hands were shaking as he wiped his brow.

"Now back to my question about your association with Stonebridge. You haven't given us an answer," said Nigel.

"Stonebridge knows the Judge in Bangkok. Stonebridge lived in Thailand several years ago and became friends with the Judge. He learned of a fool-proof scheme to launder money and approached me with the scheme. I was to setup the phony investment firm and hire someone that was an expert at cons to run the firm. I found Peters though a friend. I told Peters about the scheme. If Peters had any problems, there was a contact in Bangkok that Stonebridge said could make things happen. I assumed it was one of the Judge's people. Stonebridge gave each of the lottery winners a brochure about Secure Pacific Investments. I was to encourage the winners to go see Peters for professional advice on how to invest their winnings. That's all I did."

"How many lottery winners were involved in the fraud?" asked Mark.

"As far as I know, there were about seventy-five over the past two years. The Jenkins' was by far the largest. I never personally received any of the money. Stonebridge setup the account in Vanuatu and promised to cut me in on the total when it was safe to do so. I have no personal account in Vanuatu."

Nigel spoke, "Were you aware that Peters had control of all the money and had personally taken over a million to purchase property in Malay?"

"What? No. That little shit is a weasel. I should have guessed he would try something like that. The figures he gave me showed close to ten million was squirreled away. I didn't get into the details."

Nigel nodded at Mark and O'Hurley and they left the room. They could tell the suspect was a broken man.

"Let's go talk to Stonebridge," said Nigel. They went down the stairs to the other interview room. When they opened the room, Stonebridge was seated looking at the wall.

"Sir Rodney, we have interviewed the others associated with this case. They have given us a lot of information. It appears you have quite a scheme going here," said Nigel.

"I have no idea what you are referring to. Between running for the election and running the lottery, I have no time for anything else?"

O'Hurley bent down close to Stonebridge. "Let's start with your time spent in Thailand. It seems you and a certain judge are very close. So close in fact that you make frequent calls to each other."

"I have no idea what you are talking about. Who are you?"

"I am Inspector O'Hurley of Interpol. We have evidence that you were involved in a money laundering scheme in Bangkok. That same type of scheme is being used here to bilk all the winnings from some of your lottery winners."

"This is preposterous. I know nothing about any money laundering."

"Come now Sir Rodney. You gave the Jenkins' a brochure directing them to Secure Pacific Investments. You set up a phony investment company and used the same scheme used in the oil scam in Thailand to launder the money."

Stonebridge sat very still at the mention of the oil scheme. Nigel noticed a tic in Stonebridge's left cheek.

"Sir Rodney, we have a confession from your associate naming you as the one that brought the scheme to him. He also says you are the one that setup the account in Vanuatu. It will be very easy to get the particulars on that account," said Nigel. The tic was more pronounced.

Mark leaned forward and looked directly into Stonebridge's face. "The Judge has been arrested in Bangkok. He has a list. Your name was at the top of the list. One man is already dead. It would seem the safest place for you is here with us."

Stonebridge's hand began to shake. He swallowed and looked at each of the men staring back. "I..I don't know any judge in Bangkok."

"Okay, let's play it your way. We can just turn you lose. Let the chips fall as they will, or you can cooperate and be safe with us," said O'Hurley. "Let's go gentlemen. It's obvious the man doesn't value his life very much."

The three got up and went to the door.

"OK, I know a certain judge in Bangkok. We were business associates a few years ago. It seems he uses extreme measures in dealing out justice. What do you want from me?"

O'Hurley turned and sat down across from Stonebridge. "Explain your current association with the Judge. We already know about the Oil scam."

Stonebridge sat looked at the table top a long time. He said, "The Judge and I have several enterprises. We invest our money into various companies that have the potential to return large profits. That is the extent of our current relationship."

"Do you know Gwen Leong?" asked O'Hurley.

Stonebridge looked confused. He shook his head no. "I never heard of her."

"Do you realize that all the money defrauded from your lottery winners is not actually in the bank that Peters used in Bangkok? Gwen Leong owns a bank in Malay that has a secret branch in Bangkok. All of the accounts reside on a server in Malay. The statements are all false. Peters thought they showed balances of nearly ten million, but in fact are zero. Your friend the Judge and Gwen Leong are working together to scam the scammers. The Judge's police force brings various scams to his attention. He sends one of his men to persuade the scammer to use a certain bank to deposit their funds where they will never be traced. As soon as the funds are deposited, they are transferred to the Malay bank. The scammers are never aware until they try to withdraw the funds. Then they realize they have been scammed. Who are they going to complain to?"

Stonebridge sat and listened to this information. His tic was more pronounced. "All you have is that I am a friend of some judge in Bangkok. You have my word against anyone that says that I came up with the scam to send lottery winners to Secure Pacific Investments. That will not hold up."

Mark pulled out his note pad. He read a few lines. "Sir Rodney, we never mentioned Secure Pacific Investments, how do you know the firm? Stonebridge bit his lip. You forget we can tie you directly to the Vanuatu accounts. The money received in those accounts came directly from Secure Pacific Investments and Asian Investments in Singapore. That makes it an international crime. I work for the AG's office. I can assure you that it will stand up in court, especially the international court. I'm afraid your bid for PM is over."

O'Hurley got up and knocked on the door. A military policeman opened the door. "Take Sir Rodney Stonebridge to his cell. Take all the precautions."

The policeman took Stonebridge by the arm and escorted him away.

Nigel called Stan in Bangkok. He went over both interviews with Stan and with Doug on the extension. They told Nigel that Peters was unharmed but in a very deep depression and won't talk and demands he speak to a lawyer. Nigel said he would be returning to Bangkok to interview Peters, but it may be a few days until all was sorted out in Australia.

Nigel phoned Joyce and gave her an update. He explained that Mark would be coming to Canberra to update the AG. It may be a good idea to go with him.

§

Joyce met Mark at the airport. She was very happy with the way things went with the arrest. No violence and it seemed confessions would be forthcoming.

"I really dread seeing the AG," said Mark. "How do I tell him he was under suspicion?"

"I don't think you have to tell him that. We only took precautions in case there was a leak; due to the nature of the high profile the case was taking involving Stonebridge.

"Okay. I guess this will help the AG with his reelection prospects."

Joyce drove them to the AG's office. They went up the steps and entered the building. A security guard waved at Mark as he put his ID badge through the machine. Joyce registered as a visitor and followed Mark to the AG's office. They entered the typical government office. The AG's secretary looked up and smiled at Mark.

"Hello Mark. You're back. Are you here to see the AG?"

"Yes thank you. This is Inspector Mathews." The secretary smiled politely and spoke to the AG on the phone. She waved them toward the AG's office door.

Mark opened the door and allowed Joyce to enter first. "Sir this is Inspector Mathews. You may recall her name from my reports."

"Yes Mark. You two have a seat. I assume you are here in regards to the Jenkins' case."

"Yes sir. We have completed the case. You have not been brought up-to-date recently because of the possibility of a leak. We were very cautious and careful with all the information. We have made two arrests today in Sydney. Harry Zellman, who I think you know very well and Sir Rodney Stonebridge."

"Stonebridge! My God man, I hope you have solid evidence. And Harry Zellman?"

"Sir the arrests were done by Interpol. Their agents took over the case after it was found to involve individuals in several countries. There are actually two major cases involved. Neither is associated with the other with the exception that they were perpetrated by the same parties."

The AG was stunned to say the least. Interpol had arrested Australians in Australia and without his knowledge and one was a contender for the position of Prime Minister and the other one of the most popular TV personalities in Australia. His face took on an angry look. His cheeks turned red.

Joyce saw he was about to explode. She quickly said, "Sir, our hands were tied. With Interpol coming in and taking over the case, we were not allowed to make any reports. We came here as soon as possible. I know this is going to create a lot of publicity, but given the circumstances, it seems you are the best person to make the announcement."

The AG appeared as a balloon losing all of its air. "I…I…you are right. This should be announced from my office. You did the right thing coming here. Where are Zellman and Stonebridge?"

Mark was very relieved. "Sir, the Interpol agents made arrangements with the military to provide temporary accommodations at the military barracks in Sydney."

"Are formal charges being made?"

Mark looked at Joyce. "Sir I have copies of their arrest warrants. No charges have been made as of yet. We have one Inspector working with the Interpol agents. As soon as they have signed statements, he will phone you. I was told that may be within the hour. You may then make the announcement."

"What about the money. Will the winners bilked get their money back?"

Joyce said, "We don't know. The money was recovered by Interpol but I don't know its disposition."

"I see. Well, one thing at a time." The AG looked at his watch. "I would like to get a copy of the statements before I make the announcement. We must make our own decision as to what charges to make with regards to the laws of Australia. Mark can you see to that?"

"Yes sir. Consider it done."

"Mark, you have outdone yourself on this case. I am amazed at the job you have done."

Joyce smiled at Mark. "Sir, if it had not been for Mark, I don't think the outcome of this case would be the same. His knowledge of law, procedures and just down-right common sense are remarkable. We can use someone with his talents in the Fraud Bureau."

The AG smiled for the first time since their visit. "Inspector Mathews, I have been watching the fine job Mark has been doing. It is time I do something to show may admiration. Mark, as of today you are associate AG of Australia. I will put through the paper work first thing tomorrow."

Joyce took Marks hand in a firm handshake. "Mark congratulations."

Mark stood and shook hands with the AG. "Sir we have some

more work. We will go to my office now. As soon as word comes of the statements, I'll call you." He turned, motioned to Joyce and they left the office.

Mark's office was on the ground floor. It was like most government offices for non-elected officials, nearly bare. Joyce took a seat in the only visitor's chair. "It appears your fears of the AG's reaction were overstated. He was thrilled with the prospects of him reporting the most sensational crime solved this year."

"Yeah, but I really think before you intervened I was a goner."

Joyce laughed and nodded. Her phone rang. It was Nigel. "Hi, how's the interviewing going?'

"Better than expected and we have Peters' in Bangkok. I am sending to Mark's email copies of the statements. They reveal all. I spoke to Watson and Bloomingthal about the money in the Malay bank. They assured me the money is now in an Interpol account in London. They both think that under the circumstances, Gwen Leong will be in no position to file a complaint. After the International trial, the money can be distributed to the lottery winners. We don't know all the other parties, but there is more than enough to cover all loses to the lottery winners. The balance will go will be up to Interpol to distribute. I'll be in Canberra in this evening and go directly to the AG's office."

Chapter 44

The announcement

At 20:30, TV crews completed the setup in the AG's office. Joyce, Mark and Nigel stood against the back wall. The AG got last minute makeup adjustments.

"My fellow Australians. The office of the Attorney General has just concluded investigating one of the largest fraud cases in the history of Australia. Over seventy-five lottery winners were scammed out of all their winnings. A couple from Sydney filed a complaint a few weeks ago. The Australian Fraud Bureau, headed by Nigel Bowman and Joyce Mathews traveled to Singapore, Hong Kong and Bangkok tracing the money. The individuals involved in this case of fraud have been arrested and are currently being held for court appearance. The lottery winners will receive full restitution. The money has been recovered."

The AG read from a teleprompter. He took off his glasses and picked up a document from his desk.

"Many of you may be wondering who are these crooks. I am afraid you know both of the main criminals. Harry Zellman and

Sir Rodney Stonebridge have been arrested." There was an audible intake of breath in the room from the press and crew.

"I am proud to inform you of the team that carried out this successful investigation. Nigel Bowman, Joyce Mathews of the Australian Fraud Bureau and from my office, Mark Young. Their hard work and brilliant investigative skills resulted not only solving one of our largest scams in history but also broke up one of the largest money laundering schemes in the world. Interpol has arrested most of the international criminals. Australia is proud to have a police force that is ranked as one of the best in the world. Thank you, and good evening."

Nigel and Joyce clapped along with the entire room of press and crew. Mark was very quiet and seemed preoccupied.

"Mark are you OK?" asked Joyce.

"Yes. I'm pondering what will become of Peters."

Nigel smiled and said, "Peters will remain in custody in Tailand. He has agreed to testify if they do not extradite him to Singapore, Hong Kong or Australia."

Joyce looked at Nigel. "What about Gwen Leong and Peters' involvement in Asian Investments?"

"I have spoken to Howard Chong and he indicated they have Chung and it would be very difficult to prove Peters' involvement. I spoke to the police in Hong Kong about the misrepresentation as a lawyer by Peters. They say the case is not large enough for the Chinese to spend money having him returned to stand trial. Chong said Gwen Leong has been released by the Malay authorities. She will be very surprised to find all the money missing from her bank."

Chapter 45

Peters' Interview Plans

Nigel and Joyce arrived back in Bangkok on Wednesday evening. They checked into the Hilton Hotel on Wireless road. An envelope was waiting for them at the front desk. Nigel opened the plain envelope and read the single page.

"It's from Stan. He is going to meet us here tomorrow morning at 09:00. They have Peters in a holding cell.

"Let's get into our rooms and meet in the bar to make plans," said Joyce.

"Okay, see you in about half hour."

They went up the lift to their floor. In half an hour Nigel was seated in the bar and saw Joyce looking for him. He waved her over. The bar was quite busy this evening.

"Hi, there must be a convention going on. Lots of people in here tonight."

Nigel looked around. "Yep, looks like mostly from Asia."

The waitress came and took their drink orders. Nigel ordered an appetizer platter.

"I've been giving a lot of thought about Peters' situation. He is defiantly going to jail. Mark says that in his case he'll receive about ten years. We have lots of money we recovered from his house and the Secure Pacific Investment offices. We cannot tie any of the money to the scam. He can say he won it or found it or anything that would not be associated with the scam," said Nigel.

Joyce didn't say anything for several minutes. "What if we made him a deal? He doesn't know about Hong Kong and Singapore dropping the case against him. He has no idea that he will not be expedited to Australia until he has served his time in Thailand. If he thinks he will be going back to Australia and we indicate that we won't expedite him to Singapore or Hong Kong if he donates the funds we recovered to a suitable charity."

"But he was promised not to be expedited if he cooperated."

Joyce smiled, "But we didn't promise that. It was Stan and Doug that made that promise."

"I think I will call Stan and check in." Nigel punched in the number to Stan's mobile.

Stan answered on the second ring. "Stan this is Nigel. We have checked into the hotel. Would it be okay if we interviewed Peters at your offices? We can take a taxi down first thing in the morning." Nigel listened for a few seconds. "I see. That sounds like a real mess. Were you able to find his personal effects?" Nigel made notes on his pad. "That's great. We'll be looking forward on seeing you tomorrow morning."

Nigel clicked off the call. He made a note on his pad. Joyce was patiently waiting. The food and drinks arrived. "They have all of Peters effects and the most incriminating thing found was a journal. It starts when Secure Pacific Investments was formed, how he was hired, his role in setting up Asian Investments and the bogus Hong Kong and Bangkok companies."

"Wow that is a real find. It should be all we need to give the AG's office all facts necessary to send Stonebridge and Zellman to jail for a few years, not to mention Peters." Joyce took a sip of her drink. "When we interview him, let's let him assume we do not have the journal. If we can get him to point fingers and confirm what's in the journal, then we have a solid case."

"I agree. The tighter we can tie Stonebridge and Zellman to Secure Pacific Investments the better. I asked Mark to check out the Vanuatu bank accounts. He is flying to Vanuatu today. That will complete the circle of involvement from our perspective."

"The Vanuatu banking laws are not too keen on releasing personal information about their customers without a personal appearance," said Joyce.

"Mark mentioned that the AG has a connection within the Vanuatu government and will be granted a writ to examine the accounts. I'm not sure how many accounts they have, but according to the bank statements we uncovered at the Secure Pacific offices, there are certainly two," said Nigel.

They conversed for several minutes as they ate the variety of items on the platter. They agreed on a plan for the interview.

Chapter 46

Review of the Bangkok Raid

[handwritten annotation: They took a taxi to police headquarters]

Nigel and Joyce had finished breakfast and returned to their rooms. Nigel was in the lobby by 08:00. Joyce stepped from the lift a minute later. A taxi pulled up to the portico. The driver came into the lobby and went to the front desk. The desk clerk pointed out Nigel and Joyce seated in the lobby area.

The ride into the central city was slow. The early morning traffic was heavy. The taxi driver spoke English and apologized for the slow progress. It took close to an hour before the taxi pulled up in front of the police headquarters. ~~Nigel paid the driver and they went into the building.~~

To Nigel's surprise, Stan and Doug were waiting for them at the information desk. "Good morning," said Stan. He extended his had to Nigel. Doug did the same for Joyce. "Welcome back to Bangkok. This time we have some good news," said Stan. Doug said nothing. His arm was still in a sling.

"We have a lot to discuss and updating to do," said Nigel.

"Yes, we have a conference room reserved. It seems Doug and

I are able get just about anything we ask for lately." All laughed. Shall we proceed?"

~~Doug led the way to the lifts and the conference room on the third floor. The room had fresh coffee and pastries. Nigel helped himself to coffee. Joyce did not.~~

"I think the first order of business should be an update as to what has happened since your returned to Australia. Doug has a presentation. Doug?"

Doug stood and turned the top page of a large easel. On the pad were diagrams and names of various positions. "As you can see, we have a large network that has been operating within the Justice Department and the Police. With the assistance of the Interpol agents, we think we have uncovered all the parties involved. All are currently in the military facilities. We took no chances with how far down the network extended within the police department. The military has been very cooperative."

Nigel was impressed. "There appears to be a few individuals in the Justice Department but a great deal more in the police. How were you able to ferret out all the names and positions?"

Stan ~~stood and went to the easel.~~ explained, "Interpol recovered several bank statements that led to individuals receiving funds from accounts that were controlled by the Chief Justice. It appears that most of the police were of high rank and controlled most all investigations. Our boss and several of the Inspectors were named. They are now in the military facilities."

Doug took over from Stan. "When the raids took place, we found several references to a secret location used by the Judge to incarcerate individuals. We found Peters there unharmed. The building was well guarded. Unfortunately we were forced to use extreme measures to gain access. The military officers were very careful to use only enough force to enter the building. One of the top figures associated with the Judge was killed."

"Were you present during the raid?" asked Joyce.

"No, Stan and I were away on other business at the request of t Interpol. The Interpol agents arrested the Judge. It was without any incidents. Communications was blocked from the Department of Justice. This prevented anyone from alerting the secret ware-house and the police.

"The Judge has not spoken to anyone and refused to make a statement. He has several employees that are very vocal, especially his private secretary. We are able to connect several cases that we had no idea involved the Judge. A list was made of individuals from the interviews and sent to the Agents at the police head-quarters. The agents held back on their investigation until the list was received. The evidence recovered is under Interpol control. There were several agents sent in to assess the evidence. We were not given access to the evidence until they had it cataloged and processed."

"How were the police involved in the network arrested," asked Nigel.

"The Interpol agents and the military officers came to this building under the ruse of a conference with the top brass. They explained that a very important training program was to be held, but only for executive officers. They indicated that an invitation would be send to all concerned within an hour. All but four of the people on the list were invited to attend. The four not in the building were arrested at their homes. The arrests went without incident also."

"It appears this was well planned and executed. I'm very im-pressed. Thanks for notifying us about Peters. Without him we would be hard pressed to make a good case for the courts," said Nigel.

Doug sat down. Stan remained at the easel. He turned the page. There was a diagram of the scheme to scam the scammers. The money flowed to a phony Hong Kong investment company which made various large purchases of oil and other high profile commodities. The investment company sold off the investments to a bogus Bangkok company for a large profit. The money was transferred to the secret local branch bank of the Malay bank. The bogus Bangkok company then sold off the commodities to a Sin-gapore company for a huge loss. The scammers were unaware their funds were not actually in Bangkok, but in the Malay bank. Their statements were all phony. There were over thirty such schemes.

Joyce studied the diagrams carefully. "I have one question. How much money was transferred to Malay from the local branch?"

Doug answered the question. "According to Interpol, over One-Hundred Million US dollars."

Nigel and Joyce looked at each other. Nigel raised another question. "What will happen to the funds Interpol appropriated out of the Malay bank?"

The door opened to the conference room. Agent Watson entered with two other agents Nigel and Joyce had never met. "I'm sorry we're late. We were detained with some information that may be of great interest to this group." He looked around the room. The other two agents took seats around the table. "The Judge made an offer to one of our agents. He would talk if given immunity and would implicate the bank in Malay. He offered as a teaser that he had the password to the accounts and was willing to transfer ten-million to the agent." Watson sat down next to his agents.

"What do you think should happen," asked Doug.

"First, our protocol does not allow for deals. We must only gather facts and physical evidence. The Judge is unaware we have removed all the funds from the Malay bank that involve any of the schemes. We are certain that there is enough evidence at the local bank to support our case against the Judge. We think it appropriate that the Bangkok authorities speak to the Judge and deny his offer. This will be a large blow to his effort to escape prosecution."

"By even stating he has passwords to accounts at the Malay bank and can name others is a confession of being complicit in the scheme," said Doug.

Stan sat down across from Joyce. "I have to attend a meeting shortly with the Prince. He is about to name replacements for those arrested. I think we have explored all that took place during the raids here in Bangkok. Now if Nigel and Joyce will update us on what occurred in Australia?"

Nigel stood. "I don't have any charts or diagrams, but in a nut shell, we were prepared for three raids. Only two were necessary, we have no evidence that the AG was involved in the scheme to defraud the lottery winners. We arrested Sir Rodney Stonebridge at his office in the Lottery Board building without incident. Mark and the Interpol agents arrested Harry Zellman at his home. They were both taken to the military barracks for questioning. We have statements from both and they will used in court. We are here today to interview Mr. Fredric Peters."

Watson smiled. "I want to thank you all for being instrumental in cracking one of the largest money laundering rings in the world. We have made arrest in several countries; individuals that were conducting schemes similar to the Australian one. So far over forty-six individuals and several law enforcement personnel have been detained. We are in the process of producing all the evidence in each case for each government to use in its prosecution of their cases. The international tribunal is meeting today to decide how we should proceed with the international law as it pertains to each case. I will inform you as soon as they have made the decision."

Doug stood. "Gentlemen we are extremely satisfied with the result of your investigation. If there is anything we can do to assist further, do not hesitate to ask."

"And that goes for Australia also," said Nigel.

"If there is nothing more for me, I'm sure you have very pressing matters to attend to. We will be at our hotel until word comes as to the disposition of our prisoners." Watson and the other two Interpol agents left the room.

"Stan, I know you have a pressing meeting. Unless Doug must be in attendance, we would like him to accompany us to interview Fredric Peters," said Nigel.

Stan looked over at Doug. "Do you have anything on that you can't go with Nigel and Joyce to interview Peters?"

"No. I have nothing on at the moment. I would very much like to be present at the interview of Peters."

"Fine, we will adjourn. Doug will take you to the interview room for Peters. If possible I would like to invite you and Joyce to dinner tonight."

"Thank you Stan. I would be honored," said Nigel. Joyce nodded yes and smiled at Stan.

"Good, I will pick you up at 19:00 at your hotel." Stan shook hands with Joyce and Nigel and left the room.

"I have reserved an interview room on the next floor for Peters. I will call lockup and have him brought to the room," said Doug. ~~He used the phone on the sideboard to call lockup.~~

~~They gathered their papers and note pads and followed Doug.~~

Chapter 47

The Peters Interview

The interview room could be entered from two doors. One went directly to a hall that led to the lockup. The other door led into a control room with video equipment to record the interview. The three entered the darkened control room from a door off the main hallway. Several chairs for observers were positioned in front of a large window looking into the interview room. The window appeared as a large mirror from the interview room. The two Interpol agents that had accompanied Watson were sitting in the observation chairs. Peters sat in the next room staring into the mirror.

"Before we begin, I've been instructed to inform you that all the charges from Thailand must be satisfied before he can be expedited to Australia." Nigel and Joyce nodded approval. "I think it best if I go in first. He has met me when we made the arrest. I will begin the interview with a direct line of questions about his involvement with the Judge. Then I will leave and you two can take over," said Doug. He turned and entered the room with Peters.

Peters looked up at Doug when he entered. "Mr. Peters, I have a few questions. Your answers will determine the future of your stay in Thailand. Explain your relationship to Wo Jun Fat."

Peters looked puzzled. "I don't know anyone named Wo Jun Fat."

"Mr. Peters, we have examined your phone and there have been several calls to Wo Jun Fat's private mobile phone."

Peters' mind was racing. The only calls he made after arriving in Thailand was to Chung in Singapore and his special contact here in Bangkok. "I only have a phone number. I never knew his name. He arranged passports and airline tickets. He fixed things. I called him my contact"

"I see. When did you last speak with him?"

"I got a note from him when I checked into my hotel to leave to another hotel and to call him." Peters was sweating. "I called him and he told me that the police knew I was in Bangkok. That was the last time. I have never met him."

Doug studied Peters' face. "When was the first time you made contact with your contact?"

Peters sat still. "I don't remember the exact first contact date. It was a few years ago. I had just set up the Singapore and Hong Kong companies and I came here to setup bank accounts. I received a phone call at my hotel. The man told me he could make sure any funds deposited with a certain bank would be untraceable. I asked for his name, but he didn't give me one. I asked him how he got my name. He said his organization made it their business to assist people in my line of work. I asked him again how he knew me. He never told me. I assumed it was through the bank."

"Did you ask him how he knew your line of work?"

"Yes, but he never told me. I was curious but assumed it came from the bank."

Doug got up and left the room for the control room. He closed the door. "You heard, not much about his knowledge of the Judge."

"I think we'll will give it a go. He met us in Sydney and will be surprised to see us," said Nigel. He and Joyce went into the room.

Peters didn't look surprised at Nigel's and Joyce's appearance.

"Mr. Peters, we have all of the blackmail evidence from your home in Malay. We know about your relationship with Gwen Leong. We know you used three different names. Who is your employer at Secure Pacific Investments?" said Joyce

Peters looked genuinely shocked at what Nigel revealed about their knowledge of him. "I never met my boss. I was hired over the telephone."

"Yes, but what is his name?"

"Harry Zellman," said Peters.

"And do you know any others associated with Secure Pacific Investments?"

"No, I only dealt with Harry. He steered the lottery winners to me and I took it from there."

Nigel consulted a folder. "Mr. Peters, tell me about your relationship with Gwen Leong."

"We are friends. We met at a conference in Hong Kong several years ago. She assisted me in finding a house and we have been friends ever since."

"Did you know that she has scammed you of all your funds?" said Joyce.

Peters looked as if he was going to have a heart attack. "Wha... what do you mean she scammed me of all the money?"

"Just that, you thought you had ten million in the local bank, but in fact it was never here. It was always in the Leong Bank in Malay. The statements you receive are all phony. You sir have no money in Bangkok" said Joyce.

Peters was in complete shock. "How? I personally transferred the funds from various banks to the Imperial Bank of Bangkok. Are you saying Gwen owns the Imperial Bank of Bangkok?"

"Yes, your chance meeting in Hong Kong was not a chance meeting. She played you," said Nigel. "As I see it, Mr. Peters you don't have many options. The Interpol agents would like to ask you some questions about the scam using the race horses in New Zealand, a bogus company in Hong Kong, the impersonation of a lawyer in Hong Kong, money laundering in Singapore and of course fraud in Australia." Peters looked down at the table. "You have no money, you are wanted in four countries. What do you propose?"

"I have money, it's in Australia. I can send someone to get it. I have substantial funds in my home and at my office in North Sydney. None of that money is tied to any of this."

"Oh, you mean the money in the freezer at your house and the money in the panel behind the file cabinets in your office. We have all of that money and the letter with all the names of the people you were blackmailing. We have all the files from the hidden safe in your house, thanks to Gwen Leong. As I said, what do you propose?"

Peters looked directly into Nigel's eyes. He was sweating profusely. "I don't know. The money in Australia had nothing to do with Secure Pacific Investments. It was money I earned as fees."

"You mean blackmail don't you," said Nigel.

"You can't prove I blackmailed anyone. That letter was a threat to make sure none of the people made a move against me. The so called evidence was only some receipts, cancelled cheques, and phone recordings. It doesn't prove I was blackmailing anyone."

"Let' talk about Sir Rodney Stonebridge. You named him in the letter. Why put him in the letter if you didn't have any association with him?"

"My contact let slip once that I was fortunate to have such a powerful political person on my team and soon to be PM. I had no idea what he was talking about. I found out that Stonebridge was the chairman of the lottery board and may take a run for Parliament. That is when I figured he was also into the scam, I decided to include him in the letter."

"Okay Mr. Peters, that will be all for now.." Nigel and Joyce left the room for the control room.

Doug and the two Interpol agents smiled as they returned.

"That guy had all the angles covered with the exception that his girl friend played him for ten million dollars. Good questioning. We videotaped it all." said Doug. "Interpol would like to question him about the various enterprises he had in Singapore, Hong Kong and here in Bangkok." The Interpol agents got up and went into the interview room.

"I would like a copy of the tape to take back to Australia. Also a copy of the bank records that you have connecting Peters to the whole thing," said Nigel.

"No problem." Doug turned to the officer seated at the control panel. "Make a copy of the tape for Inspector Bowman."

"It looks like Zellman and Stonebridge will be spending a few years in jail. The Jenkins' will get their money back and the Australian government will get a large payout with the "blackmail" funds," said Joyce.

"I don't think Mr. Peters will ever see Australia again," said Nigel.

§

Afterword

This novel is based loosely on real events that took place in the late 80's in Australia concerning the Football Pool. When I started writing this novel, I was not sure if I should follow the actual facts. I decided not to.

All of the characters are my creation. I added many scenes that took place in Singapore, Hong Kong and Bangkok that are from my own imagination.

Interpol never played a part in the solving of the real case. The famous TV celebrity did in fact serve some jail time, but maintained that he never received any money from the scam.

Chuck Lumpkin

October, 2017

Made in the USA
Columbia, SC
26 November 2017